**Books by Talia Wall:**

*The Nightshades*
*The Bleeding Hearts*
*The Oleander*

# THE NIGHTSHADES

## Talia Wall

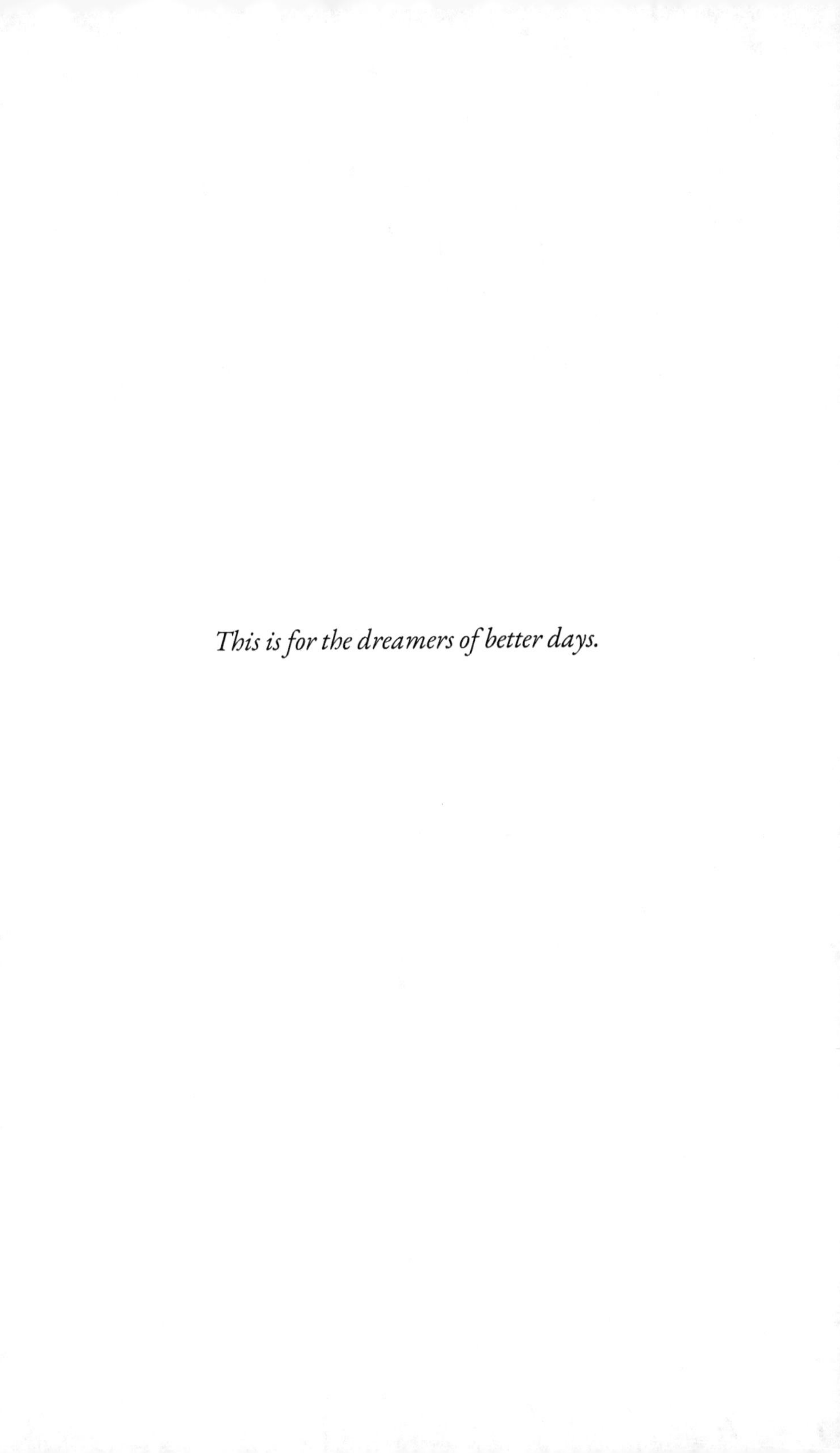

*This is for the dreamers of better days.*

# 1

# DRAVEN

ASHES FELL FROM THE BUTT OF MY CIGARETTE AND FLUTTERED into the man's eye as he squirmed under my boot. He blinked wildly and coughed as the smoke surrounded him. His short fangs glinted under the pale moonlight as he hyperventilated. I leaned forward on my knee, pressing my foot harder against his chest. A whistle sounded from miles away, indicating a train would soon cross the tracks behind the dilapidated brick alleyway.

"Still waitin' on that money, Arlo." I pulled the cigarette from my lips and tapped the glowing ash over him. I thought about searing the cherry into his leathery cheek. Judging by his skin texture and his fangs, he had gone days without blood. I smirked.

"Tell ya what. I'll take a quarter of your debt tonight, and I'll give you a bag of juice. Otherwise, you'll be chained up to that pipe over there 'til dawn. If the sun won't bite, the Sun Dwelling cops sure will." I cocked my head, waiting for his answer. I had all night to hear it. The man's pallid lips trembled as sweat trickled down his heavily rippled forehead, and his hands shuddered against my ankle as he tried to alleviate my boot's pressure.

"I-I..." I felt a knot fall in his throat. A forced swallow. "I don't got it, s-sir—"

I drooped my head with a sigh and lifted my boot from his chest. I straightened and cracked my knuckles, slowly shaking my head.

"That ain't what I wanna hear. Boss ain't gonna accept that neither. You and I both know that. It's been six months, Arlo." I rolled up the sleeves of my black t-shirt, revealing the black and red dragon tattoos spiraling up my arms. "Neither of us can show up empty-handed, and I'm gonna look out for myself."

"I can't! It's not enough time! I-I'm in the process of selling my house. I just need a little more time," Arlo stammered.

I sighed and snatched him up by the collar. Arlo released a yelp when I slammed him against the brick wall. The train was still a little ways away, but its bellowing groan along the creaking tracks was gradually growing louder.

"You're out of time. If you knew ya couldn't come up with the money by now, ya shoulda sold your house! Not only that, but you couldn't take the deal? Don't say I ain't try to bail ya out!" I growled. "Now, which is it? A pinky finger, a toe, or an ear?"

"Wait, wait, wait—wait!" Arlo started to scream as I held him up with one hand and, with the other, pulled out a dagger carrying my clan's initials carved into its silver hilt.

"Pinky it is." Just as my curved blade kissed the base of his little finger, the train howled next to us, masking his chilling cries. I released his collar, letting him fall roughly on his side. Arlo gripped his wrist as tears streaked his face steadily. I flicked the blood off my hand after wrapping his finger in a handkerchief.

"Ah, calm down, man. It'll literally heal in five minutes. It won't grow back, sure, but at least it ain't gonna hurt no more." I stepped over his body and trailed to the blacked-out limo with purple under-lighting that waited for me at the end of the alley. I flicked my hand again, disgusted by the scent of Vampyre blood. It certainly didn't carry the sweet aroma of human blood, but being able to differentiate between the two also made me sick. I thought I'd grow out of it but, after thirteen years, it was safe to say I wouldn't.

I got in the limo and walked hunched over toward the farthest backseat. Across from me sat my friend and right-hand man, Caspian Bishop. He always kept his snow-white hair in a spiked hairstyle, and his crimson eyes were stark against his pale skin. He always wore copious amounts of black leather, and looked fused to the limo's seats.

"Did he give you any of it?" Caspian didn't look up from his phone. Probably playing one of his stupid games.

"Does it look like he did?"

Caspian glanced at me from under his white eyelashes as I held up the handkerchief with just the tip of Arlo's finger poking out of it. His nose scrunched.

"Gross. Well, at least you're not empty-handed." Caspian shrugged.

"Yeah, can't say the same for Arlo, though." I leaned back, sifting through my jogger pants' pockets for another cigarette. I groaned when I realized I'd used up my last one.

"Hurry it up, will ya?" I cupped my hands around my mouth to shout at the driver, Hartley. His handlebar mustache quirked in the rear view mirror, but he didn't respond. He was slender in stature and always wore suits while he was on the job, and also a man of few words.

"Somebody's irritable," Caspian mumbled, focusing on his game as he held the phone closer to his face.

"I used my last smoke. Not only that, but the sun's about to be up," I grumbled.

"Ah, we'll make it back to Uriah's in no time," Caspian said. "They're cancer sticks anyway."

He mumbled his last statement, though I heard him perfectly. I sucked my teeth as his phone chimed in a negative tone, then smirked as he lost whatever level he was on.

"Well, I ain't trying to get burned. Ain't tryin' to get arrested neither." I glanced out the heavily tinted window.

The sky was entering civil twilight, its inky abyss vaguely brightening to lavender. I felt a tinge of bitterness enter my chest. Not because the daylight gave us sun poisoning ten times faster than Sun Dwellers—otherwise known as humans—but because it was once the time where my heart belonged, where I found joy.

Joy. Ha. What was that? It was just a word on a page, dandruff on someone's shoulder, an ant at my boot—three little letters with mythical meaning. I, for one, should've found whatever joy meant in the comfort of midnight's black cloak.

"Draven?" Caspian's low voice intercepted the low music reverberating through the limo's speakers.

"What?" I rolled my eyes, as if being addressed was an inconvenience in itself.

"You know Uriah probably would want more than just the finger, right? He probably expected the head," Caspian warned.

"Yeah? Shoot, I forgot. Let's just tell Hartley to turn us around." Sarcasm saturated my tone. I got it—Caspian always hated to bear witness of Uriah's reprimands—but it was always annoying whenever he tried to play big brother.

"You can't keep giving people second chances. It makes us look weak," he droned.

"I ain't weak," I snapped. The limo fell quiet, with only the dubstep bass pounding like a heartbeat through the speakers.

When we reached the estate, the sun was leaking over the horizon behind Uriah King's Mediterranean-style mansion. The palm trees rustled gently in the briny morning breeze. It wafted the smell of salt water, sand, and sunscreen from the ocean over the cliff behind his house. Caspian hissed when the light hit his skin as he stepped out of the limo. He rushed inside with a hand shielding his face. I stood outside the limo a moment longer, ignoring the burning sting on my skin to admire the beauty I was forbidden from indulging in. It felt like I was holding my face inches over a fire, but the sunrise was always worth it.

The foyer was open to the grand, curved marble staircase that led up to the wrought-iron railing lining the mezzanine, which wrapped the entire perimeter. The second floor was supported by several columns and arches that served as gateways to different sections of the house. The chandelier glittered above us with a warm welcome, though past these doors it would be the only thing that held warmth.

Multiple servants milled about carrying trays of food, towels, and décor. I groaned quietly, realizing I had forgotten that tonight was one of Uriah's parties for the "family." Caspian's ear twitched slightly, and he glanced at me.

"You forgot, didn't you?"

I rolled my eyes.

"Yeah, whatever," I sniffed, then crossed the foyer and headed up the staircase to Uriah's office. It was one of many doors lining the wall upstairs. His office, however, was the only one hidden behind a pair of arched mahogany doors centered between white roaring lion statues on either side. I raised my fist to knock but paused. I couldn't help but hear Caspian's warning in the back of my mind.

*I'm not weak.* I frowned, then rapped my knuckles against the wood.

"Enter." Uriah's voice had a tang of annoyance and I clenched my teeth to brace myself for everything that could happen. He was already in a questionable mood, so this interchange could go either way.

"Ah, Hawthorne! Always nice to see you." Uriah's back was turned. He was looking at a map of the Nocturne District of Neo-terra behind his desk, but he already recognized my scent the second I entered.

"You too," I muttered. I stuffed my hands in my pockets, my right hand brushing against the wrapped finger. I'd forgotten I even had it.

"So, did you collect?" Uriah finally turned toward me, his metallic arm intertwined with his healthy, fleshed arm as he crossed them over his chest.

"I tried—and failed, so I took his finger as a message." I pulled the handkerchief out of my pocket and rolled it out on his desk. By now, the finger was rigid and purple.

"Hm." Uriah looked down at it, then up at me with lips pressed in a thin line. His blood-red eyes pierced through my soul as his pupils shrunk to pinpoints.

"I don't have to tell you that this needs to stop," he said with a huff.

"What?" I knit my eyebrows together and tilted my head.

"All these pitty-pat punishments. I trained you well, so I know you're capable of a lot more... *impactful* actions." He folded the handkerchief over the finger to conceal it, then sank into his red velvet wing-backed chair. I scoffed and pointed at the lumpy cloth.

"Hold up, are ya saying the finger ain't enough?" I asked with a wry laugh. "He said he was tryin' to sell his house."

"What difference does that make? People say anything nowadays." He grabbed a bottle of whiskey and two glasses from the corner of his desk. "While I'm busy with this party tonight, I want you to go to his house and burn it."

"I don't under—"

"Think of it as helping the man out. Burn the house down, he gets the insurance money, and we get our money." Uriah smiled smugly as if he'd created the most diabolical plan of the century. "I don't mean light a match, since they don't cover arson. Get creative and make it natural."

"Fine," I seethed. There was no use in arguing with him. I didn't exactly feel like getting whipped in front of everybody again anyway. Arlo was never a friend, just a nuisance. I wondered if I could give him a heads-up so he'd know.

Nah, I don't care anymore.

"Thank you." Uriah spoke with his lips inches away from his glass. I turned away and walked out without a word or a single sip of the second glass he'd poured for me.

Caspian was halfway up the staircase when I started to head downstairs.

"What did he say?" he asked, arching a pale eyebrow. I brushed past his shoulder without any regard for his presence. My words made my stomach turn sour.

"You were right."

# 2

# BRIAR

I SWIVELED SIDE TO SIDE ON MY STOOL AT THE CASH REGIS-
ter, chewing old gum and scrolling through my phone. It was the
dead hour of the day and one of those moments where I wished I
had taken on a fast-food job rather than retail. At least I'd be busy
during the lunch rush. I mean, who would want to shop for clothes
in the middle of a workday?

Ultimately, I wished I was rich and didn't have to contemplate
any of it.

The closest to entertainment I'd had so far today was two wom-
en bickering over who stepped in line first. Since I was looking at my
phone before they approached, I wasn't able to be their mediator.
They argued for five minutes before one of them threw her clothes
on the counter and stormed out of the store. I tuned out during the
other woman's incessant ranting as I processed her transaction.

Shortly after those women left, a group of three high school girls walked in.

"Welcome to Katie's Kloset," I yawned. One of them was glued to their phone and the other two sounded like they were talking about some sort of beach party later in the afternoon.

"Do you think this would catch Jeremy's attention?" The girl with bright, wheat-blonde hair held the cropped shirt up to her chest for her friend's judgment.

"Oh, for sure, Stacey. Without a doubt!" The mousy, brown-haired friend beamed.

I wanted to cut in and say the yellow color of the fabric made her complexion appear sallow, but I didn't want to deal with them. They perused a little longer, piling up outfits in their arms.

"Hey, worker girl, I'd like to use one of your fitting rooms," the blonde called. I looked up from my phone and my eyebrow twitched.

"Of course." I forced a tight smile as I grabbed the keys from under the register. I pursed my lips tightly to keep the snide remarks at bay as I led them to the back. The brown-haired friend tossed a bunch of her clothes at me, and I caught them out of reflex.

"I changed my mind about those," she said. I huffed in disbelief.

"Hey, how about you actually use some manners? My name is Briar, if you can read name tags. Also, it only takes two seconds to show basic human decency and ask me questions nicely," I reprimanded. The blonde girl scoffed and stepped in front of her friend.

"What are you, like forty and working in a place like this? If you want manners maybe you should've done something with your life," she sneered.

I laughed. "You know what? I forgot that the fitting rooms are closed for cleaning." I relocked the door. "Maybe you three should go back to whatever summer camp you crawled from."

The blonde took a threatening step toward me, but her friend put a hand on her shoulder.

"Let's just get out of here. There's a store with cuter clothes, anyway," she said. Then they dragged the third clueless friend away. I mentally replayed the exchange to figure out where it went wrong as I cleaned their mess for the next hour. Once I finished, I returned to the register and went through my phone to try to take my mind off of it.

My boss, Emilio Stevenson, limped with his cane to the register, his lips drawn in as if tasting something sour.

"Get back to work, Briar! All you good-for-nothing kids do these days is stay on those phones," he snapped, briefly raising his cane to point at me. My shoulders jolted as I stifled a laugh.

"I already did everything," I said as I lifted my gaze from my phone and swiveled in his direction.

"You put away the returns?"

"Yeah."

"You refolded the clothes on the displays?"

"Yes."

"Updated the mannequins?"

"Obviously."

Emilio narrowed his eyes at me and started to walk around the store. His cane thumped slowly—almost maliciously—from section to section as he tried to find something I could've slipped up on.

I was always a good worker when I had a ton of tasks. Whenever

I finished them, I'd do whatever to pass the time until a customer would bother me for the fitting rooms or to check out. With the amount of rudeness I had to deal with day in and day out, and the number of times I bit my tongue no matter what in the name of "customer service," I figured it was a fair trade as long as I did my part right. Not only that, but I always managed to do the job of three people in a matter of three hours. Emilio would've never given me the credit, despite being unable to carry a box of t-shirts himself.

It took him about twenty minutes to inspect everything. I watched him the whole time, and merely smirked when all he did was grunt and walk back into his office. It wasn't a surprise that he wouldn't apologize. Managers could never be wrong, after all. I returned to my phone, then paused for a moment.

Why was I taking any of the unnecessary attitude from him or customers? It was never an issue for me to get a job and I could easily move on elsewhere.

I didn't realize I was picking at my black nail polish while I lived in my head. I glanced up at the clock over the exit leading to the mall. I still had four more hours left. I pursed my lips with a nod and stood, squaring my shoulders. I snatched my name tag off my shirt and left it on the counter. I closed my till and grabbed my miniature book bag. I walked out without warning. The weight melted off my shoulders as I crossed through the metal detectors. A rush of euphoria hit me so hard that I didn't know if I wanted to start skipping or crying. I reached up and pulled my hair tie, letting my wavy, cotton-candy-pink hair pour over my shoulders. Nothing could've made this day better.

✳

I tied my hoodie around my waist and slung my bag over my shoulders as I neared the mall's exit. I scanned the parking lot for my motorcycle and waved a hand over my phone to unlock the bike. I grinned as the chrome edges of the motorcycle's curves came to life with lines of glowing pink LED lights, fading in and out as if the machine breathed. It took me three years to save for that motorcycle and add turbo boosters, all because a dagger-wielding human thug in a ski mask had stolen my car in broad daylight.

I glanced up at the sky with a heavy sigh. The sun beamed with aggression as it hovered at its zenith. With four hours to spare, I decided I would be somewhat productive and get my monthly blood donation over with. It was mandatory for every human to donate for the Vampyres' sake, and I'd procrastinated long enough. I once forgot to go back in high school, and I was escorted out in the middle of class by an officer for involuntary donation. I'd never truly experienced embarrassment until that moment.

I drove to the medical district. The traffic was heavy because of the lunch rush, and once I arrived, I had to circle the parking lot twice before I found a spot. The line stretched outside the doors and slinked around the building. I spit out my gum in a nearby trash can, then walked briskly to the line as I saw another car pull up. One less body between me and the front.

The line slowly crept forward. I flipped through apps on my phone until my neck started to hurt, then leaned against the brick wall. I dragged the back of my hand across my sweaty forehead. I thought about coming back another day when it was less crowded. I could also risk forgetting again. I occasionally pulled out my phone to check the time. I forced myself to stop when I realized I was checking every two to three minutes.

Two hours passed, and I was finally inside the building. After another half hour, I was able to sit in the lobby. Then, for another three hours, I waited. I would've gone home, but after all the waiting I did outside, I felt too invested to give up. Once my name was called, I showed them my ID, went through the millionth medical questionnaire I had to fill out each visit, then was brought to the back.

I was out well past the time I planned. I examined the gaudy, neon gauze wrapped around my elbow. The cotton ball covering the needle puncture constantly rubbed against my jacket's sleeve. The sun was weighed down from the day's exhaustion and the moon was already appearing next to a few jet streams that streaked the sky.

The clouds were swirls of ruby, amethyst, and topaz. I wanted to watch the full sunset, but I had to hurry home before the police started their patrols to enforce the Check-In. I huffed a quick sigh before putting on my cat-ear helmet.

I mounted my motorcycle and slowly drove out of the parking lot before speeding into the mildly busy street. I weaved in and out of lanes to pass cars driving exactly the speed limit or ten under. They were more than likely Vampyres already getting an early start to their night.

The roads were gradually emptying as most people were deathly afraid of the monsters that came out after sunset. I'm not talking about the freaks like pedophiles and traffickers, but rather the evolved human population that had become immortal. The type that survived off of blood, bones, and brutality because their bodies stopped processing normal food like the rest of us. Old movies and books from the twentieth and twenty-first centuries called them vampires. Some were beautiful, others were diabolical. Back then, they were a myth. Today, as of 2120, Vampyres were the reason why we were legally chained to the sun, and they were chained to the moon.

I'd never actually *seen* a Vampyre in person. I knew they were real of course, otherwise the laws wouldn't exist. Yet I couldn't help but feel a gnawing curiosity nag at me like gnats. Do they still look human when they bite someone's neck or do they turn into total monstrosities? Since it was illegal to hunt humans, and they used our donated blood, did it taste different, like how a turkey burger differed from beef?

I came to a screeching halt at a red light. I was so deep in thought that I almost ran it. Red and blue lights flickered over the end of the street. Yellow tape squared off the perimeter of a grocery store parking lot next to the neighborhood I needed to pass. I cursed under my breath and made a U-turn. A roadblock like that could get me arrested or executed if I was a few minutes late to Check-In.

As the sky sank into a deeper saturation of jewels, I could see the city's neon lights gradually cut on in my rearview. It always seemed like the city slept during the day and came alive at night. There were vibrant hues of pink, blue, and purple emitting from the skyscrapers for all the nightlife. The far northwest side was illuminated by malevolent neon red lights—that region was known as the Nocturne District, where the most dangerous Vampyres lived.

Sometimes I envied the Vampyres for the freedom they must have. Of course, they weren't allowed to go out during the daylight either, but it was safer for them to blend in with humans than for us to try to walk among them. They also didn't have to deal with Check-Ins, which were mainly implemented for humans' protection. Police officers would go door to door with an electronic tablet and check off every resident within the home that was present. Whoever wasn't home in time or missing at the time of Check-In would be flagged, and whenever found, could be arrested or shot on sight. Human police officers generally had more patience for human civilians than Vampyres. We could explain ourselves before they pulled out their guns, but I didn't want to risk being at the end of a barrel in any circumstance.

The road sloped into a steep hill, heading toward the more rural area of Neoterra. The hill blocked the view of the city and the moon was my only guide until the ground eventually flattened into endless farmland. In the distance, the warm honey windows of my home flickered in the middle of the sleeping fields. It was the only yellow house for miles, the closest I could get to the vibrant colors of the city.

I pulled into the driveway seconds after an officer did and removed my helmet. The officer began to step out of his car, wearing the mandatory dark blue mask that covered the top half of his face. They were all required to wear Columbina-styled navy blue masks to protect their identities while in uniform. Their masks were always matte with antiquated Venetian carvings, but lacked any jewels or feathers like typical masquerade masks. He narrowed his eyes as I ran to the porch and waited by the door.

The second I noticed the officer's head barely clearing the roof of the vehicle, I knew he wasn't my brother. This particular officer was small-framed and brown-haired. Even behind the mask, he looked too young to wear the uniform. My brother was tall and muscular because for the past two years, his second home was the gym when he wasn't working overtime.

The officer stalked down the driveway and stopped at the bottom of the porch stairs.

"State your name," he demanded. He'd already pulled the electronic tablet out. His voice was light and young, but it sounded like he tried to put bass in it to be more authoritative.

"Briar Shaw." I pursed my lips to hold back a laugh. He scrolled through and glanced at me sharply before sweeping his gaze across the porch. My younger, nineteen-year-old sister, Astoria, was already sitting in the white swinging bench on the porch. She waited until he approached before standing and stating her name too. I kept a wide distance between myself and the officer.

"There's one more that's supposed to be at this residence. Sterling Shaw. Where is he?" He asked curtly.

"Working with you guys, I guess. He's probably doing overtime again." I stood in front of Astoria and crossed my arms. His tone no longer amused me; I certainly didn't like that he questioned my brother's presence.

"Explain." The officer spoke with such a flat yet demanding tone. He flicked his eyes up at me before turning them back to the tablet.

"He's an officer. He's essential personnel and he's cleared to work after hours. You must be from a different department or a rookie." I waved at Astoria to follow me inside.

"Briar," she chastised and shook her head, planting her feet firmly in place.

"When is his shift over?"

"I don't *know*. Like I *said*," I spoke slowly, drawing out the words he seemed to have missed, "he works *overtime*. Why don't you just call the precinct and *verify*?" I rolled my eyes. I waved my hand dismissively. The officer's dark brown eyes narrowed behind the mask. A corded vein in his neck seemed to pulse as if he'd explode at any moment. He rested his hand on his belt, near his gun. I could hear my own blood rush through my ears, my body tensing as I prepared to dodge an oncoming bullet, no matter how impossible it might be.

"Have a nice night, ladies. Lock your doors and windows." He turned away in a quick jolt, stomping back to his vehicle. I watched him drive off before going inside, only to hear my sister lecture me.

"You know, maybe if you weren't so rude, he would've been easy on us," she said, throwing a hand up. I pressed my tongue against the side labret piercing on my bottom lip and shrugged.

"Any other officer we had for Check-In didn't question us when Sterling was out late."

"Yeah, well, you were a minute late... he could've technically drawn his gun on you and—" Astoria choked on her words and shook her head. "Sometimes it's best to just shut up, okay?"

"But he didn't, so don't worry." I smiled at her as I slung my book bag and helmet on the couch, shortly plopping myself next to them. "Anyways, guess what I did today?"

"Ugh, what, Briar?" She grunted as she settled into Sterling's favorite recliner.

"I quit my job. Just walked out without saying anything while

Emilio was in his office."

"You... *what?*" Astoria's jaw dropped.

"Yeah, customers were giving me crap all day and Emilio was the last straw." I continued to pick at my nail polish.

"Well... as long as you're happy," Astoria said as she leaned back in the recliner. I glanced past the sheer white curtains that blew gently against the living room windows.

"You know you're not supposed to have those cracked, right?" I gave Astoria a small smirk, somewhat surprised that she'd break a rule. Astoria's cheeks flushed and she leaped to quickly shut and lock the windows.

"I'm so sorry, I completely forgot!" She covered her mouth, her other hand at her throat. "What if that officer saw it? We could've been arrested!"

I shrugged.

"Good thing he didn't, I guess. He was too busy trying to figure out if Sterling was allowed to be out this late." I pushed myself up from the couch and dragged my feet to the wooden staircase. "I'm gonna go shower."

My heart sank. Was it... disappointment? I didn't want to be the only one in the family who lacked respect for the government and its arbitrary rules. I was hoping she was starting to cross over. Then again, our mother didn't have respect for the government either... and that wasn't exactly the role model I wanted to emulate.

Ah, our beloved mother. Vivian Shaw. A woman with a big heart full of alcohol. A woman who loved her needles more than her children. A woman who I, for one, referred to by her first name rather than the term of endearment, whenever I had to speak to her.

Depending on my mood for the day, whenever someone asked me where she was in my life, I'd either say dead or in jail. The real story was that she was in prison, and Astoria was the only one who bothered to visit her and still called her Mom despite her scars from extension cords. I couldn't spite Astoria for it, though. Her heart—unlike Vivian's—was too big to fit in this world. She'd probably forgive a serial killer if she knew one.

I quickly showered, washed my hair, wrapped it in a towel, and plopped on my bed with my phone. I glanced at the window, feeling a small itch at the back of my mind to open it. The Check-In was completed... no one would really come back around in the countryside for the rest of the night—and there was a nice balanced, humid breeze. I paced a few times in my room before I cracked the window ever so slightly. I sat on the windowsill bench, listening to the bristling tree branches and the owls.

While I yearned to roam the streets at night in the city, I did enjoy the serenity of the country. There was something about the lack of any activity that seemed... freeing.

I raised the blinds and peered up at the sky, occasionally glancing at the road whenever a car rolled by. None of them was my brother's unmarked car. I always felt a rush of relief whenever he walked in the door, and crushing despair when he left. My phone's screen lit up with a needless advertisement notification, revealing the time to be a quarter past midnight.

I yawned, then picked up the remote to turn on my television. It was already on the news, which ordinarily I'd ignore but... there were bold letters stating there were four missing people—two women and two men in their twenties—with their pictures posted. Before I could even process the fact that they were abducted in broad daylight, the news cut to another issue that lit the screen with vivid red, orange, and smoke.

Flames engulfed a house as fire trucks and two ambulances nearly blocked the footage. Several cops were sweeping the area and—

*Sterling.*

I saw a mess of copper hair behind another mask... the only officer I knew of with that natural blazing shade of red. I snatched my phone off my nightstand.

I checked my brother's location, which I'd secretly activated the second he announced his promotion as a detective six months ago. It looked like he was exactly where I feared. I pushed my bangs back as a sting started to build behind my forehead. I stared at the screen until the GPS map grew blurry and thoughts had raced hundreds of laps through my mind.

I stood up quickly and put on a pair of black leggings and a baggy black rock band t-shirt with sneakers. I put on a hoodie and my helmet, then climbed out of my window, onto the balcony, and down the column. On the way down, I caught a glimpse of Astoria in her room reading a book in bed. Of course, if I took my motorcycle, she'd immediately know I'd snuck out. So instead, I put the gear in neutral and rolled the bike into the grass to avoid the crunching gravel in the driveway. I walked it down the street until I was comfortable with the distance, then rode the rest of the way into town, following my brother's location.

The closer I got to the city, the more I saw electronic billboards and neon storefronts. They were even brighter in person. It was so much to take in at once that I wasn't sure if I could drive straight.

Police patrolled a lot more frequently during the night. People were walking around the streets as if it was the lunch rush at high noon, going in and out of bars, stores, and restaurants.

Not people—Vampyres. Many of them held their heads high and shoulders back, and walked as if they owned the streets. Few held their heads low under hoods, and some wore sunglasses despite the sunless sky with a confident swagger in their gaits. Others had the grace of prowling lions and the poise of models.

My mouth went dry as I slowed my speed. I pulled over in an alley and concealed my bike behind a dumpster. I was only a block away from Sterling's location. As I crouched next to my bike, my chest tightened. It was finally hitting me how much I risked my life being here after hours. Being on foot was both the smartest and dumbest idea I had, but at least it drew less attention. Not to mention that some police officers during the night shift were also Vampyres—they could all see and smell humans a mile away. At the very least, I had to keep my helmet on.

There was no way I wouldn't get caught. I was running out of chances to turn around and go home, but since the camera wasn't angled on any of the first responders, I had to see what the media wasn't showing.

# 3
# DRAVEN

As Hartley sped through the city, lights, buildings, and trees appeared as smeared streaks against the deeply tinted limo windows. Once again, I was slumped in the farthest back seat, fumbling with my lighter while Caspian played more games on his phone.

"You seem extra brooding today." Caspian glanced at me.

"Well, I didn't exactly start the night thinkin', 'I wanna burn a guy's house down tonight,'" I quipped. Of course, sometimes I wanted to burn Uriah's house down, but I'd never tell Caspian that.

"You won't have to deal with Arlo anymore after though." Caspian put his phone away and lay across the seats on his side, clasping his hands over his chest as if he slept in a coffin.

"I will, though. Once the insurance is claimed, we gotta get the money from him before he blows it on gambling. For some reason,

Uriah never wants to get it himself."

"That's because he already did all the dirty work to get to where he is now." I flicked my eyes pointedly in his direction, tightening my jaw. It took every bone in my body not to slap him. He always had an answer for everything.

Caspian raised his arm and extended his long fingers, staring at the ceiling. I shifted my gaze to the black duffel bag of supplies we'd packed. Why I didn't take the time to buy more cigarettes, I didn't know. I probably wouldn't have been as irritable and "brooding," as Caspian pointed out. Hartley refused to stop anywhere, and my pride refused to beg for it.

I leaned my head against the window and watched the passing buildings gradually turn to townhomes, then houses as we grew closer to the suburbs. I imagined myself somewhere else, playing my guitar and writing songs, maybe even living in one of those houses. I growled lowly to myself and closed my eyes. So immature. I gave that up when I learned as a kid that Vampyres and Sun Dwellers were like oil and water.

"Hate to do this to you guys, but you know the drill," Hartley called from the front. I sighed and crouch-walked across the limo to grab the duffel bag. Caspian stepped outside after me.

Hartley drove off the second we got out. We stood outside the entrance of a mature neighborhood named Pelican's Crossing. Large pine trees shrouded the homes. Most windows were dark, indicating either slumbering Sun Dwellers or empty homes. Street lamps provided small golden pools of light spaced evenly along the shadowy street, only illuminating trash bins, mailboxes, and the occasional parallel-parked car.

"Ya ready?" I whispered as Caspian started walking. He nodded, then leaped high in the air and landed silently on a nearby roof.

"It's best if we stay out of the street. People these days have cameras everywhere," he said as he reached into the pocket of his black leather trench coat for a pair of sunglasses. I jumped right behind him, landing with a louder thud. I couldn't be graceful to save my life.

Caspian and I jumped from roof to roof until we caught Arlo's scent. I dropped to the grass and set the duffel bag down to put on latex gloves. Caspian landed behind me, then quietly crossed the porch to start picking the lock on Arlo's back door.

The floors didn't creak until I stepped inside. I gritted my teeth, and Caspian swung his head in my direction with a sharp glare.

"Sorry," I silently mouthed. I couldn't help that I was the size of a boulder. Uriah honestly should've made Caspian do it alone.

I scanned the kitchen, curling my lip upward. Clutter was everywhere. Dishes piled in the sink and across the counter, the dining table was covered in mail, and empty blood pouches and liquor bottles. I suddenly didn't feel quite as bad about burning the place down. I carefully sat the duffel bag on Arlo's table and rummaged through it.

"How the hell are we supposed to make this look like an accident?" I asked in a harsh whisper. Caspian only chuckled softly, carefully surveying the house and all its chaos.

"Well, if you bought cigarettes, you could've used that."

"Yeah, that would've been a great idea if the guy actually smoked." I frowned as I pulled out a 100-watt incandescent light bulb, an old lamp, and some paper. I glanced at Caspian with my nose scrunched up.

"Here, give it to me. You go check on Arlo and make sure he's able to escape in time." I tossed the bulb to him confidently. He caught it swiftly and gently enough that it didn't break. Perks of being an anemic, night-stalking creature.

He wrapped paper around the light bulb before screwing it in the lamp and plugging it in. I raised my eyebrows slightly, having never thought of overheating a bulb. The paper would instantly burn too. Once again, I wondered why Uriah didn't make Caspian do this by himself.

I crept up the stairs and cringed when they creaked.

The stairs led to a narrow and dark hallway. Picture frames of a woman and children lined the walls like a gallery. I stopped in front a few photos, briefly distracted. A woman with golden curls, a round face, and a rotund body smiled brightly with a pair of brown-haired boys who appeared to be twins. That same muddy brown hair that desperately clung to Arlo's balding head. I pressed my lips in a tight, thin line and snapped my eyes away from the photos before my stomach could turn sour.

There was a door slightly ajar at the end of the hall. Diffused moonlight poured from the crack in an open window. I slowly opened the door and peeked through.

Vampyres don't sleep. Yet there Arlo was, skin still tough as hide from a lack of blood and snoring with an empty bottle of gin barely hanging from his fingers. I sighed quietly and crouched in front of him at the bed. I pulled the bottle from his hands.

This could work... potentially. A drunk accidentally triggering an electrical fire in his house was plausible. But... if we got him out of the house, how could he explain his escape in this state without the cops inevitably searching for the mysterious Good Samaritans? Alcohol dulled Vampyres' senses much worse than it did for Sun Dwellers. He wouldn't even be able to smell the smoke, let alone be sober enough to get out successfully.

We could risk letting him die in the fire. Uriah wouldn't get his money, but at least Arlo wouldn't be a thorn in my side anymore. I preferred dealing with the clients that actually paid up. Caspian would never agree with that, and I wasn't so sure I'd be able to live with it on my conscience either. Although I was tempted to test it.

Arlo groaned, moving his head side to side. He struggled to raise it, blinking slowly.

"Hey." I slapped him in the face. "Wake up. You need to get out of here. There's—"

"Wh-why?" He dropped the empty bottle and looked at me, then his eyes widened, and he scrambled across the bed to get away. "Get out! Out, out, out! *NOW!*"

"Arlo, you don't underst—"

"Draven! Let's go!" Caspian shouted from downstairs. Sirens were distant, but rapidly approaching.

Burnt rubber. Wood. I quickly stood and sniffled, looking toward the door, then back at Arlo. I reached for his white sleeve, but only tore a piece of fabric as he snatched his arm away.

"No! Get away! I'd rather *die* than leave with you!" he shrieked. I ran around the bed and lifted him, just to feel something as hard as iron strike me in the jaw. White light briefly blinded me. I stretched my jaw and let go of him. I wasn't sure if it was those Vampyric knuckles that had struck me or something else. I huffed air roughly through my nostrils, my breaths growing quicker with each heave as my vision threatened to close into a red box of rage. My knuckles cracked as I clenched my fists, and I bared my teeth, my fangs growing thicker, longer.

"I'm trying to help ya," I growled, then stopped when Arlo reached unsteadily under his bed and pulled out a shotgun. The barrel wobbled and I hissed furiously at him before sprinting out of his room.

Smoke swept over the stairs like morning fog over a lake in autumn. Caspian stood in the living room with the duffel bag over his shoulder and his hands in his pockets, as if he weren't surrounded by Hell itself.

Caspian adjusted the duffel strap and took long strides to the back door. I took one more look at the fire rapidly growing in the cluttered living room as it licked the carpet, curtains, couches, and piles of junk. The flames were quickly traveling toward the staircase, but at least he was awake enough to get himself out once he realized what was happening.

I sprinted out of the house as smoke blanketed the rest of the second floor.

# 4

# BRIAR

My fingertips were white as I gripped my phone. I was still following the GPS to my brother's location, each step heavier than the last. My heart sank into my stomach and seemed to boil in the acid. My breath became thick as my chest ached, and then it hitched when police cars sped down the street at the other end of the alley. A soda can clattered behind me. I spun around quickly but saw nothing. I didn't want to go back in that direction, but seeing as how there were police nearby, I had to get back to my motorcycle. I had a better chance to blend in with Vampyres on wheels. I realized that keeping a low profile on foot wasn't as smart of an idea as I thought.

I lifted my chin to see if anyone was perched on the fire escapes above. I'd seen enough horror movies to know that attacks from above were possible, especially with creatures like Vampyres. I ran to my motorcycle, each step threatening to be my last as my knees turned to water.

As I mounted my bike, I thought about how this was probably my only chance to go home in one piece. I gripped the handlebars tightly. I could trust Sterling was okay and support Astoria at home, but that sickening feeling kept gnawing at my chest, mind, and soul.

*No.* I looked back down at my phone. That blue dot was still there, still begging the question of whether or not he was okay. I didn't waste another second contemplating—I just drove. As much as I wanted to speed to get there, I couldn't afford to draw any attention to myself and risk getting pulled over, arrested, or killed.

As I drew near, the orange glow in the night sky became more vibrant. Soon, I was able to see flames whip, churn, and fold into each other as they engulfed a house. The firefighters flogged the house with a column of water. I slowed to a stop at the end of the street and snuck through backyards until I could duck behind a neighbor's fence and peer through the slats. My eyes widened; the street was full of first responders and Vampyric onlookers. I scanned the police officers for Sterling, but he was nowhere to be found. Even with their masks, I'd always know him from his hair color. My palms went clammy as I began to worry he'd run inside the house for someone. How many minutes ago was that? Ten? Fifteen? He was *just* outside near the reporters. He couldn't have been that stupid... not with firefighters out there already, right?

Once the fire was under control, white smoke coated the air and burned the back of my throat. I watched a body with an oxygen mask over its face get strapped on a gurney and rolled into the ambulance by paramedics. The body's clothing was burnt and tattered, and I caught a brief glimpse of marred skin. I narrowed my eyes and strained to see if it was Sterling or a resident. It would've made sense for him to get himself hurt. He'd run into a burning building for anybody. Idiot. *Idiot!*

My hands trembled as I pulled out my phone. The ambulance backed out of the yard and drove off with frantic sirens, and I watched the blue dot on the GPS leave with it.

Still crouched in a neighbor's backyard, I saw two men run past, yielding little details. One had white hair, pale white skin. The other had shoulder-length black hair, shaved on one side, and golden-tan skin. Both wore all black. Both looked up to no good as they leaped on a neighbor's roof with a duffel bag and dashed away in a supernatural streak of black and white.

Vampyres in the neighborhood began to whisper among themselves about smelling a human, so I ran back to my motorcycle as fast as I could. Thankfully, the fire served as a big enough distraction and no one was curious enough to investigate.

I drove along a different route to get to the nearest hospital. Even if I got arrested, or a police officer shot me to remind the public never to break curfew—even if my blood would paint the world red—I had to know my brother was still breathing. I cursed under my breath, wishing I could've seen more of the two men for a better description.

I was halfway to the hospital when I pulled over on the shoulder of the street. I removed my helmet and wiped the tears from my eyes. My entire body trembled. I kept seeing my brother's face on the hospital bed, charred, the EKG monitor completely flat. What would I tell Astoria? How would she finish college with the burden of her brother possibly dead? I put my helmet back on and beads of sweat pearled on my face. I wanted to faint.

I shut my eyes with a deep breath and told myself that Sterling was fine. Maybe he hitched a ride in the ambulance to question the victim if they were conscious. Maybe he had already been sitting inside and that was why I couldn't see him in the crowd.

*He's not dead. He's fine. He's not dead. He's fine. He's not—*

Sterling was highly trained in Vampyric situations, a skilled fighter, and one of the strongest officers known in Neoterra. He climbed the ranks so fast that he became the youngest detective in the city because he'd solved so many cases as a rookie. He *couldn't* be dead. *He's fine.* The world needed him. *I* needed him.

The hospital was one of the neutral zones for patients of either species, but I could get in trouble for being here past curfew without a life-or-death emergency. Even if I lied about being sick, I wasn't in a condition that warranted being out here at this time.

The stark white hospital building was covered with hundreds of windows, exposing the offices and corridors inside. The lights weren't a warm amber like home, but rather harsh like floodlights, washing the life out of anything that fell under its rays. My motorcycle's robust growl lowered to a quiet rumble as I slowed in the parking lot. The ambulance was already in the drop-off zone, but three police cars were also in the lot. It was saturated with danger, but I had to at least try to get a sneak peek of the body before it disappeared inside.

A line of bushes divided the edge of the parking lot from the gentle slope that led to the sliding glass doors. Thick, wide cream columns held up the portico. I kept my helmet on and quietly ran across the parking lot, ducking behind one of the columns. I peeked around the corner warily. The police officers were heading inside while the paramedics unloaded the ambulance. I craned my neck a little more to see who was on the stretcher, but the paramedics' bodies blocked the view of their head.

"Do you smell that, Zane?" One of them sniffed loudly. I quickly tucked behind the column, going rigid as I held my breath.

"Yeah, it's probably the Sun Dwellers in the waiting room."

Once they were rolling the gurney through the front glass doors, I darted to my motorcycle and mounted it. I needed to get out of here. I couldn't continue to risk my life while achieving nothing.

As I drove home, I called Sterling at every red light. Each attempt cut me straight to voicemail. I clenched my fists tighter over the handlebars and shook my head with a sigh. I just had to accept that if there were any bearers of bad news, they'd show up first thing in the morning. I was useless... in every way possible. I didn't have enough information on those two men, and I couldn't check up on my brother, through the phone or in person.

I pushed myself to move forward. The only thing that kept me from wrecking was trusting that Sterling was okay and just busy with other things, despite my gut warning me otherwise.

The triple-lane street eventually shrunk to a single, two-way country road winding around the hills. The windows of our yellow house were pale, like tiny stars sitting at the end of the road. A huge part of me hoped Astoria was still in her bed, engulfed in whatever fantasy her book provided.

When I was halfway to the house, I put the gear in neutral to roll the bike back home like I did when I left, then quietly entered through the front door. I gritted my teeth when the door squeaked. I took off my helmet and wiped my damp eyes. My heart jumped when I turned around and saw Astoria glaring at me from the couch with her piercing, topaz-colored eyes.

"Glad to see you're in one piece." She scowled and stood up quickly with her phone in hand. The screen was illuminated with our brother's contact on there, her thumb right next to the call button. Her shiny cheeks were bright red and her bottom lip quavered. "Do you have any idea what you've done?"

"I'm sorry, Ria..." I held my hands out to try to comfort her, but she reeled back. "I went out to look for Ster—"

"Do you have a death wish? Since when do we go out looking for him when he's out late?" Astoria spoke rapidly, her voice quaking. My mouth hung open and I just stared at her. She wasn't wrong, but I never heard her yell like that before. If only she'd let me explain what I saw on the news—

"Ria—"

"Don't you dare! When he gets home, he's gonna know." She spun around and stormed upstairs. I lurched forward and snatched her wrist midway up the stairs as a flurry of tightness overwhelmed my chest and the dam of tears broke.

"You can't! Please!" I pleaded. I tightened my grip as she tried to jerk away. She raised her other hand to strike me, and I quickly let go. I pressed my palms together.

"He can't find out that I did this, okay? Please?"

*We don't know if he's even coming back,* I wanted to say, but I couldn't bring myself to. She had classes tomorrow—normalcy—I couldn't ruin that, not when there was still hope that Sterling would indeed come home tomorrow.

Astoria's lips were twisted upwards in an angry grimace as she narrowed her eyes. She looked away from me, chewing her inner cheek. "Fine, but if you do it again, I'm not gonna hesitate." She whirled around, whipping her waist-length hair behind her as she continued her heated path upstairs. I jerked my head back to avoid getting slapped by the inky tendrils and released a shaky sigh. I clenched my fists, but they felt weak.

I wanted to be angry, but Astoria had a valid point—it wasn't the first time he'd stayed late. However, it was the first time I'd seen him on the television in front of a burning house and his location moving straight to the hospital. Maybe I wasn't thinking right. Even if he were in a tough situation, what could I have possibly done to help him, especially if Vampyres were surrounding him? Besides... if he needed it, he was trained to call for backup.

I retreated to my room but left the lights on. I kept my phone plugged in and constantly checked for notifications from Sterling, the hospital, one of his colleagues—anybody. I wished he'd check in with one of us. Then again, when would he have the time to do it in the heat of the moment? He could've once he was in the ambulance...

Was I being unreasonable?

Crumbs of nail polish littered my bed sheets as hours went by. Before I knew it, the sun was already rising again, filtering through the fibers of my black curtains. I took one last look at my phone, its edges blurred by the tears in my eyes.

Quiet, soft dragging down the hall indicated my sister had woken up to get ready. If only those footsteps were a little heavier—a little lazier—then I'd know Sterling was safe at home. I wanted Astoria to skip her college classes today and come with me to the hospital, but I couldn't bring myself to ask her. Besides, if I were to find out any bad news, I wasn't sure if I would be ready to share it with her anyway. She needed to focus on her studies. I was twenty-three without a degree, and now without a job. Both of us couldn't be failures.

I let my body fall listlessly on my pillows and stared at the ceiling. As I attempted to will myself to sleep, all I could think of was that fire, the body on the stretcher, and my brother's GPS tracker leaving with the ambulance. No phone call meant he could be alive though, right?

No news is good news, as someone in some book said somewhere.

"Going to class! Don't be stupid, love you!" Astoria shouted from downstairs, her words followed by the loud creak and heavy thud of the front door. I peered out my window to watch her stroll down the driveway to get in her car and drive off with an audiobook blaring. I never understood how she could drive to a book rather than music... it always put me to sleep whenever I rode with her.

As soon as her car crossed into the street, I leaped out of bed. My body felt anchored to the floor, but my magnetic desire to find out about Sterling was strong enough to pull me to my motorcycle and speed deep into Neoterra.

# 5
# DRAVEN

Caspian and I ran from the scene just as the house was surrounded by firefighters and cops. I was racked by coughing for a few seconds before my inflamed throat returned to its normal state.

My steps faltered when my eyes flashed to a small-framed person in a cat-ear motorcycle helmet crouched behind a fence in the neighbor's yard. It looked like the body of a woman, and as Caspian and I flashed past, I could've sworn I caught the scent of a Sun Dweller. Regardless, I knew I had to remember that scent.

We waited on Hartley a block away from Pelican's Crossing near an old grocery store that had shut down. The parking lot was unkempt, cement splayed with weeds growing through the cracks to reclaim the grounds.

I chewed on my bottom lip as I stared out the limo's window. I didn't realize how narrowed my brows were until Caspian spoke.

"What's the matter?" he asked, for once not on his phone. "You should be relieved of yet another clean getaway."

"No, I just... well, I don't think it was as clean as ya think." I faltered.

"Why is that?" Caspian questioned.

"I saw somebody watching us." I leaned forward in my seat, suddenly feeling nauseous from the limo hugging the rocky road. "A girl."

"A girl? Okay, and? She wouldn't be the first you smoked." Caspian shrugged coolly.

"She smelled human." Every word that came out of my mouth felt like jabs in the gut.

"At this time of night? You're kidding. They stopped breaking that law a long time ago." He laughed a little, but his face fell slack when my expression was unchanged.

"You're not joking," he mumbled.

"No. But... we ain't gotta tell Uriah," I said, sliding my clammy palms over my pants.

"Why not?" Caspian asked, raising an eyebrow and folding his arms.

"It'll be better if we take care of this quietly instead of dealing with his, uh, *disappointment*." I ran a hand through my hair with a sigh, then slumped in the seat, the leather squeaking. Caspian's phone just sat in his lap with a black screen, his eyes glued to the polished leather loafers he wore.

Now would've been a good time for not only a smoke, but a drink too. . Caspian looked like he also needed a drink after I gave him the news.

I would've told Hartley to take us to a bar, but they were all about to close for the night.

※

Red plastic cups littered the gardens and pool area. Wrung towels were sprawled all over Uriah's mansion, probably from drunken fools attempting to clean spills. Uriah's servants were scattered across the estate cleaning after the party. Even though Caspian and I spent most of the night committing arson, I was glad to have missed the pressured "mingling" and body-guarding I always had to do during events.

There was one thing that bothered me, though. It was enough to take away my admiration from the burning sunrise, enough that I wanted to vomit. That charred body... was it Arlo, a firefighter, or a cop? That Sun Dweller... why was she out there? If she lived in the neighborhood, why would she risk being close to so many Vampyres and cops, where she could've been either attacked or arrested? She could've watched through a window.

If Arlo was dead, that meant the entire plan was for nothing. The money would go to the state since he didn't have any next of kin. I should've knocked him out, maybe tried harder to get him out of the house. If I didn't get so *angry*...

If it was a cop, there would be a heavy investigation that could bring the Nightshades into the light. If it was a firefighter, well, it would be the same result.

Either way, I was certain Uriah was back in his study, waiting for a report from Caspian and me with a bottle of scotch from last night.

Caspian and I took slow steps up the staircase. We were both stalling. I kept trying to think of ways to discuss what happened without involving the Sun Dweller or the fact that I left Arlo to his own devices.

When we reached the lion statues that guarded his door, we exchanged glances.

"You go first," I mouthed silently. Caspian shook his head and elbowed my arm.

"No, *you*," he whispered. I frowned and pushed his shoulder.

"You boys going to keep standing there or are you going to come in with an update?" Uriah's voice drawled from the other side. Of course, he caught our scents, and we were just fooling around like a couple of idiots.

I shut my eyes tightly and took a deep breath before stepping inside. Caspian followed behind me and stayed near the door when I approached Uriah's desk.

Just as I predicted, he had a bottle half full of scotch opened and his breath was coated with it.

"We did it," I said curtly. I looked to the side of the room, at the window that filtered out the sunlight. I squinted. The light stung, but the curtains prevented the sun from affecting our skin.

"That's it?" Uriah ran his metal fingertip around the rim of his glass, his cheeks flushed.

"We burned the house down. Arlo was, um... *drunk*, I mean... I don't know what kinda info ya lookin' for. It was pretty cut and dry." I raised my hands, shrugged my shoulders, and let them flop back at my sides. Uriah chuckled softly.

"That's good. Where is he now?"

"Well..." I glanced back at Caspian, hoping he'd step forward and take over. He was always able to deliver the bad news better than me. Somehow, we could say the same exact sentence and he wouldn't trigger Uriah's rage like I would. Caspian cupped his hand behind his neck and stepped forward.

"Well?" Uriah's eyes drooped sleepily, as if he was already bored with the conversation. He tilted the glass around its bottom, testing the balance with his fingertips and watching the liquor within to see if he could keep it from spilling.

"We don't know. He was in the house. Authorities were on the scene quickly, so we didn't have time to stay and see if he survived the fire. Draven and I were going to visit the hospital to see if it was him they took." Caspian held his hands behind his straightened back as he gave the information. A good ol' soldier.

"You... *don't know?*" Uriah chuckled again. I folded my arms and looked down at my shoes, waiting for the other shoe to drop. "How fast could they have possibly arrived if you guys didn't have the time to *force* him out of his house?"

"I think it would've been suspicious for the insurance company if the house was completely empty anyway." I lifted my gaze. "If the house catches on fire with no one inside, don't ya think they'd suspect arson quicker, especially if there ain't any evidence of gas leaks?"

I watched Uriah's metal fist clench, each joint groaning as he tightened his grip. He shut his eyes tightly, but his frown loosened once he took a sip of scotch. He pinched the bridge of his nose and opened his eyes.

"Caspian... Draven... is there anything else you want to tell me?" he grumbled.

We exchanged more glances. Caspian's lips were pressed in a tight line as he turned back to Uriah.

"No, sir. That was all that happened," he said, then headed for the door.

"You're lying, Caspian," Uriah intoned, stopping him midway through turning the handle. He smiled maliciously. "What did Draven do?"

I looked back at Caspian over my shoulder and for once, his face wasn't slack or hardened to stone. Instead, the stone appeared to have tiny cracks around his subtly squinted eyes. I gave him a nod and turned back to Uriah, sucking in a breath and holding my head high as I took my hands out of my pockets.

"I left him there. Arlo was drunk, refused my help to get him out, and threatened to shoot me. I left him. It's my fault we don't know who was on that stretcher."

Uriah nodded and rubbed his fleshed hand over his face. He stood and grabbed the bottle of scotch by its neck. He tested its weight and hurled it at my head. I shut my eyes tightly and let the glass slice my skin. I could dodge it but doing that in the past had ironically landed me with more injuries.

Before I could open my eyes, Uriah's metallic hand was clamping over my neck, and I was slammed onto my back on the floor. My breaths were strained into wheezes as the air forced its way out of my chest.

"Caspian, go get the whip," Uriah said breathlessly, and then he started to strike me repeatedly in my face.

"Sir, please—"

"*Now!* Unless you want to join him!" Uriah bellowed, and all I

could hear was the gust of wind left behind as Caspian rushed to follow his orders. My eyes were swollen, but every time they started to
open back up, I was met with more metal crunching against bone.
Pain... pain I knew all too well but could never get used to, even with
the rapid healing.

"Uriah—" My voice was a gurgling, mumbling mess.

"What? What was that?" Uriah snatched me up by the collar
and slammed me into the floor again.

"I'm sorry," I forced between gasps for air.

A rush of cold air again. Caspian returned with the whip in his
hand and gave it to Uriah. I turned weakly onto my stomach. As the
swelling in my eyes shrunk back, and the burning, crawling pain of
my bones fusing back together in my face abated, Caspian looked
down at me with an agonized grimace. He turned away and reached
for door handle again, but Uriah stopped him.

"No, you don't get to leave. I want you to remember this next
time you decide to try to hide any information for his sake." Uriah
gripped the whip tightly in his metal hand. Glass from his shattered
scotch bottle crunched under his boots and repeatedly cut through
my clothes as I tried to crawl away. I hissed at the first strike on my
back as it ripped through my jacket and lashed my skin. I bit my lip,
my fangs stabbing deeply as I held back my scream. For every wail
would come an additional ten lashes...

"You! For-got! That we! Have! Con-se-quen-ces! A-round
here!" For every word and syllable, he struck me, and my nails sharpened to claws and dug deep scratches into the wood floor. The whip
wrapped around my face, struck my neck, ears, head, back, over and
over and over and—

I looked to Caspian, pleading with my eyes for him to do something, *anything*, to get Uriah to stop, but I knew he couldn't. None of us could. Uriah was the Alpha of the Nightshades, and anyone who dared to challenge him met their maker.

I lost count of the strikes. Smears of blood smudged against the oak floor. I flinched at the sound of the whip dropping on the floor and clenched my eyes, preparing for more.

"Fix this Arlo situation and make sure he's not dead." Uriah spoke breathlessly, but more calmly, as if my pain was enough to douse the fiery rage within him. "You two owe me a new bottle of scotch. And clean this mess up before my floors are completely ruined."

I gave him a weak nod and watched him push past Caspian to leave the study. I twitched as the cold air stung my open wounds, which began slowly stitching themselves back together one by one.

※

By the time I left Uriah's office, Caspian was nowhere to be found. It was silently agreed that neither of us wanted to address what happened earlier. It was normal for everyone to disappear during the day, though. We never slept, so we were always cursed with the task of passing time. After what happened, I just wanted to curl in my bed and hide. I felt like my fourteen-year-old self again, crying for my mom after nightmares and instead waking up in the basement, getting whipped by Uriah for it.

*I'm not weak*, I reminded myself as I walked around the manor with shame. Caspian was the only one that watched, but everyone that resided in the King Estate had good enough hearing to recognize the rhythmic sounds of the whip cracking against flesh. Since

I was always the problem child, I was certain everyone always assumed it was me getting flogged.

I peeked around the corner into the kitchen. When I saw it was empty, I went inside and opened the fridge. It glowed rubellite as the light reflected off the bags of blood stacked on each other. I stared at red liquid and numbly grabbed a bag. I'd gone a week without eating, which was generally the limit for me before I'd get unbearably ravenous, develop dulled fangs, and the same leathery skin Arlo suffered near the train tracks. We heal, but at a much slower rate without blood for long periods, and we eventually decay like rotting corpses. My back still burned, and I would've healed completely by now had I decided to go on a fast another time.

I couldn't count how many times I'd considered starving myself to death, but if Uriah ever found out, he'd get four men to hold me down and force-feed blood to me until I healed. Might as well just keep taking care of myself at the bare minimum.

I wish I could remember what it was like to only survive off junk food, meat, and vegetables. To have so many available options. Where a juice box had actual juice, and it wasn't a blood donation bag.

The bag wobbled in my palm, cool and soft like gel. I stared at it, then slowly twisted the cap. The seal cracked, and my nose was instantly greeted with a sweet aroma. My mouth watered before I brought the bag to my lips and drained it in seconds.

"Finally eating again?" My skin snatched from my bones as I whirled around to see who'd snuck behind me in the kitchen. Delilah Maison leaned against the archway with her arms folded and one ankle crossed over the other. Her skin was like the flawless night sky, a rich umber full of depth. Her long, microlocs were pulled back into a larger, singular braid. Her full, bright red lips stretched into an alluring smile, revealing strong, bright, healthy fangs, but then it shrunk as her eyes scaled me from head to toe and saw the tattered clothing.

"Yeah, I guess I felt like breaking my fast." I relaxed my shoulders and tossed the bag in the biohazard trash can. Delilah pushed herself from the archway. She stopped inches from me, brushing her hands against my shoulders as if wiping off lint. It felt forced, like she had to try too hard to ignore my appearance. It was a fat elephant in the room, my whipping. I knew she heard it. She *had* to. I looked at a random cabinet just to avoid her concerned gaze.

"I heard about what happened last night." Her voice dropped to a whisper. She pushed some of my black hair to the side, gingerly hooking it behind my ear. She tapped my chin. "I'm sorry you have to keep being bothered by it."

"Yeah, well, Arlo's always been a thorn in my side." I cleared my throat. "How was the party last night?"

I was tired of poking and circling the subject. She looked at me with soft eyes, raising her eyebrows slightly as if she held a tinge of pity. Rather than argue, she played into my attempt to change the subject.

"It was fine, I guess. We got a few new fledglings and celebrated their official graduation from initiation. I spent the entire night listening to rumors about some sort of experiments going on at White Fang." Her eyes swept over the rips in my clothing.

"What sort of rumors?"

Delilah merely shrugged and traced her fingertips along the collarbone that poked just above my t-shirt collar, over my chest, down my waist—

I grabbed her wrists gently with a ragged exhale.

"I miss spendin' time with ya, but... I got a lot to do today," I said softly. "Uriah ain't gonna make any exceptions." I caressed her silky skin gently, then leaned down to kiss her forehead. I walked through the archway to exit the kitchen and crossed the foyer, then headed upstairs to my room to mentally reset. I could've sworn—if my ears didn't deceive me—that Delilah sighed with disappointment when I walked away. If I'd bothered to look over my shoulder, maybe I would've seen her face.

✳

I remember when I was around fourteen years old, and the curfews were much more heavily enforced with 'round-the-clock police patrols, Uriah would declare "ownership" of about five Sun Dwellers that were either homeless, felons, or otherwise at some disadvantage in society to be a part of the Nightshade clan. He called it the "Mandrake Assistance Program." Their sole purpose was to provide blood if we ran out of donation bags and run errands during the day so we wouldn't have to worry about skirting cops or burning in the sun. After those humans died from "wear and tear"—as Uriah liked to put it—we bore the burden of handling everything ourselves, day or night.

Today was the first day I even thought about those men and women, wishing I could've delegated this assignment to them instead.

I stared at myself in the smudged mirror in my bathroom, thinking about how I'd dress myself to blend in with the Sun Dwellers, avoid the burn, hide from the cops, and manage to get this thing done. Uriah was too impatient for us to go at night.

I reached into my drawer full of razors, shaving cream, and cologne, and removed a contact lens case, then slipped on a pair of dark brown lenses. I took another look in the mirror with a heavy sigh. The man I saw now was who I would've been if my parents had never died in a car crash and Uriah had never taken me in and turned me.

After I showered the blood off my healed skin, I rummaged through a pile of clean clothes until I found a black hoodie and a worn pair of jeans. I threw the large hood over my head, allowing it to cast a shadow over my face, then left the comfort of my room to wait in the foyer for Caspian.

I chewed on a toothpick nonchalantly, aimlessly searching for distractions. I scrolled through social media on my phone as I sat on a bench near the front doors with one hand in my pocket.

"Are you ready to go?" Caspian's voice sounded above me. I looked up from my phone and straight at his shoes, polished leather Oxfords that contrasted with my dirty black-and-white Converse. How he found the time to keep his life together while also being a Nightshade member was beyond me. He wore a black suit with a white undershirt and sunglasses with a black ascot hat that provided little shade over his eyes and ears.

"How do you expect to blend in like that?" I jerked my chin at him.

"How do you expect people to assume you're not a thug dressed like *that*?" Caspian shot back. He adjusted his hat and walked outside. The tips of his ears instantly began to redden as he stepped away from the protection of the awning. I stood with a grunt and walked out the door behind him. I could feel the heat seep through my sleeves, the prickling burn on the tip of my nose, and the instant craving for blood as my strength already began to decline. Hartley waited outside a large black SUV this time, standing under an umbrella that provided a protective circle of darkness around him. He wore sunglasses as well, his dark brown mustache curled to flawless points like an animated character.

"Not the limo today, Hart?" I asked as I rushed into the backseat. Caspian and I always had a silent agreement that he'd get shotgun. I never liked sitting in the front anywhere.

"You know just as much as I do that this is low profile, Draven." Hartley waited until we were both inside before getting into the car and starting it up.

Caspian's red ears instantly faded back to alabaster. Hartley turned on jazz music, as if it were a cure for the growing anxiety between us. Maybe it was for him, but all I could think about was how this toothpick wasn't cutting it, and I still needed more cigarettes.

# 6

# BRIAR

I could still smell burning flesh in my nostrils. My mind was plagued with thoughts of the body on the stretcher, Sterling's GPS tracker, and the two men running away from the scene.

The traffic was thick with people heading to work. I slammed my brakes. My fat front tire nearly tapped the rear bumper of the car in front of me. I took a shaky breath and flipped my helmet visor up to allow some air in. I closed my eyes briefly, savoring the briny humid air against my sweat. It was a hot summer for sure, but it was nothing compared to the sauna in my helmet. I probably should've considered saving up for a car instead of a motorcycle.

I flicked my visor down and started to drive along the yellow dashed line between cars. Some of them honked their horns at me, but I flipped them the bird and kept it moving—until I saw a nearby patrol car and skirted back into a lane. I was able to pass twenty cars, so I figured it was worth the risk.

The hospital was just outside of the road work zone. I parked in the visitor's lot and took off my helmet, shaking my hair. I patted my pockets to make sure I didn't have any pepper spray or knives on me before I entered. I went through security, who confiscated my phone like everyone else's, then went straight to the front desk.

A woman in burgundy scrubs chewed gum nonchalantly and peered at me over her cherry red-framed glasses.

"How can I help you?" She spoke in monotone, as if she was already tired of repeating the same question. Rather than letting it brush me the wrong way, I assumed she was at the tail end of a night shift.

"I'm here to see if my brother was checked in last night. A possible burn victim—"

"Name and date of birth," she droned as she set her hands on the keyboard. I clenched my jaw with a wry smile.

"Sterling Shaw, born November 20, 2090." I flattened my tone to mock her subtly. I almost hoped she'd notice. She merely scrutinized me over those gaudy glasses.

"He's not a patient here."

"Well, he's a police officer, so is there any way—"

"I can't give out that information. Why don't you just text him since you two seem so close?" The phone trilled and she snatched it, swiveling her back to me as she answered. I scoffed and scanned the lobby. To my right, a couple of nurses holding clipboards were gossiping. To my left, an elderly man in a wheelchair hooked to an oxygen line was signing papers. Directly in front of me? A stack of visitor passes.

I occasionally glanced over my shoulder as I walked along the endless corridors. Doctors, nurses, and techs were all busy in their own worlds. I followed the signs until I reached the trauma wing, then stopped at a set of closed double doors with warning signs all over them. It was appointment only, with instructions on sanitation and getting in contact with the unit's nurse and other rules. Even though the receptionist said Sterling wasn't checked in, I convinced myself that she only did half of her job and told me whatever yielded the least work on her end.

I didn't read the rest of the signs and pushed through the doors with a grunt. The burn unit was open, with each bed divided by curtains. Some had the curtains wrapped around the beds while others were open, showing patients covered in gauze. I didn't recognize Sterling as any of the exposed patients, so I moved forward to check behind the curtains.

"Hey!" A gruff male voice barked just as I was reaching to pull one of the curtains. I whipped my head in the direction of a human nurse with buzzed hair and sky-blue scrubs stalking toward me.

"Who are you? I wasn't notified of any visitors here." He scowled as he jabbed his finger at me.

"I'm just here for my b—"

"I don't care, this area needs to remain sterile! We have procedures for this! Get out and properly check in or I'm calling security!" he chided.

"Alright! Jeez, alright!" I quickly held up my hands and started to back away toward the doors. I tore the paper name tag off my shirt and tossed it in a small trash can near the door. "I'm gone," I seethed. I reentered the corridor, the nurse exasperating just before the doors slammed shut.

I started my way back to the lobby. I'd get my phone back from security and hopefully, if his phone was still on, I could check to see if Sterling was finally back at home, the precinct, or to my horror—a morgue. I kept my eyes low until I rammed my shoulder into something solid, followed by a grunt.

I looked up at the man I'd run into, and what little color I had in my face to start with completely sopped out. He towered over me by a foot and a half. His gilded face hung ominously underneath that black hood, the details of his tattoos around his neck barely visible beyond the dim shadows. He smelled of cigarettes and vanilla, and his eyes were like two coals waiting to ignite and burn my soul. For a brief second, we locked gazes, and his nostrils flared. I quickly averted my eyes and walked faster. The skin around my neck seemed to tighten. I felt like he continued to watch me, but I never bothered to look back to find out.

# 7

# DRAVEN

When Caspian and I arrived at the hospital, I passed security with ease. However, the guard's eyes lingered over Caspian's scarlet ears as he walked through the metal detector.

"Excuse me, sir." The guard put his hand on Caspian's chest and nudged him back in line. Caspian looked down at the guard's hand. The ball of his jaw feathered subtly.

"I'm going to need your sunglasses off." The guard put his hands on his hips, and I kept an eye on the hand near his gun. My shoulders tensed as I tried to deny the possibility the man would open fire in the middle of a hospital lobby. Caspian removed his sunglasses and gave the man a piercing glare. The guard folded his arms slowly with a grunt after seeing that Caspian's eyes were as brown as mine.

"I need to see some ID."

"You're holding up the line," Caspian muttered, but I knew it was only to conceal the tornado threatening to form within him.

"Better get it out fast then, boy," the guard hissed. Caspian reached in his inner suit coat for his wallet and pulled out a fake ID, which all Nightshades owned. Neoterra's identification cards always had the holder's species listed underneath the birth and expiration dates. With the help of some of the Vampyric police Uriah kept in his pocket, they simply replaced "Vampyre" with "Human." We were all issued fake IDs for daylight business.

The guard examined Caspian's ID for what felt like three minutes. He turned it in his palm carefully, held it in the light, and even pulled another security guard aside to look at it. The second guard pulled out a detector gun and scanned the back of the card just for the screen to turn green. He shrugged and handed it back to the one that kept hassling Caspian.

"You're free to go. But don't think I don't know what you are, boy," the guard growled.

"You have no idea." Caspian gave the man a thin, malicious grin as he took his card back and tucked it away in his wallet, then back in his suit jacket. We finally moved on to the front desk, where Caspian took several slow deep breaths to tame his icy rage.

We got our visitor passes for Arlo through a lady with large, flamboyant red glasses and a bad attitude. He was in the burn unit in critical condition, but was otherwise stable. Our kind healed rapidly, but anything with fire or sunlight stunted the rate, so it was understandable that he'd have to spend a day or two in the hospital.

I was able to breathe once we were walking down the hall to meet him.

*At least he's alive,* I thought. There was a sour tang of guilt that tried to scratch its way through my chest. *It was just orders, nothing personal. I tried to help.*

*I tried to* help.

We followed the signs, taking several turns through the labyrinth of corridors. We were about to take a final turn when something knocked the air out of me. I looked down to see a girl with long pastel pink hair, a stud nose piercing and lip ring, and bright but frightened light grey eyes. Dark rings hung under her eyes. She held a matte-black motorcycle helmet with short cat ears under her arm. I squinted and sniffed subtly, catching a familiar cedar scent. She quickly looked away and continued rushing down the hall without so much as an apology. I just stared right after her, in disarray. Caspian clicked his tongue and shook his head.

"How rude," Caspian scoffed. "Typical human."

"Yeah…" I trailed off and followed him inside the burn unit, where a nurse stopped us at the double door's threshold. Behind him was an open bay of beds divided by curtains, some occupied and others empty.

"I need you two to wash your hands for twenty seconds and put these gloves, caps, and gowns on. Also cover your shoes." I groaned under my breath but didn't protest when he pointed at the section we needed to be in. "I know it's a lot, but we need to keep this place sterile."

"I guess," I grumbled. I scrubbed my hands, silently counting down the seconds. Once we were dressed in the required uniform, Caspian and I examined each other.

"We look like a couple of idiots," I grumbled. He smiled, laughing subtly and then turning his attention to the room to find Arlo.

I had lost interest in finding out his current condition... in fact, it was safe to say that he was alive and well. I wanted to follow that girl now, but I knew I'd have to go through the whole sanitation process again.

Caspian stopped five curtains down. I caught up with him, assuming he'd found Arlo. I curled my lip upwards in disgust. Arlo's skin was melted, mangled, and peeled. Some pieces of dead skin were still caked with soot. His tired red eyes widened, but I couldn't decide if it was with fear or anger.

"We're just here to check on ya," I said. "Woulda brought flowers, but the sign said ain't nothing allowed in here."

"Would a gun be hidin' in the stems?" Arlo retorted. "You two here to finish the job?"

"On the contrary, we're here to see how you're doing." Caspian smiled thinly, but it didn't meet his eyes.

"I'm doing peachy, now get out, North Side trash," Arlo hissed. I chuckled softly, glanced over my shoulder to see the nurse distracted with another patient, then inched closely to him.

"I hope ya know that burning ya house was to help ya get the money sooner, and you wouldn't be in here if ya weren't so stubborn. Uriah's next step ain't gonna be so merciful if ya fail this time and I ain't gonna bail you out," I whispered darkly, then backed away with a saccharine smile.

"Get well soon." Caspian turned away and headed for the door, removing the hair net, gown, and shoe covers. I gave Arlo one last dirty look. He bared his fangs.

＊

As we walked down the halls, Caspian called Uriah. I drowned out their conversation and homed in the strange scent of that girl with the pink hair. It trailed outside with us, and as we waited for Hartley at the patient pickup zone, I was deep in thought. I sniffed the air again, trying to pinpoint if she smelled like citrus, sandalwood, or roses.

"You know what? I think I'm going to hang around the city for a bit," I said as I shoved my hands in my pockets. I stood partially in the sunlight, partially under the portico. Caspian was completely in its shadow. His snow white eyebrows furrowed behind his sunglasses.

"What for? I'm sure whatever you want to do can be done tonight," he said.

"Nope, it can't. Don't wait up." I started walking along the sidewalk that wrapped around and sloped downward toward the street.

"Draven, come on!" Caspian called. I waved my arm dismissively without looking back.

I crossed the street to a gas station, purchased a pack of cigarettes—finally—and then whistled for a cab at the edge of the parking lot. My first order of business was to follow that girl's scent, find out where she lived, and well...

I kept my head low to shield myself from the sun when the cab pulled over. I slumped in the backseat and gave the driver vague instructions to follow the road. I cracked the window, allowing the wind to drift her scent through. It was strong, as if she was just a couple cars away. Being exposed on a motorcycle left her vulnerable to my senses, and I wondered how she'd survived sneaking out that night if that was her only form of transportation. Her blood seemed to blend in with the cedar and roses as if it was just as sweet as whatever soap she used. The only thing I could think of was that the acrid fire had probably masked everyone's senses at the crime scene. She was just awfully lucky.

"Rough night?" the driver asked, breaking the silence. I gritted my teeth and folded my arms, leaning against the window.

"Somethin' like that," I said stiffly. I wished he'd fill the silence with the radio instead of his grating, nasally voice.

"You just look like you're hungover, son."

"And you look like ya runnin' the meter drivin' ten under the speed limit." I tried to be mindful of opening my mouth, keeping my lips partially opened to keep my fangs concealed. I shouldn't have drunk that bag this morning... at least then they could've passed closer to a Sun Dweller's incisors.

"Tch." The driver sucked his teeth and fell silent, slightly speeding up. I peeked from under my hood out the window. We were long gone from the hospital and the heart of Neoterra.

The condensed apartments and town homes were gradually spreading out into neighborhoods, subdivisions, and soon, fields. The scent was still strong, and as the traffic thinned out, I saw a motorcycle speeding down the road up ahead.

"You can stop here." I sat up quickly.

"It's nothing but an open field—"

"I said *stop here*," I growled, and the driver jerked the cab onto the shoulder. I threw a wad of cash into his front seat through the plastic dividing window and got out. I reached into my hoodie's pocket for another toothpick and then started walking.

The fields stretched for miles. It might've been difficult to blend in after that blood bag earlier, but it sharpened my senses. I could see a yellow house roughly a mile and a half away, and the motorcycle that pulled into its driveway.

# 8

# BRIAR

I swerved into the driveway, kicking up gravel dust, and nearly let my motorcycle slam on its side when I saw Sterling's unmarked car parked next to Astoria's. I barreled through the front door and immediately screamed his name.

Astoria jumped from the couch, her book flying across the room.

"Briar, what the hell?!" she snapped as I stormed into the kitchen, filled a glass of water, then stomped upstairs. She ran behind me.

"Whoa, slow down! What's wrong?! You need to calm down!" I felt her tug at the hem of my shirt and I slapped her hand away. I was a raging bull chasing a red cape, determined to run down anything that stood in my way.

I burst into Sterling's room and threw the glass of water on him. He writhed wildly, tangled in his sheets.

"WHAT THE F—"

"You couldn't have taken *two seconds* to call or text either of us last night *or* this morning? Too busy trying to play hero, huh?" I paced back and forth at the foot of his bed, spatting a mile a minute. Sterling wiped the water from his eyes and glared at me.

"Excuse me? I don't have to tell you anything! It's official police business, Briar! That doesn't give you the right to come in here and wake me up after a long night shift, splashing water on me!" He flung the covers off the bed and jumped up.

I looked around the room, searching for something to either throw at him or break. I paused and took a shaky, deep breath.

"We live in a world of Vampyres, Sterling." I lowered my voice. "You of all people talk about how dangerous they are more than anyone."

I put my hands on my hips and took another deep breath to try to steady my voice. "You and Astoria are all I have. I get it, your job is intense, but—"

"How would you even know what's going on in the first place? What made last night different from any of the other late shifts I had?" he demanded. Astoria shrunk by the door.

"I saw you on the news. That fire was something serious and I know you're always trying to be someone's savior." I took a step back as he crept closer. The truth was right at the tip of my tongue, so I pursed my lips in a thin line to keep it from escaping.

"Really? You dump water on me for not answering a text—because of the news?" He folded his arms. The clouds moved away from the sun and the light exposed his freckles and leaked into his angry, honey eyes.

"I thought you were dead." I dropped my voice lower when I felt my throat quiver.

"Well, here I am." He knocked his shoulder against mine as he pushed past me to go to his bathroom. He grabbed a towel and started to wipe his face before narrowing his eyes. Tiny pearls of water still dripped from his mess of autumn curls. Small hairs started to curl back from his forehead.

"I'm sorry, next time I'll just not worry about anything," I grumbled, storming out of his bedroom. I went across the hall to mine, slamming the door in Astoria's face when she tried to follow me.

I lay across the bed with my back toward the door and stared out the window. I gazed at the open fields and the tiny pricks of distant, hazy skyscrapers. The door creaked open, and I turned my head expecting to see my meek sister poking her nose in my room, but it was Sterling instead. His eyes were sunken—probably exhausted from last night's events. I woke him up out of a deep sleep, yet I didn't want to apologize for it.

"I know you're always worried, but... I can't have my phone attached to me at all times," he said, sitting at the edge of my bed.

I kept looking out the window, debating on whether I should answer.

"Shouldn't it be, though? You'd need it for backup." I scrunched my face.

"It's not that easy." Sterling chuckled lowly, shaking his head. "Besides, we use radios to communicate."

"Well, it should be easy enough to send a 'hi' or something quick like that just so I know you're alive and able to use your hands." I rolled my eyes and shook my head. I was beating a dead horse. "I don't even know why you took this night shift anyway."

"Well, that's where the best cases are, and it pays a lot more."

"Yeah, that money sure would be useful if you died," I grumbled. "What do you think, you'll be able to go to the grim reaper's shopping mall?"

I briefly glanced out the window and saw someone walking along the road in all black, but they were too far away for me to see who it was. I had a fleeting moment of curiosity. No one ever walked out here.

Sterling nudged me with his elbow, snapping my attention away from the sauntering figure.

"I'm sorry." Sterling looked dead into my eyes, his jaw subtly twitching. "I'll do better, okay?"

I swung my feet back and forth at the edge of the bed, keeping my eyes glued to the rug below. I gave a short nod. I was still mad at him, but I appreciated the apology that I so rarely received.

"We good?" He tilted his head and lightly flicked me in the shoulder.

"Sure," I said quietly, fidgeting with my nail polish. He paused for a second, then stood.

"I'm gonna go back to sleep... we're all gonna have dinner a little early tonight because I have work."

"Right," I said through tight teeth. "I guess you're officially a night-shifter now, huh?"

He gave a slight nod. Despite the cold shoulder I gave him, he still gave the courtesy of closing my door.

※

When the sky turned blood orange and fuchsia, the same officer from the last Check-In pulled into the driveway, the gravel crunching slowly beneath his tires. Astoria was already on the porch with her identification. Sterling was in the kitchen prepping the "early dinner," which realistically was probably just frozen lasagna or Salisbury steak thrown in the oven.

I sat at the windowsill in my room a couple moments longer. I wanted to test how long it would take for that weasel to cross the line and try to push his way inside. I stood when I saw him hold three fingers and wave them aggressively at Astoria, then point at the front door behind her.

"Sterling!" I shouted as I rounded the railing at the bottom of the staircase. Astoria flinched when I swung the front door open, and I placed a soft hand on her shoulder.

"You're late again. Is this going to be a problem?" He hooked his hand over his belt. I glanced at the handcuffs and gun that hung from it, then back at him.

"Late? I was already here." My eyebrows knit.

"You need to be on this porch ready with your ID before I get here," he chastised.

"You like bullying young girls to feel powerful, little man?" I sneered. He took a threatening step forward just as Sterling came outside with his badge and put an arm between us.

"Whoa, back up, Officer!" he snapped. He stumbled one step off the porch.

"Apologies, Detective—"

"What's your name?" Sterling demanded as he jerked his chin

upward and puffed his chest.

"O-Officer Kent." The man shrunk back until he was standing in the gravel.

"I heard you gave my sisters problems when I wasn't here. You get reassigned to another district for Check-Ins and never come back here, or I'll have your badge."

With every word, Sterling took a step closer until they were inches away from each other. I couldn't hide the smug grin on my face while Astoria fidgeted with her thin gold necklace. Officer Kent nodded quickly as he logged our names. His retreating car kicked up a cloud of dust, rocks spitting into the grass from beneath the tires.

"Thanks," I said flatly. I had forced my smile away. I didn't want Sterling to think we were totally okay, because I was still mad at him.

"There's nothing I hate more than cops like him," Sterling grumbled, then went straight to the kitchen. I helped Astoria set the small square table that rested under the dim, yellow chandelier. Every time we sat under it to eat as a family, I'd look at the cloudy crystals and tell myself to clean it, only to forget moments after.

Sterling set the food and three serving spoons at the center so we could all serve ourselves at once. I ate a little, then pushed my food around the plate.

"Are you going to switch to night shifts completely?" Astoria asked. Her light voice somehow managed to make the air heavier. I froze with my fork in hand. Sterling eyed me warily.

"I might. Things have been taking a turn for the worse in the Nocturne District," he said. "There's a couple cases I promised I'd help with."

I sucked my teeth, chuckling wryly and returning to my food.

"What? You got something to say, Briar?"

Sterling frowned. His fork clanked against his plate as he dropped it. I shrugged and shook my head, leaning my cheek into my palm. Astoria's head swiveled between us.

"I said what I wanted to say already. Now, I'm bored."

"Guys, please. We really shouldn't fight..." Her voice was quiet, but I could hear the trembling.

"I'm curious." I twirled my fork in the sauce, "If Vampyres are as dangerous as you say, how do you even manage to come home in one piece?" I watched him with an unwavering gaze of ice. I refused to crack first.

Sterling scoffed and broke our stare-down to look at his watch, then stood up, the chair screeching loudly against the wooden floor. He sighed, giving his lips a final wipe with a napkin.

"I'm heading to work. Stay out of trouble." He walked off with wide, irritable strides. The statement was for both of us still at the table, but the message was addressed to me.

I got up to watch him leave. He carried his mask in hand as he headed to his car. Bile crawled up my throat.

I clenched my fists as he drove away.

"Briar... you really shouldn't fight with him so much. This is his career, and we never know when seeing him could be our last." Apparently, Astoria had followed me. Her steps were always so quiet, so feline.

"Don't you think I know that?" I snapped. "Why do you think I keep trying to convince him to switch to something else, or at least just stick with the day shift?"

"Yeah, but still... at the end of the day, he's a grown man with his own choices. Life is too short."

"That's fine. I got choices too." I shrugged. I went back in the kitchen, Astoria still hot on my tail.

"What's *that* supposed to mean?" She frowned.

"Nothing, Ria." I started to clean the dishes while Astoria cleaned the table. She fell silent. She didn't push me, so I knew she was deep in thought.

I was too wrapped up worrying about Sterling safety last night to fully enjoy the city lights. I'd seen a brief moment of beauty, but I wanted to experience it without the threat of my brother being burned to ash hovering over me. There were plenty of Vampyres walking the streets that could've stopped me in my tracks last night, yet they minded their own business just as my people would. After all, the whole reason I had a motorcycle was because a human had carjacked me three years ago.

I decided I was going to go to Neoterra again that night. Everyone claimed they were dangerous, but after last night—I needed to see it for myself.

# 9
# DRAVEN

THE WALK DOWN THE WINDING COUNTRY ROAD WAS ENDLESS but soothing. I texted Caspian that I'd be gone for the rest of the day. I stayed in the shade of an oak tree in a field near the yellow house. I leaned against the tree trunk, smiling contentedly as I watched the sunset slowly arrive. What was once blistering heat at high noon was cooling down to a nice, neutral temperature. I reached in my pocket for my lighter and peeled the plastic off a fresh pack of cigarettes.

I took a long draw and savored the minty burn in my throat, observing the leaves and branches winding into each other. A gentle wind passed through the leaves, creating a soft tremor. I closed my eyes and inhaled deeply, then exhaled a long column of smoke. This was the most peace I'd had in a very, very long time, and if I were human, I would've definitely fallen asleep.

I never experienced the outskirts of Neoterra like this. My heart ached as I wished I'd had the chance to experience it as a kid. I lowered my hood and enjoyed the burn of the sun, pretending for just a moment that I was human again for the sake of the sky's fickle beauty.

But I had more important things to do.

The slow and steady pace of the country was lulled to sleep by the birds' evensong. The blinding light of day became crystal clear night. The previously grey windows against yellow siding now glowed amber.

A police car arrived, and the officer harassed one with long black hair to the verge of tears. Then another girl—the one with the pale pink hair from the hospital—came out and stood in front of her protectively. Sisters, perhaps. Cops always harassed us Vampyres any chance they got. It was fascinating to see they did it to their own species too.

The girl foolishly spewed an insult at the officer, and he reached for his belt. I leaned forward slightly to see if he'd shoot, although I doubted it given that they were the same species.

My ears twitched when a tall man finally came out of the house and flashed a gold badge in the officer's face. It glinted against the setting sun.

"Whoa, back up, Officer!"

"Apologies, Detective—"

*Detective.* I forced a swallow. The girl who'd witnessed us at the crime scene was either dating, married, or related to a cop. I smothered the cigarette and replaced it with a toothpick, then jumped onto a sturdy tree branch to surround myself with leaves.

Could this situation get any worse?

The cop—Officer Kent—left in a hurry after the detective threatened to get him fired. There was loud, sharp muffling through the house shortly after—possibly more arguments. Roughly thirty minutes later, the detective got in his car and rolled out of the driveway, heading north toward the metropolitan area of Neoterra.

I dropped out of the tree and put my hood back on. I crept toward the house slowly. The closer I got, the more I regretted keeping Caspian out of the loop. He could've kept watch of the younger girl while I handled the other one. Now, I had to make sure they weren't near each other.

What a *mess.*

I couldn't just kill her, though. There had to be some sort of fatal accident; otherwise, if word got out a Vampyre had killed someone dear to a detective, war would be unleashed on not only the Nocturne District, but all Vampyres.

I jumped halfway across the field and landed with a quiet thud on the house's roof. The more I mulled it over, the more delicate I realized this situation was. I'd tell Caspian since he was inherently smarter than me, but I didn't want Uriah to know this was an issue in the first place. Lying had never been his strong suit.

I quietly walked down the roof, then stopped at the edge. Music started blasting right beneath me and a yellow-orange glow poured over the balcony below. I never knew how Caspian did it, but he always landed with a cat's grace. Now would be the time I learned how to, especially considering the window was still open and the music wasn't quite loud enough to mask my landing. Thirteen years of being a Vampyre and I still hit the ground like a fledgling. I looked down at my dusty black sneakers and loosed a sigh.

I crouched and gripped the edge of the gutters before letting my body dangle. In a reverse pull-up, I lowered myself to the balcony just to the left of the window frame. It was a quiet thud, if not only because I was tall enough to hang a foot off the ground.

The music volume magnified.

I kept my back against the wall and peeked over my shoulder into the room. The girl's bathroom door was open, steam wafting into the bedroom. She was wrapped in a pale blue towel, her hair twisted into another bleach-stained towel. A toothbrush hung out of her mouth as she stopped to check her phone. Her hips swayed subtly with the rhythm of the music. She had a thigh tattoo of vines and flowers that poked from underneath the terrycloth. My eyes wandered, but I snapped my head forward. I took a deep breath, staring at the empty road for a couple moments before looking back into her room. In those short seconds, she had already dressed in a baggy band t-shirt tucked into black ripped jeans, boots, and a cropped leather jacket. I blinked and my shoulders tensed.

I had been under the impression that she was getting ready for bed, but upon further inspection of her outfit, and her dancing as she padded her cheeks with makeup—I instantly knew she was preparing for an illegal outing.

I was so entrenched in watching her sway, shimmy, and occasionally bob her head to the music that I didn't realize that I, too, was nodding my head to the beat. Her playlist consisted of several forms of rock—metal, hard, soft, classical, grunge, and indie. Most of which I recognized, songs I could've sung with ease back when I was into music.

The gritty songs that rattled my bones and made me itch to

dance were the same ones that moved her to pick up a hairbrush and sing into it and bang her head, her hair flying in every direction. She ran and jumped toward her bed, near the window. I flinched, but my shoulders fell again as she started to play air guitar. I smiled softly to myself. To have just had to deal with Officer Kent and a possible argument with her family earlier, she sure seemed to be having the time of her life. It was a raw joy I hadn't seen in a long time. I was curious to see if she really had the nerve to sneak out and was confused as to *why* she would even want to be around my kind at all. Her clothes certainly didn't look like a work uniform.

Once the song ended with a fading guitar chord, she jumped off the bed, combed her fingers through her hair, grabbed a small, black book bag and her helmet. She turned to look at the window.

I turned to stone.

# 10
# BRIAR

I kept the music going. I let it flow through my bones, serve as an anchor holding me down in the present, fuel to keep me going. I stared at the window, where my reflection filled the black space beyond the glass. My fingertips went numb, my palms clammy. This was different from venturing out for my brother's sake. This was rebellion.

I gripped the straps of my book bag tightly. I kept the music on, even though it drove Astoria crazy, because it would at least make it easier for me to sneak away. I took a step closer to the window. I could do this.

*What would I even do?*

No, I'd figure it out once I was there.

*I could do this.*

Fear rippled across my face by the time I was inches from my window sill.

*I survived it once; I can do it again.*

I pursed my lips tightly and released a thick exhale through my nose. I shoved my window open and heard a scraping noise above. I frowned and poked my head through the open space. I didn't see anything on the balcony, and when I looked up, small pebbles fell near my face. A squirrel scurrying across the roof, perhaps. I paused for a moment and took one last deep breath before I raised one leg over the sill, then the other. I drank the humid night air, taking in the earthy smell of damp grass. Fireflies flickered slowly across the yard and fields, mimicking the stars above.

Once I climbed over the balcony's white vinyl railing and slid down the column, I rushed to my motorcycle and rolled it out of the driveway just as I did before. I could still hear the music from the house. I waited to mount my motorcycle until I couldn't hear it anymore. Then, at that point, there was no turning back.

✳

I parked my motorcycle at a meter. It was shut off, with a schedule posted on it. I clicked my tongue and shook my head. Of course, humans would be the ones to have to pay quarters for an hour of parking, but the Vampyres had unlimited, free parking.

I crammed my hands in my cropped jacket's small pockets and walked down the street. Vampyres were going in and out of restaurants, bars, clubs, stores. Their activity matched the human activity during the day. Without the distraction of my brother's safety weighing on my shoulders, I was able to really soak in Neoterra's nightlife.

I grinned. I knew my scent had to be glaring among them, but they were so captivated with their own lives that I was insignificant to them.

The soles of my shoes scraped against the concrete as I came to an abrupt stop in front of a hair salon named Sundance. I snorted at the name. The large display window exposed its interior with the same aesthetic as a tattoo shop. There was a collage of paintings, drawings, and sketches along the black walls. The floors were polished cement, reflecting the large vanity light bulbs illuminating each station. There were men getting their hair cut and beards groomed, and women getting hair dyed, trimmed, styled. There were a couple of women toward the back with curlers sitting under hair dryers, giggling and looking at each other's nails. My eyes fell out of focus and I saw my reflection in the window. I grabbed a few strands. My hair had a lot of split ends, for sure.

Someone brushed past me with a deep inhale and a chuckle. I flinched with a gasp and scurried inside the salon without even looking to see who it was. In the moment, it seemed safer inside than on the street.

As the door swung open, a bell rang, and all the stylists paused to look at me. Red eyes of many shades stared into my very soul, many with pinpoint pupils. Pale faces, flared nostrils, tense bodies poised to pounce. My ears went muffled as sweat immediately formed around my neck and forehead. My chest tightened as the walls seemed to close in. In my mind, I took steps back to the door, but in reality, I didn't move at all.

"Welcome in." A tall, slender woman with flawless bronzed skin, diamond studded earrings, and a gold septum piercing greeted me with a sweet, fanged smile. Her teeth were stark white, almost artificial. Her hair was in braids gathered together to form a Mohawk. She extended her hand with an ethereal grace. She could've been a model, if it weren't for those piercing, menacing eyes.

*What am I doing?*

I finally stepped toward the counter. She looked down at me, her smile settling into a soft grin. I avoided her gaze, my eyes scanning the rest of the salon and the appointment sheet on the counter. I looked anywhere but her, just so that I could forget she was a Vampyre.

"What brings you in here?" she asked in a professional tone, but something told me it wasn't supposed to be a customer service question.

"I, um... I, uh." I spotted a list of their services posted high on the far wall near the bathrooms. I squinted.

"I'm here to get a trim, maybe get a new hair color too. If you take walk-ins, anyway." I dared to give her another look before turning my focus back to the paper.

"We do, actually." She flipped through a binder. "Jocelyn can take you." She pointed toward a vanity near the hair washing station in the back.

"Thank you," I mumbled, and started walking back there. Midway through, I started to worry if the receptionist had heard me. Then I remembered they were all Vampyres, and the entire salon probably heard me.

Jocelyn was sweeping hair at her booth. She didn't look up. Her hair was tied back in a French braid with two chin-length strands framing a round, pale face. She wore bold winged eyeliner, vibrant blue eye shadow, bright scarlet lipstick, dimple piercings, and a lively black-and-yellow sunflower sundress with fishnet tights. She was almost half the height of the receptionist, but still beautiful like everyone else in Sundance.

"Hey, go ahead and sit down, I'll be right with ya!" she lilted, then disappeared in the back. I sank in the seat, savoring the cool touch of leather against my clammy palms. It brought me back to the present, gave me a sense of clarity. I started picking at my nail polish again, which was chipped so badly that it was basically non-existent.

I jerked my head up when a flash of black flew over my head. The protective cape floated down over my body as Jocelyn tightened the collar around my neck.

"Relax." Her voice shook subtly as she stifled a laugh. "Is this your first time out after Gloaming?"

"Gloaming?" I echoed.

"It's twilight, the hour the Sun Dwellers run for Check-In, and we're finally allowed to come out."

*So that's what they call us,* I thought.

She started to comb through my hair gently. I stared at myself in the mirror. Even with makeup, I still paled in comparison to the Vampyres in the salon. Maybe it was the concealer, since it wasn't doing its job to hide the dark circles under my sunken eyes, and the rust-colored eye shadow that made my eyes appear inflamed—as if I had been crying.

Many bad choices have been made tonight.

"What are we looking to get done, hon?" she asked as she continued to comb through my helmet-mashed tangles.

"I guess just... freshen up the hair dye and trim to shoulder length?" Through the mirror I watched her nod and pull supplies from her drawers.

"So, why are you out at this time anyway?" she asked.

I shrugged. "It gets boring doing the same thing every day. Seeing the same faces, doing the same routine, being locked away and getting yelled at by some cop every night."

Worrying about Sterling every night...

"You do realize the stakes, right? You can get killed, arrested, or Turned." She raised her manicured eyebrows.

"Yeah, I don't really care." I was terrified. But seeing the city lights at night and feeling the buzz, the adrenaline of the fear... it was how I imagined skydiving would feel. It was the lightning bolt that would strike my body each time I sped down the country road. It made me forget the world I was in and helped me enjoy the moment.

"You've got a pair on you then, girl." She busily started cutting my hair. What was once below my shoulder blades was inching its way up the top of my shoulders.

"Is it true what they say?" I asked.

"What's that?"

"That Vampyres will kill or Turn a human on sight if we're out after dark?"

She giggled, a little too sweetly, and shook her head.

"Oh, darling. If that were true, you'd be dead before you even set foot in Sundance."

I swallowed tightly but eased my shoulders a little. She reached over and turned on a small personal fan. It blew gently on my face, drying the sweat that lightly coated my skin. Jocelyn had a point, but... there was a reason the government had to set such strict curfews for us to live among each other.

"Now, which shade of pink are we talking?" She opened a cabinet full of different hair dyes and my eyes widened at the choices. It was just the icebreaker I needed.

✳

I left Sundance running my hands through my fresh silky, wavy hair. I picked a shade of rose pink to contrast with black roots so that whenever my hair started growing back, it would blend in a little more. I gave Jocelyn a nice thirty-dollar tip, after which everyone in the salon seemed to loosen up in my presence. They even bade me farewell. It wasn't at all what I expected, but I left there feeling revitalized.

I walked down the strip, passing various restaurants, tattoo shops, and stores. I stood at a crosswalk, waiting for the light to switch from the hand to the walking stick man. My eyes kept swinging back and forth along the streets like a metronome. Would these Vampyres be just as tolerant as the ones at Sundance?

A crowd started to form around me, blocking out the humid breeze that had been blowing through my hair. I took a step back to give myself space but ran into a brick wall. I looked back, and it was just a tall, broad-shouldered man who I refused to look in the eye. He released a low growl.

"Sorry," I muttered, then turned back around. I fought the urge to dart across the street too soon.

The light turned, and everyone stepped off the curb. They

moved just as gracefully as Astoria, their footsteps as silent as an owl's wings. I was a sheep among wolves, but I locked my gaze on a food truck called Chen's Den on the other side of the road. The smell of brown sugar and smoked meat floated through the air. It brought me back to my childhood days in the festivals. My mouth went watery as I approached the truck. Two men slaved over a stove behind the clerk hunched over in the window.

I didn't realize Vampyres ate anything outside of blood.

"Welcome, young la—"

The scrawny, stringy blonde-haired cook stopped in his tracks. He sniffed a couple times, adjusted his hair net and frowned. "Human?" He scrunched his nose.

"Ah ha, yes..." I laughed nervously.

He eyed me carefully, then leaned down to poke his head out of the narrow window. "You're lucky there's no cops 'round here," he said quietly. "Hurry up and get away from my business before you get me shut down."

I scoffed and waved my hand dismissively at him.

"Whatever, your food is probably nasty anyway." I curled my lip up and stormed away.

I shoved my hands back in my pockets and walked further down the street toward a glowing red light that shone from an alleyway. Electric guitar music and a haunting, ethereal voice weaved through the air from that direction. It was definitely some kind of rock I'd add to my playlist at home, but I'd never heard of the band. A line hung at the edge of the alley, people talking among themselves and clinging to a red velvet rope. I inched closer to the line. I peered up at the neon sign, the source of the red light, and it was a bar named The Nightshade. I hung around the periphery and observed everyone's outfits. The men were either dressed in sharp suits or grungy leather—there was no in-between. The women were in elegant silk, rhinestone, velvet, and chiffon dresses that I could never dream to afford. I felt like I was six feet underdressed.

I approached the bouncer and sucked in a breath. He looked like Death himself, with ghostly white skin, sunken cheekbones, deep-set eyes, and a strong browbone made of steel. He had a long scar across his cheek on one side of his lips, as if it were an extended smile.

"Where do you think you're going, *Sun Dweller*? This is a Vampyre Only establishment." He spat my species like an insult. I frowned but held my tongue because he looked like a Vampyre who probably would kill me without hesitation.

"Ha, sorry, I guess I got the wrong place." I rubbed the back of my neck with a sheepish smile.

"Right, you got your hours mixed up, too?" He folded his arms, tilting his head aggressively. He bared his teeth, his fangs extending to poke his bottom lip.

"No, I'm—" A heavy arm plopped itself over my shoulders.

"Ah, there ya are, babe. I was just at the ATM gettin' cash. Sorry it took so long." A deep, husky voice with the richness of honeyed whiskey brushed my ear.

I went rigid. Whatever heat I felt in Sundance instantly turned to ice. Without moving my head, I slid my wide eyes to look at who stood next to me. My bottom lip trembled, and I held it in my teeth to conceal it.

A toothpick hung between a pair of full, alluring lips. The side of his cheek was pricked with a dimple and a small freckle like some classic starlet. He pulled me closer, and the bouncer stepped to the side.

"Sorry, sir," the bouncer said with a slight bow. Whoever was standing next to me... if he could make even Death apologize... then I feared all the wrong things.

"Thanks." The mysterious man pulled me into the bar before I could regain my senses to run.

# 11
# DRAVEN

HER FRAME WAS SMALL AND FRAIL AGAINST MY SIDE. AS I CURLED my arm over her shoulders, I knew I could easily crush her right then and there, but what made me falter was the warm, earthy scent of cedar drifting from her more vibrantly dyed and cut hair—and the rosy nectar of the blood running through her veins. And of course, her personal dealings with a detective.

As we stepped inside Nightshade, red light washed over us like a blood moon. I felt her tug away and instinctively tightened my grip as the music pounding through the walls grew louder and clearer. I couldn't tell if she was shaking, or if the entire building was vibrating from the music. We finally entered the dance floor, greeted by strobe lights sweeping over hundreds of dancing Vampyres and the "Until Dawn" band at the front. Most of the patrons were here for the band's live performance, but many among them belonged to the

Nightshade clan like me.

There was an underground floor I would usually go to, where all our members would gather. There was a chance Caspian was there, but an even bigger chance Uriah was.

"Alright, you can let go of me now!" she shouted over the music. She pushed my side with as much force as she could, but without impact. I frowned and straightened, towering over her. Big, round, mascara-laden eyes stared up at me. Her mouth hung slightly open, and she took a step back, as if I was already baring my fangs to rip her throat out.

Without a doubt, she was the one that saw me and Caspian running from Arlo's house.

And she remembered.

"You—" She took another step back until she bumped into a dancing couple and came back forward. I flashed her a smirk, twirling the toothpick between my teeth. Such a bold chick to be out here after Gloaming, yet she cowers in my presence.

"I haven't seen you 'round here, why don't we get a couple drinks?" I drawled.

Those thick, arched, manicured eyebrows sank over her brow in a frown. She pivoted on her heel and turned away, pushing through the crowd and quickly getting away from me.

It was hard to catch her scent among so many moving bodies, but I managed to follow the faint roses. I squeezed between people until I reached the bar, where I saw her sitting at the counter with a drink already in hand.

"You don't waste any time, do ya?" I shouted over the music, sliding into the space between her and some guy on the next barstool over. She curled a lip at me, then back at her glass, clicking her nails against it.

"I didn't accept your invitation to drink with *ya*." She mocked my southern drawl and spoke lower, knowing I could hear her beyond the music. I began to wonder just how much experience she had being around my kind.

"You don't have to, it's a public bar. I'm just here gettin' a drink for myself." I gave her a cheeky grin and waved for the bartender's attention. I caught her rolling her eyes as she brought the glass to her matte mauve lip, and chuckled to myself.

"What did ya get?" I leaned on the counter as I waited for the bartender.

"Nothing for you to roofie." She downed it, then set the empty glass down firmly, almost in a slam.

"You're somethin' else. Sure is a lotta smack comin' from the same girl that was shakin' like a leaf a minute ago." I moved closer to her ear and she leaned away. "I know ya heart is racin'... being in here among predators."

"What is your deal? Leave me alone!" She stood from the barstool and stormed back into the crowd. I let her go this time. In a den of lions, I knew she wouldn't get far.

I slid into her seat as the bartender, Stella, approached me. She smiled sweetly at me.

"What can I get you tonight, Draven? The usual?" Stella's scarlet eyes flicked beyond my shoulder, possibly in the direction of the girl.

"Yeah." I clasped my hands together and pressed my lips in a thin line. How would I kill her without triggering the next war between Sun Dwellers and Vampyres? It'd have to be during the day, when the likelihood of a Vampyre attack was extremely lessened.

"What's on your mind, Draven?"

She placed a hand on her hips and released a puff of air, blowing away stray strands of straight golden hair. She ignored men and women waving cash and credit cards for her attention. I smiled softly at her. It always warmed my cold, immortal soul when she prioritized me over anyone else, despite our relationship never extending beyond the counter.

"I got a sticky situation," I said as I rubbed my temples.

"Business?" She arched an eyebrow as she poured my drink.

"Yeah."

"Isn't it always sticky?" She chuckled slightly.

"Yeah, but this time I think I'm drownin' in quicksand."

Stella's eyes softened and she leaned against the counter with a sigh. "I feel you. She got closer to the band, if you're still looking for her. If you need anything else, you know where to find me." She slid the glass toward me and left to tend to her other customers.

I downed the amber liquid, then swiveled on the stool to scan the crowd for that human girl. It was a big club, and the Nightshade VIP section was heavily guarded... I just hoped her curiosity didn't lead her to that deadly rabbit hole. It'd be impossible to hide her from Uriah at that point.

I quickly stood and started sifting through the crowd for her, heading toward the stage as Stella had indicated.

"Do I need to call the cops?" The girl threatened louder once I approached her.

"Go ahead, I'm sure you'll have tons of fun explaining to them why you're out past ya Sun Dwellin' Hour." I gave her a smirk.

She turned her gaze back to the band, muttering under her breath. Judging by the shapes her lips made, she mumbled obscenities. It didn't take long for her to ignore my presence. There was a twinkle in those grey eyes, like starlight, as if she was a shooting star full of unfulfilled wishes.

I sucked my mouth inward and shifted my weight with a sting in my chest. I knew that feeling all too well, with the rough guitar strings vibrating underneath my previously calloused fingers. I didn't say anything else, I just watched, and then allowed a few dancing Vampyres to separate me from her. She was still in my sight, but I wanted her to at least experience the euphoria of the band before I killed her, when the day came.

The girl danced for a while, getting caught up in a group of inebriated Vampyres that didn't bat an eye at her. She seemed comfortable, as if she belonged to this world as much as I did. She broke away from the group and went back to the bar. I watched her take a few sips of a new drink, check the watch on her wrist, and swivel on her stool to watch the band from where she sat.

I flinched—a clenched fist ready to strike—when a hand touched my shoulder, but I relaxed when I saw Caspian. His hair was ruffled up, the top button of his blouse freed. It was only safe to assume that he snared a willing Vampyress in his trap.

"Hey, man, where have you been? Uriah was asking about you. We got a clan meeting about something big soon," he shouted over the music, vodka weighing heavily on his breath. Caspian was not a huge drinker, but I supposed the past couple days had pushed him to the edge for the first time in a while. I guess even the man with a bottomless chalice of patience could still run out. I winced at Uriah's name.

"I was tryin' to clean up the mess we made with the witness. You haven't told him about that, have ya?" I pointed at the corner of my lips. "You got something smudged there."

There was smeared lipstick on his mouth, cheek, and neck. I rolled my eyes. While he was having the time of his life, I was having to strain my brain figuring out how to kill a cop's girlfriend, or whatever she was to him. Caspian used the back of his hand to wipe the red stain away with little success.

"No, I haven't," he insisted with a pout. "I'm honest but I'm not *that* honest."

I laughed, but my smile faded when I noticed the very top of the girl's pink and black hair move within the crowd, toward the exit.

"I'll catch up with you, alright? Tell Uriah I'll be down there in twenty minutes or so."

Caspian nodded and headed toward the glowing topaz light of the VIP underground lounge entrance when a girl in red lipstick snatched him by the collar and smashed her lips against his. The security guard moved away from them uncomfortably, but stayed near the Nightshades' VIP entrance. I laughed and shook my head, knowing he'd forget our conversation in a matter of seconds because of her. I turned my focus back to the Sun Dweller, who was nowhere to be found. I went outside, where her cedar-rose scent was strongest, and followed it through downtown.

# 12
# BRIAR

I LEARNED THE BAND PLAYING SUCH ATMOSPHERIC, EVOCA-tive, gothic alternative music was named Until Dawn. I hoped they had their music on Treblesome, the subscription-based music app that had pretty much any song anybody's heart desired available to download. I would immediately add them and track down their concerts.

The Nightshade was probably the most fun bar I had ever been to. The drinks weren't watered down acid, the music was amazing, and no one attacked me. I wanted to stay longer, but that weird guy kept hovering most of the time. Not only that, but that black hair that hung over his shoulder, the half-shaven head, and those neck tattoos...

*No.* Neoterra couldn't be *that* small, where I'd run into the guy who might've burned that house down. Besides, it was dark, and they were running so fast. I easily could've been mistaken from the start.

But he followed me a great deal through the bar, as if he'd seen right through my helmet that night and knew *exactly* who I was... or maybe I was just being paranoid.

I forced a deep breath and crossed the street. I drank in the open night air as my chest tightened from my spiraling thoughts. I passed Sundance, which looked busier than earlier in the night, and eventually found my motorcycle. I froze at the edge of the space reserved for diagonal parking as my bones turned to ice.

Two men crowded my bike, trailing their fingertips along the black paint and chrome accents. The one with long blonde hair pulled into a messy bun had high cheekbones and a wide neck covered in tattoos, like the guy at the bar. The other, with dark russet hair, had a thick beard that only slightly concealed his fangs when he smiled at me.

"That—that's not—"

I didn't realize how terrified I was until I tried to speak. My words were choked, as if one of them already had their hand around my throat. They cocked their heads like dogs.

"I don't recognize you, girl." The blonde man took a step closer and his nostrils flared as he inhaled deeply. "You got a nice bike... for a Sun Dweller."

His friend's eyes lit up with fascination. "She's kinda cute, maybe we should take her with us."

The brunette man reached to grab my helmet and I slapped his hand away. I took a step back and clenched my fists in my pocket, wrapping one of them around a bottle of pepper spray.

"That's my bike," I finally managed to get out. "I was just heading home."

"Yeah? Well, I want your bike."

The blonde crept closer and gripped my shoulder. I snatched the pepper spray out of my pocket with a yelp and sprayed it, but it ran down my sleeve.

"You should've stayed home after your little cop friends checked on you. And you certainly shouldn't have tried *that*," the blonde snarled. I flinched as he tightened his grip, his claws digging through the leather and into my skin.

"Is that any way to treat a lady?" A third voice—that familiar huskiness—sounded behind me and I whirled my head in that direction. I swallowed, but my mouth was so dry that it felt like sand scraping against my throat.

*Not him too.*

The men bared their teeth at the guy from the bar. He leaned against a light pole, unfazed by their malicious growls.

"Let her go." He spoke lowly, his tone a lethal warning even as his toothpick danced around his lips. What was once a mischievous flicker in his eyes turned into bloodlust.

I winced again as the blonde's claws retracted out of my shoulder. I held my arm close to my side, biting my lip to stifle a cry.

"Two against one, brother." The bearded man stalked toward the newcomer, and I slowly crept toward my motorcycle. The blonde licked my blood off his fingers and snarled with a smile.

"One against none." The guy with the toothpick stretched his shirt collar downward, exposing a tattoo of a lion skull encircled by nightshade flowers as the mane. The two men went rigid, backing away and then taking off in a sprint. I was already mounting my bike and putting my helmet on to get the hell out of there, but he flashed by my side and put a hand over one of the handles.

"Please," I pleaded quietly as I flipped my visor up so he could see my face. "Whatever you want—"

"I wouldn't offer that to a Vampyre," he purred, and pressed a finger through the torn hole of my jacket's leather. He pulled his hand back and rubbed his crimson-coated fingertips together. My cheeks heated and I looked down at the handles of my bike. Even if I was able to drive away, he would catch up to me in seconds.

"What do you want from me?" I rasped. The rock in my stomach felt just as heavy as when I thought Sterling was on the stretcher, if not more so. The guy stared at my blood on his fingers, then, with a willpower made of steel, wiped them on my sleeve. I loosed a shaky breath.

"For starters, never set foot in that club again," he breathed. I paused, lifting my gaze to meet his. I didn't expect those words from him, considering he'd been following my every move.

"Why?"

"Secondly, a thank you would be nice."

I scoffed and shook my head with a scorned chuckle.

"Third—if you know what's good for ya, you'll keep your mouth shut."

I blinked, frowning. Could he be referring to the crime scene or what just happened? I could still be paranoid, but I wasn't going to admit to anything for clarification.

"Don't pretend ya don't know what I'm talkin' about. The game you're playing, being out here, in that club, is very dangerous.

I don't want to have to kill ya if I can avoid it."

"*Kill* me? Why not just let those two guys do it for you? Why even help me? Why would I report anything to anyone when I'd just get in trouble for breaking curfew in the first place?"

He paused, squinting his eyes nearly imperceptibly, as if considering my logic.

"Go. Home," he quietly commanded, then backed away before vanishing in a smudge of color and shadow.

I looked frantically over my shoulders for any more Vampyres, closed my helmet's visor, and sped out of the parking lot. My shoulder burned as my jacket slapped against my punctured skin. I could feel the warm blood creep down my arm, so I drove with it held close to my chest so I wouldn't leave a trail along the road.

I wasn't entirely sure if I should even go home. The Vampyre seemed to have finally left me alone, but I still worried he'd follow me. Then Sterling and Astoria would be left vulnerable.

I pulled onto the shoulder of the road, surrounded by fields. At a somewhat close distance, I could see the yellow house enveloped in the night's navy blue. The lights were off and the music was quiet. Deep periwinkle leaked along the horizon as morning crept on. Sterling's car was still gone, so at least there was that. It was a quarter to five, so he still had another couple of hours before his shift ended.

I wanted to go home and be surrounded by the comfort of my bed's blankets. My shoulder ached and burned, but I didn't think anything would hurt worse than being confronted by Astoria again. If she went in my room to turn the music off, then she'd instantly see I'd snuck out again... and something told me that her threat to tell Sterling wasn't an empty one. I cursed myself. Why didn't I consider any of this before I left? If I was bored, why didn't I just go out and get another tattoo or piercing or new pair of shoes?

I rolled my motorcycle the rest of the way home, each step closer curdling the contents of my stomach more.

✳

The house was completely still. Before heading upstairs, I went down the hall across from the living room to Astoria's bedroom. I turned the knob completely before silently cracking the door open. She was curled against a body pillow on top of her comforter, still in her clothes from the night before. A pile of crumpled tissues was near her pillows. Her hair was a midnight mess that veiled her face, a few strands shifting with each shallow breath. I gnashed my teeth tightly, looking away with a heavy cringe. While I was out having reckless fun, she was practically pulling her hair out. Rightfully so, considering two Vampyres could've seriously hurt me if that stranger hadn't stopped them.

I opened the door wider and tiptoed into her room, painted sage green and beige. She surrounded herself with plants, books, and wicker. But even the coziness of her bedroom couldn't bring her comfort.

I eased myself onto the edge of her bed, running my hand through the white furry throw blanket folded neatly at the bottom of it.

"Hey," I whispered.

"Ria?" I spoke a little louder and she snapped awake, instantly sitting up. She raked her fingers through her hair to get it out of her face and looked at me. There was a flicker of happiness, but only for half a second before it was snuffed out. All that remained was fury.

"How could you?" Her voice was hoarse, either from sleep or crying. Maybe both.

I opened my mouth, only to close it again. What excuse did I have this time? I certainly didn't leave for Sterling's sake. I wanted distractions. I wanted to *live*, no matter the risk. I survived the first night searching for Sterling, so I felt like I could survive another.

"How could you? *How could you!*"

She asked again and again until it was unintelligible screaming, and she was throwing all fifty million of her pillows at me as hard as she could. With my good arm, I kept blocking them and dodging. She froze in place, her last pillow raised above her head, to stare at the caked-up blood on my hand and the torn holes in my jacket.

"W-what happened?" She crawled across the bed and reached for my shoulder, but I jumped away.

"Nothing, I fell off my bike on the way back. I had a couple of drinks," I said quickly. "I just... listen, I just came to say I'm sorry. You said life is too short, so I wanted to live for a night." It was wrong to flip it on her, to make it seem like her words were what drove me to madness, but it was the only thing I could think of.

"Life is short, yeah, but you're going to go and try to make it shorter?"

"Turns out Sterling was just exaggerating anyway," I grumbled. Sighing, I pinched the bridge of my nose and then pressed my palms together.

"Please... *please* just keep it a secret between us," I pleaded.

"You want me to keep it a secret? From *Sterling*? After you almost *died*?" She pointed at my injury.

"If Sterling can arrest our mom for drugs, he can arrest me for breaking curfew without blinking an eye. If you want me to go away for life or get executed, then fine." I turned away. "I'm going to go fix my shoulder, now."

I could hear the quiet thuds against the carpet as she rushed to follow me. She reached out, and I jerked away as I headed for the staircase down the hall.

"I can handle it myself, thank you," I snapped. I didn't want her to see deep punctures instead of scrapes.

Astoria retracted her hand and stayed at the bottom of the staircase. I glanced back at her, then quickly looked away when I noticed a glint in her glassy caramel eyes.

I sat on the closed toilet seat with the first aid kit opened on the counter. The door was locked, the fan running. I tossed my leather jacket and shirt carelessly on the floor. I figured I'd cut the sleeves off both the t-shirt and jacket to make a tank and vest. I didn't believe in wasting or giving up on anything, even if it was supposed to be permanently broken. Except for Vivian Shaw, of course.

As I painstakingly cleaned my wounds with cotton swabs doused in peroxide, I thought about that guy's words.

*Never set foot in that club again.*

I frowned, angrily ripping the bandages open. I ignored the sting in my shoulder from the spastic motion.

*I don't want to have to kill ya if I can avoid it.*

A small part of me wanted to run into him again, just to see if he meant it.

I had such limited information about the burning house. Even if I wanted to risk my freedom and tell Sterling about it, I couldn't have a clear conscience reporting him as a potential suspect. That guy *did* save me from those creeps. Plus, if he wanted to kill me, he had ample opportunities to do so. All the Vampyres did. I spent the entire night among hundreds of monsters, yet only three gave me trouble—and the third saved me from the other two, so he only partially counted. That tattoo he showed them... I wondered if it was some sort of gang symbol. It made the men run for their lives, as if the tattoo itself would come to life.

I stood in front of the mirror in a black spaghetti-strap tank top and looked at my first aid. I raised my arm up and down, then rotated it all around to make sure the bandage wouldn't peel off. I stared at my reflection a little longer, his words still echoing through my mind.

He said I was playing a dangerous game, yet the risk of being out past Gloaming and getting attacked didn't seem much worse than being out during the day and getting carjacked in broad daylight.

I cut the light off and made sure the first aid kit was put exactly where it had been. I went to my room, then collapsed on my bed. I welcomed dreams to take me anywhere, but was only met with nightmares.

# 13
# DRAVEN

I RETURNED TO THE NIGHTSHADE BAR, THINKING ABOUT THE beating I'd had for leaving Arlo in the house. All I could think about was Uriah finding out about that girl and maybe taking one of *my* fingers. I certainly hadn't made a wise choice.

I chewed on my inner cheek as I contemplated the situation. In the history of the Nightshades, witnesses were always Vampyres and always terminated, but that girl raised a valid point—she was already at a disadvantage to say anything.

I didn't know how to handle that.

I finally descended to the basement, where the security guard didn't even give me a second glance as I entered the underground VIP lounge. No one ever challenged me unless they didn't know me like those two fiends outside, but every fledgling clan member, or new employee was given a rundown of all clan members.

The underground lounge was much bigger than the club up-stairs. The ceilings were made of human and animal skulls. Vines and nightshade flowers wove among the skulls and wrapped around the poles of spherical pendants filled with liquid light that churned like golden lava lamps. The lounge had tufted, half-circle section-als of violet crushed velvet , mahogany tables, and warm amber un-der-lighting at the wide, hexagonal bar that resided at the center.

"Draven!"

Caspian threw his arm over my shoulders and rubbed his knuck-les rapidly in my hair. My eyes widened and I blinked, rubbing my head once I pulled away.

"How much have ya had to drink?" It baffled me how a man with the skin of a Greek limestone sculpture managed to have flushed cheeks.

"I dunno," he slurred, somehow still walking with grace and sta-bility as he moved to the velvet couches.

"When's the meetin'?"

Caspian shrugged, his lips moving clumsily in search of the skin-ny straw in his glass that seemed to run away from him. I pinched the bridge of my nose with a sigh and pulled out my phone to text Hartley. It was *my* job to be the mess, not him. I guess I could un-derstand why Caspian was always so snappy with me whenever I was inebriated.

I put my phone in my pocket just as Uriah approached me with a cigar in his hand and a couple of men in suits trailing behind him. I'd never seen them before, but my guess was that they belonged to other clans Uriah was attempting to ally with.

"Ah, there you are. You've been gone all day. Doing what,

exactly?" Uriah's metallic arm whirred as he stretched his fingers before grabbing a drink off a silver platter.

"Clearing my head," I said.

"Hard to clear it when you have to watch out for the copperheads, isn't it?" He tilted his head slightly. "Anyways, I'm glad Arlo is going to be fine."

"Yeah, me too." *Glad you beat me for nothing too.*

Uriah himself was dressed in a maroon suede suit with a black blouse, flawlessly pressed. He spent thousands on his suits, with many of them custom-made for him. If his corpse was dressed in anything cheap in a casket, he'd haunt the living for it.

"There's going to be a very important meeting at the King Estate this morning. Things are going to change for us Nightshades. Matter of fact, things are going to change for all Vampyres."

He blew smoke into my face before approaching a round table full of more unfamiliar faces. I frowned and watched them for a minute. Despite the smile on Uriah's face, I couldn't help but feel anxious with the news.

Within the next hour, the underground lounge and the bar above cleared out. Sunrise was quickly approaching. As soon as fresh air slapped Caspian in the face, he was hurling his guts behind a dumpster in the alley.

"Now I remember why I rarely drink." He reached in his pocket and pulled out a handkerchief, wiping his mouth. "Is this what Sun Dwellers feel like? Why would they do this to themselves?"

I shrugged. While I wasn't born a Vampyre, I was too young to have ever experienced a drop of alcohol or its effects as a human. I had zero answers for the man with all the answers.

I looked both ways down the street, waiting for either the SUV or the limo. I wasn't sure which direction Hartley would come from, but I waited in stoic silence.

"Hey, are you okay, man? You disappeared earlier and then again tonight... what's going on?" Caspian slid to sit on the dirty concrete, leaning his head against the wall. He pulled his tie loose and let it hang sloppily around his collar, then propped his arms on his bent knees.

"Uriah, that girl, just... everything."

Caspian paused, raising a wary eyebrow. "What about the girl?"

I didn't respond, just waved at the recognizable SUV heading our way. The birds were starting to awaken and the sky was subtly brightening, though the stars and moon still dominated.

"Draven... what did you do?"

Caspian stood with a grunt, using the wall for support. He dragged his feet into the backseat once Hartley pulled up to the curb. I groaned as I slid into the front seat. The only reason I'd let him sit in the back was because he felt sick.

"You're not answering my question," he whined as he hung his head over the edge of the seat.

"How about you just focus on keeping your vomit in?" I leaned my head against the window with a sigh.

Hartley gave me a sidelong glance, his eyebrows raised slightly. "Rough night?"

"You can say that." I winced when a sharp pain stabbed my forehead. I closed my eyes, pretending to sleep, pretending to be human, pretending to be anything, anyone, anywhere but here.

❋

The King Estate was shrouded in morning gold. Calm waves rolled up the shore below the hill. I would often forget about its existence in Neoterra's heavily urban terrain. There wouldn't be any bodies of water for miles, but if anyone went to the Nocturne District and kept driving, it would be as if they'd reached the edge of the world.

Once Caspian and I made it inside, we retreated to our respective rooms. I showered, brushed my teeth, and collapsed on my bed. As always, I wondered why I even had one, considering it was never used for its real purpose.

The meeting was supposed to take place at noon in the basement. It was a vast room, probably the same size, if not bigger, than my old apartment when I was child before the farm. The ceilings were smooth, exposed concrete with warm, modern recessed lighting and geometric pendants. One side had a clear, turquoise pool that gently rippled like silk, a hot tub nestled beside it. The small waves spider-webbed reflections along the walls and ceiling. The other side of the room had a large sectional, plush wing-backed chairs and ottomans, a chaise, two pool tables, a poker table, a kitchenette and bar. If there was anything Uriah loved, it was to entertain.

The basement was the only place in the entire mansion that mismatched the regal Mediterranean aesthetic everywhere else on the property. It was also the only place where Uriah would do anything illegal if it wasn't feasible to handle it elsewhere. Behind the bar was a hidden room, where the shelves slid back into a pocket door to reveal five cells and a torture chamber. The only people who knew that room existed were those of us that lived at the King Estate— about ten of us. Anyone who Turned—including myself—spent their fledgling phase in those cells.

Caspian was drinking a large glass of dark crimson in one of the chairs. His skin was back to its normal color of white stone, which was healthy for him, but his eyes still hung heavy with exhaustion.

"Sorry for whatever I said or did last night. I can't remember half of it," he grumbled once I'd approached him. I grunted as I sank into the sectional, then kicked my feet up with a smirk.

"You ain't done nothin' offensive. Except maybe not get that girl's number," I teased.

"What girl?" He scrunched his nose.

I laughed, but it faded as the rest of the estate's residential clan members came pouring downstairs to take their seats. A couple of guys took it upon themselves to pass time with a quick game of pool.

Delilah soon arrived, her black-and-white striped locs pulled in a half up, half down hairstyle. She wore a fitted royal blue cocktail dress that hugged her shapely hips and narrow waist. It seemed to glow against her deep hickory skin. She looked around the room of Vampyres until she found my lingering gaze, then claimed a spot next to me on the couch.

"How are you feeling?" she whispered.

"Fine," I said with a short nod.

She placed a tender hand on my knee and laid her head on my shoulder. Why did I get the sickening feeling that all she felt was pity toward me? Every glance, every touch felt like an act of charity rather than the passion we once had. I couldn't tell if it resulted from knowing so little about my thoughts, or from my possibly broken ego, or from her truly just seeing me as a pitiful man.

Uriah was the last to enter, and he locked the door behind him.

I exchanged an equally puzzled glance with Caspian.

"Thank you all for taking the time out of your day to join me," Uriah announced. "Many business deals are being made. Deals that will guarantee us a brighter future." He started heading for the bar but didn't grab a single bottle or glass.

Everyone gravitated toward that side of the room, and I slowly rose from the couch. Delilah followed, with Caspian shortly after both of us. I hung behind everyone and stuffed my hands in my pockets.

Uriah's hand hovered over a button hidden among the bottles on the shelves. He pulled his hand back and turned to face us with a tight smile.

"How many of you are tired of the Sun Dwellers dictating our lives? Tired of them feeding us stale donated blood bags and looking for any excuse to shoot us down like dogs?"

Everyone muttered in agreement, some raising their hands, others nodding. I looked down at my shoes. This would just be another meeting to zone out.

"How many of you are ready to see the sun again without pain?" Uriah continued.

I kept my head down but looked up at him from under my brow.

"Well... none of it could happen without this," he said, then opened the shelves to the cellar. The shelves made a quiet grating sound as they retracted into the wall, revealing four blindfolded humans tied and gagged in chains on the concrete floor.

# 14

# BRIAR

I had a fitful sleep. Ironically, my nightmares were mostly of me getting either shot or arrested. I had a nightmare of the Vampyre who stalked me, but it paled in comparison to the one of my brother killing me because of the secrets I kept. They flipped through my sleep and raked through my mind like a horror montage that I couldn't shut off. I woke up just as the sun was preparing to sink into the sky. I groaned, realizing I'd screwed up my sleep schedule and would have to retrain myself.

Unless I managed to land a job that allowed me to work the night shift. I *needed* a job... two days of no responsibility had already driven me to do stupid things. I realized that work served as a distraction—no matter how dull it was—to keep my recklessness in check.

With a long, dragging yawn, I looked at the clock that hung

crookedly on the wall above my door. It was ten minutes before seven in the evening.

I leaped out of bed, quickly tied my hair up into a small ponytail, and put on a baggy graphic tee with sleeves that reached the crook of my elbow. I didn't want any indication of my injury exposed to Sterling.

As soon as I opened my door, the smell of pancakes and bacon swirled upstairs. I smiled softly. Breakfast for dinner meant that Sterling had taken the night off, and we'd finally hang out after months of him constantly working. Hopefully, the night could be pure enjoyment—no fighting.

Once again, Astoria was first on the porch, identification card in hand. She stared out at the horizon, toward the city, swinging slowly on the bench. She glanced at me when I came out and her face hardened for a second before it returned to its pensive softness.

I leaned over the porch railing and looked down at the azalea bushes. They were misshapen and wild, but the fuchsia flowers still held true. I told myself I'd try to remember to tend the yard.

Wind howled as a vehicle sped down our road. I moved away from the railing and watched the distant patrol car draw near our house, and silently prayed that Officer Kent had followed my brother's demands.

As the car rolled into our driveway, Astoria silently shuffled to the porch steps. Sterling leaned against the front door with his arms folded. The car continued to hum when a female officer stepped out instead. Her platinum blonde hair was pulled into a tight bun. Behind the mask was a pair of piercing, sky-blue eyes. I glanced at her badge as it caught the light of the dying sun, searching for any indication of it being fake. All judgment disappeared just as quickly as it came when I saw my brother's face light up. They exchanged hugs, and the woman smiled brightly as they pulled away from each other.

"Cyrene! What a pleasant surprise, I guess I don't have to show you my ID."

"Nah, I'm going to need your birth certificate too," she teased, her voice sweet like honey. Astoria started to fidget with her necklace again, holding her card tightly behind her back. I just rolled my eyes and shuffled to the bench, since they were probably going to be a minute.

"You can have my social security number too."

Sterling gave her a cheeky smile and she just laughed again, waving her hand dismissively. She pulled out her tablet and tapped the screen, I assumed to check off Sterling's name.

"I didn't know you lived way out here," she said, lifting her gaze to sweep over me and Astoria. "Briar and Astoria?"

"Yep, those are my sisters."

"He talks so much about you guys at work! All good things, I promise!" Cyrene called out. She checked off our names and put away the tablet without even examining our cards.

I smiled softly. Maybe this switch would make our lives easier.

"Well since you know where I live now, why don't we go out for dinner some time?" Sterling tilted his head, amber eyes shimmering like gold.

"Not in a million years, hon." She smiled teasingly as Sterling put a hand over his chest, feigning getting shot.

"So you're saying there's still a chance if I became a Vampyre?"

"Haha, you're so stupid. Have a good night, Sterling." She giggled, then disappeared in the patrol car and drove off. Sterling waved after her and she honked her horn as she drove down the street.

"She's so out of your league," I teased, standing up from the bench and stretching. I shuffled back inside the house and went straight to the kitchen to make a cup of coffee.

"Not a chance. She wants me, I'm just playing the long game."

"How many times have you asked her out?" I quipped.

"None of your business," Sterling retorted.

"That means *at least* three," I snorted, shooting my hand up to my mouth to stifle heavier laughter.

"Shut up, Briar." Sterling nudged my shoulder and I winced, biting my inner cheek to keep myself from crying out.

"Oh, sorry, I didn't mean to push you that hard." Sterling's face fell as he reached to rub my shoulder and erase the push, but I pulled away before he could touch me.

"No, no, you're good. I just slept on it wrong." I swung my arm in a circular motion with a sheepish grin. I glanced at Astoria, whose gaze was of sharpened knives. Without a word, she headed toward the kitchen table and started to pile her plate with food.

"Well... sorry to irritate it more." Sterling followed behind Astoria. I stood in the kitchen a couple moments longer, waiting for the gnawing sting to fade before joining them.

I sat across from Sterling as I always did, but kept my focus on my plate.

"You guys up for a movie night?" Sterling said even as he stuffed his face with pancakes. Astoria pushed her chair back with a loud grating against the floor.

"Actually, I think I'm going to cash in early tonight," Astoria grumbled. Just as quickly as she stood from the table, she was out of the kitchen, her plate untouched. Sterling frowned, his lips poking out in a subtle pout.

"What's her problem?" he asked.

"Girl problems, I guess," I said with a nonchalant shrug. I knew exactly what her problem was, but it was better this way. Any mention of menstruation always made our brother uncomfortable and he'd leave it alone. The only risk was that he'd probably dote on her with heating blankets, chocolates, and anything else she'd need. He always did the same for me.

"Well... do *you* still want movie night?" His eyes glimmered like a puppy's.

I didn't.

"Sure." I gave him a small smile, and after we ate, we shuffled to the living room.

Sterling scrolled through streaming options for a solid thirty minutes before we settled on an action movie. I was laying down on the sectional, propped on an elbow with my cheek resting in my palm. Sterling was in his favorite recliner, the television's light dancing across his buttery brown eyes.

We were about an hour deep into the movie, a montage scene of serene music with no dialogue playing, when Sterling suddenly spoke.

"Do you ever think about Dad?"

I frowned. "Not really. He left us and that landed me and Astoria in foster homes until you were old enough to take us."

"No he didn't." Sterling adjusted in his recliner.

I laughed. "Where is he, then?"

Sterling shifted his gaze to me, his face heavy.

"Why do you think I'm in this line of work?" he asked, his forehead crinkling subtly.

"Death wish, I guess?" I squinted, trying to focus on the movie as the characters started to talk again. "Vivian shooting up?"

He didn't react to my remark, just looked at the TV screen again.

"Dad broke curfew trying to look for her that night. A Vampyre killed him." Sterling lowered his voice, but I could still hear it tremble.

I slowly sat up, my voice suddenly choked out of me. Why didn't anyone tell me? Did Astoria know? Most importantly, why was he telling me this *now*? Did he know that I'd snuck out?

*That* night. I was only eleven years old, Astoria was seven. I could vaguely remember a red-eyed woman in a pantsuit who came into the roach- and mouse-infested house to take my sister and me away after we spent a week with Vivian nowhere to be found. The same social worker had tracked Sterling hanging out with his friends and brought him to meet with us at her stale office. That was the day Dad disappeared too. We were all separated from each other for a year after that. Had our father stayed... none of us would have had to experience that. I spent years burying any memories of him, thinking he abandoned us when actually... he was dead.

I wasn't sure which was worse.

I hugged my legs against my chest on the couch. The images on the TV screen blurred together. I flinched when I felt a hot tear hit my cheek.

"I didn't tell you guys then because we had bigger problems than grieving. I wanted to carry that burden. Just like the ones I carry now because you two are all I have." Sterling tightened his grip on the armrests of his recliner.

"I know how you get, Briar," he surmised.

"How's that?" My voice came out in a sickly croak.

"Well, you get bored easily, and when you get bored, you do things. You do the same under stress."

"I haven't done anything." I cleared my throat and wiped my cheek.

Sterling inclined his head toward me, narrowing harvest-moon eyes that seemed to dare, *lie to me again.* "Sneaking into a fraternity party and getting drunk underage, the tattoos, the piercings, suddenly chopping half of your hair off several days ago—"

"Why are you telling me about Dad now?" I snapped. I wanted him to uproot the bush completely, not beat around it.

"You quit your job. You've been sleeping during the day when I come home from work, so I know you're up all night. I just want you to look me in the face and tell me you haven't been going out past Check-In."

His eyes bore into my soul. At this point, he paused the movie and the silence was so heavy it felt like my chest would cave in. I frowned slightly, held my chin high, and simply said, "I haven't."

But I had, and my shoulder ached for it, and the smell of my blood lingered downtown, and I had been inches away from the fangs of a man that burned a house down. I'd never felt so much fear, even in the hands of strangers when I was forced to live in foster care. Even when I lost control of the fruit punch, surrounded by college students. Even when that man held me at knifepoint for my car. Fear that was so terrifying but wildly exhilarating after having survived it all.

Sterling's face slackened.

"I haven't," I repeated, much more firmly.

"Well, I don't need to tell you not to think about it," Sterling said.

"You know... humans can be monsters too."

I pushed away the memories of the two Vampyres that had confronted me. Instead, my memories swelled with the grey afternoons of hiding from my volatile mother and the beatings in foster care, then with the pleasant memories of Sundance and the breathtaking music of Until Dawn at Nightshade. The neon lights of the city, the delicious smell of human snacks at the food truck—despite insulting the cook and never tasting it. The amused smirk on the stranger's face as he creepily prowled after me, then saved me.

That's what made me still crave more despite the dull ache in my shoulder, the blood spilled, and my bike nearly getting stolen. It was the first time in a while that I'd entertained a *feeling*.

"Humans *can* be, but Vampyres *are*." Sterling glanced at his watch and yawned, then straightened his recliner before standing. His bones cracked as he stretched.

I scoffed and shook my head. If they were such monsters, why didn't a hoard of them attack me?

"I'm going to go ahead and catch up on sleep while I still can." Sterling said as he dragged his feet across the wooden floor with a sniff.

I glanced at the clock on my phone. It was just turning to midnight.

I felt... torn. Torn between the desire to feel the cool night air against my skin and my brother's warnings. Torn between the adrenaline of breaking the law and the threats that I should've been more bothered by. And I felt guilty for lying to my brother's face twice in a matter of seconds.

I lay on my side again, curled up in a ball. I stared at the frozen TV, one character pointing a gun at the other. My eyes blurred again as I came to a damning realization.

I was a horrible person, just like our mother.

# 15
# DRAVEN

THE TEMPERATURE IN THE ROOM DROPPED TEN DEGREES. Every sound, smell, and taste vanished until I felt like a mass of dead flesh standing in the middle of the basement. I gaped at the humans writhing in our presence.

"Before any of you say anything, we are not bringing back the Mandrake Assistance Program." Uriah walked deeper into the cellar and stood behind them so we could have a full, unobstructed view. "You all may have heard rumors about experiments at White Fang. Well... I'm proud to say they're true."

"What's this got to do with the Sun Dwellers though?" a woman asked impatiently.

"They're... test subjects." Uriah said, then beamed.

"I thought you said White Fang was doing it. I don't understand!" A male voice rang out and echoed, but I didn't bother to see who'd spoken. I was too busy locking eyes with the victims. All their faces were wan, their skin caked with dirt and their lips chapped.

"The White Fangs have a lab where they have been working on a way to cure our blood dependencies, but I suggested they start a new project that cures our sun sensitivity. If we can go back into the sun, we can retake the city, and maybe even the world."

Uriah took out a small pocketknife and pulled one of the young girls' hair, forcing her neck back. He made a small cut, triggering many growls and hisses from our brethren. Even I, with all my strength to resist blood on any given day, felt saliva coat my mouth at the sight and smell of it.

"It'll be our turn to force them into the shadows and treat them like the cattle they are." He let go of her hair roughly, and her head jerked forward like the snap of a rubber band.

"I just wanted to update everyone on our project. There's a large search going on, but right now the police are looking for human suspects since the abductions have been during the day. We had to take this many in a short period because that was part of the White Fangs' terms to work with us."

There were more murmurs, gradually growing louder into more agreeable tones. Uriah's smile gleamed as he stepped out of the cellar and closed the shelves. The Sun Dwellers screamed desperately, but they were shut out to complete silence once the wall completely sealed. Even with advanced hearing, the walls were so thick that no Vampyre would hear them above ground.

"If anyone has any questions or concerns, I'll be in my study. Everyone's dismissed!" Uriah announced, then walked to the door to unlock it.

Most people left, with a couple staying to lounge around. I followed Uriah to his study.

"Can I talk to ya for a second?"

"I suppose. I didn't think you'd have any concerns, considering this would allow you to go out any time," he said with an exhausted sigh.

"No, I think it's great to work toward a cure, but... do ya really think partnering with the White Fangs is a good idea?" I asked.

"I don't see why not. They have the facilities to complete our goal, and we both have the same interests." Once he settled at his desk, he wove his fingers together and leaned forward.

"Nightshades and White Fangs have a long history of rivalries and betrayals. Time and time again we've tried to partner with them just to get stabbed in the back. They might have the facilities, but we have enough money to build our own."

"Look at you, knowing your Nightshade history," Uriah chuckled. "Yes, we have the money, but to build takes a lot of time and logistics." He cracked his knuckles, then leaned back into his chair. "Any other concerns?"

"It also seems like an impossible experiment, and forcin' us to kidnap those four humans in a week's time seems more like a setup to get the cops' attention. How do ya know they're not trying to bring us down?"

Uriah was silent, tapping his metal fingers against the wooden desk and subtly nodding.

He narrowed his eyes. "What else?"

"Nothing." I averted his malicious gaze. Perhaps I wasn't sounding supportive enough for this little project. Either way, I didn't care enough to risk another beating.

"Well, in case you've forgotten, Draven, Arlo's situation is still a priority. Any other business matters we tend to will have to be during the day—as much as possible—so Vampyric activity isn't suspected first while the police are on high alert."

Arlo.

That friggin' *girl*.

I gave Uriah a nod and started to head for the door.

"Oh, and Draven?" he called. I paused with my hand on the handle. I kept my back turned.

"Keep an eye out for more human test subjects. The profile is between twenty and thirty years old. All blood types are welcomed, but they must be healthy."

I swallowed dryly.

"Yes, sir," I mumbled, then left his office in search of Caspian.

* * *

Caspian was outside in the shade of a veranda that overlooked the sea. Thick vines wove through the wooden slats. His expression was deadpan. I followed his gaze and saw several Sun Dwellers littered across the sand in the distance, many frolicking in the sea's crystal-blue waters.

"I don't know how to swim," he said as I approached. His snow-white eyebrows knit together behind his sunglasses. "I'd like to learn someday."

"What's stopping ya?"

"Sharks come out at night."

"So do we."

"We're not at the top of the food chain in the sea," Caspian retorted.

I pursed my lips tightly and fell silent for a moment. I never thought Caspian really wanted to do anything. His loyalties, hopes, and dreams always seemed to revolve around the Nightshades.

"Why not just swim in the pool?"

"It's not the same." Caspian sighed and shook his head. "Anyways... I know you didn't come out here to listen to me complain, so what's up?"

"Oh, right." I sank into a wicker chair and watched the waves, and a distant surfer dominating them as if he owned the sea itself. "That girl I mentioned before... I let her go."

"*What?*" Caspian turned his attention away from the ocean and straightened in his seat. "You had an opportunity to kill her, and you *didn't?*"

"She lives with a cop." I winced at the words.

"Then let's do away with the cop first, make it look like an accident." Caspian leaned forward, staring off into space as his gears turned.

"Yeah, 'cause that worked so well the last time."

Caspian anxiously ran a hand through his hair.

"She, um... she snuck out and was around Vampyres all last night."

I had never seen anything like it. The closest I had ever seen Vampyres and Sun Dwellers be around each other in harmony were essential night-shift workers. There were never Vampyres with authorization for day shifts because of our physical limits, but there were plenty of humans with night authorizations.

"What do you mean?" Caspian curled his lip upward.

"She was casually hangin' out at The Nightshade bar. Not an inklin' of fear came from her." The more I spoke about it, the more fantastical it sounded.

"Seriously? How did I miss her?" Caspian scrunched his nose.

"Maybe because you were plastered and makin' out with random chicks."

He rolled his eyes and waved his hand as if to shoo away the topic.

"So, what now?"

"Uriah told me to tie up loose ends tonight and to keep an eye out for more human subjects. That means gettin' Arlo's money. I ain't gonna risk bringing the girl here as a test subject when she might blab to Uriah about witnessing the fire. So... I'll handle her too."

*Even though she'd raised a very valid point.*

"Yeah, not if she's casually hanging out with Vampyres like that." Caspian took off his sunglasses and rubbed his face. "She could be with another clan like the Mandrakes we kept. Could she be White Fang?"

"No, she still seemed unfamiliar with stuff," I said quickly. White Fangs were deep in the northern Nocturne District anyway. The rural areas were in the polar opposite direction, and she couldn't have been living with her family if she was their "pet."

"What makes you so sure?" Caspian rasped.

"Like I said, she lives with a cop. They're way out in the country." I didn't realize my leg was shaking up and down during the conversation until Caspian rubbed his temples, a nervous tic he so rarely expressed.

"I need a vacation," he said with sigh, then rose to his feet.

"Yeah, me too." I stood right after and leaned back, cracking my back with a grunt.

We stalked back into the house with our heads hanging low.

※

After the Gloaming period, Caspian and I made a deal to split up. He agreed to deal with Arlo, and I would handle the girl. Of course, we probably should have switched places, considering how much I'd messed up giving people second chances lately... or he should've handled both himself.

I hung around the oak tree in the middle of the bare field near the girl's house. The unmarked car was there, right next to the motorcycle. The cop and the girl were both home, and at the very least, in the living room watching TV. A pale blue light emitted from the front and side windows, shifting colors as the scenes changed.

Around midnight, the silhouette of a tall, muscular figure crossed one of the windows, and then disappeared from the living room. I crouched low next to the tree, waiting for the right moment to launch across the field in one fell swoop. The kitchen light cut off and all that was left was the TV screen.

I made my move.

The girl with the pink hair was partially visible from the side window, lying on the couch and staring at the paused TV screen. Her eyes were a dull gray, like the matte clouds on a rainy day. Those were the days the sun burned the least, but also the days that made me feel the heaviest.

The sparkling diamond irises, the pure joy that had rested upon her face before... it was nonexistent as she twisted to lay upside down on the cushions, her legs dangling over the back of the couch. She stared at the ceiling, her cheeks puffing out as she forced air past her tightened lips. She ran her hands over her face before sitting up and heading upstairs.

I jumped to the second-floor balcony that stretched across the front half of the house. I checked each window until I reached her room, then put on a pair of gloves before testing if her window was locked. I slowly slid it open, and the muffled sound of running water became clearer. She was in the shower, listening to quiet music full of angst. None of them were headbangers like the other night.

That emptiness on her face—it reminded me a lot of Caspian. A stone wall built to conceal whatever resided inside, with curtains to cover the cracked windows that sometimes mistakenly let emotion pour out.

*Killing her is an act of mercy.* I started to silently chant the same mantra I always told myself before confronting a difficult target.

*Death is the gateway to freedom.*

I silently climbed through the window, entering her dimly lit bedroom. I closed it behind myself, then reached in my pants pocket for the dagger I'd used on Arlo.

*You will send her unfortunate soul to a realm of peace.*

I moved to the darkest corner of her room, near a bookshelf full of movies, records, and a retro record player. There wasn't a book in sight, just layers upon layers of music paraphernalia. I tucked away in the nook between the bookshelf and the wall.

*Nightshades will always come first.*

I tightened my grip on the hilt of the dagger. She opened her bathroom door, steam rolling as she came out dressed in a spaghetti-strap tank top and old volleyball shorts. My gaze swept over her body before I frowned at the bandage over her shoulder. My mind flashed to the night I chased the two Vampyres away and my grip started to loosen.

*Why would I report anything to anyone when I'd just get in trouble for breaking curfew in the first place?*

She shuffled to the window and opened it halfway. She sat at the bench built into the wall at the windowsill, then stared longingly at the skyline. She seemed to yearn for something she couldn't have, and I knew that feeling all too well.

Something within me broke, and I put away the dagger.

"You really have no regard for the law, do you?" I spoke in a low whisper as I moved out from behind her bookshelf.

She gasped, launching from the window cushion. The color was snatched from her skin, her bones chattering. She yanked a small lamp from her nightstand and wielded it like a bat.

"Hey, hey," I whispered, facing out my palm to her. "I... came to say sorry."

*She's the last one. No more second chances...*

She didn't have leverage. She never would. I was willing to bet she didn't tell that cop anything that had happened either, because then he'd have the legal obligation to arrest her.

"*Who are you?! Why do you keep following me?!*" she hissed in a whisper. Her eyes were wild, darting around the room as if there were ten more intruders. Her hands still shook on the lamp. It wasn't necessarily *comfort* with the Vampyres she had that night. It was naivete. After all, she still thought a lamp could do anything to me.

However... the cop, who had endless Vampyric defense training, was probably only a wall or two away from us.

I took a moment longer to stare at her holding that stick of a lamp, then grinned with a soft chuckle.

"Call me Draven."

# 16

# BRIAR

My heart slammed against the wall of my chest so violently that it hurt. The air in the room grew thick, my every breath plodding through my lungs like molasses. The cool metal pole of my lamp quickly warmed against my clammy palms.

"Draven." It was all I managed to get out in a single, forced breath. He took small steps toward me.

"I-I never went back to Nightshade, I swear!" I stressed as I stumbled backward until the wall hit my back. Even if I called out for Sterling, Draven could easily rip my throat apart and be out of the window before Sterling could even flip the covers off himself. I slid down the wall and sank to the floor when my legs felt too weak to hold me up.

"You ain't hear me? I said I came to say sorry." Draven tilted his head slightly, that thick, wavy noir hair sweeping over his shoulder.

Up close, in the dim light of my other lamp, I could've sworn there was a hint of dark purple. He smelled like a mix of subtle tobacco, leather, and vanilla.

"Sorry for what? Saving me?" I asked hoarsely.

"Threatenin' ya," he whispered.

From the floor, he was a towering pillar of pure, lethal strength. In the darkness, his eyes seemed to glow, something in his irises swirling like water. His face was gentle rather than contorted in malice or aggression. As I stared longer, the muscles in my body seemed to relax, the fear fading as if a cold cloak had been removed from my shoulders. He seemed... genuine enough.

I slowly stood, hooking my hair behind my ears with a deep breath.

"You ain't tell me your name." Draven jerked his chin at me, folding his arms expectantly. He smirked, but his eyes didn't meet it.

"Why should I?" I shifted the weight on my legs and mirrored Draven's folded arms.

"I gave ya mine, which puts me at more risk than you giving me yours." He wiggled a finger at me.

I rolled my eyes with an exasperated sigh and pushed my tongue against the inside of my lip piercing. I considered it for a moment, eyeing Draven carefully in his faded grey jeans and black t-shirt that hung over his broad chest muscles. Tattoos of black and red Chinese dragons spiraled over his bronzed, corded arms, reminding me of the chest tattoo he'd flashed at those Vampyres to make them go away. His neck tattoos were a collage of nightshade and chrysanthemum flowers, skulls, and small geometric shapes, and they seemed to stretch over his shoulders. He reached in his pocket for a toothpick as he waited.

"I don't know you," I said in a sharp whisper.

"Duh. Ain't nobody born knowin' names. That's the whole point." The toothpick twitched with each word.

"What does your chest tattoo mean?" I raised an eyebrow.

Draven's eyes widened and he coughed as if the question physically knocked air out of him.

"It's... uh, just a warning for some of us Vampyre folk." He unfolded his arms and slid his hands in his pockets with a shrug.

I tapped my foot against the wood and looked warily at my bedroom door. I glanced at the clock. It was two in the morning.

*If you know what's good for ya, you'll keep your mouth shut.*

Draven still hadn't mentioned me witnessing the fire. Maybe it really wasn't him and he was just referring to the stalking or the run-in with the other two Vampyres. Perhaps whoever stood before me could be more of a friend instead of a predator. After all, if he really wanted to kill me, he would've done it sooner or left me out to dry with those two Vampyres. He saved me. He *saved* me.

"My name—" I sucked in a breath. "—is Briar."

"It's nice to meet ya."

Draven smiled, that poor toothpick at the mercy of his thick, pointed fangs. He extended his hand and I hesitantly shook it. He slid his hands back in his pockets. I hugged my arm to my side and looked around uncomfortably, waiting to see if he'd finally leave. I shifted my gaze to the window, not necessarily giving him a hint, but looking at the glowing skyline buzzing with life in the distance. If he apologized for the threat, then did that mean...

"Alright, well, uh—" He shuffled toward the window, and

something struck within me. I grabbed the hem of his shirt and pulled him back.

"Wait—" I took a step back, quickly letting go of his shirt. He looked back over his shoulder, the pupils of his red eyes expanding slightly.

"What?"

"Would you be willing to... um... help me explore the city more?"

I rubbed the back of my neck with an uncomfortable chuckle. It sounded even crazier aloud. I had to keep reminding myself that he had prioritized saving me over killing me. He'd even wiped my blood off his fingers rather than trying it like the Vampyre who'd hurt my shoulder.

I kept replaying the logic in my head so I didn't feel as foolish for asking that of him.

"Are you serious?" He raised his eyebrows, then turned to face me entirely.

"You belong to that world, I don't. If you're not going to kill me, why not help me?"

"Help you be stupid?"

"Help me be free."

Draven fell silent, considering. My heart started to quake as I felt hope balloon inside my chest.

"Briar? Are you talking to somebody?"

I spun around when I heard Sterling's voice drawl behind the door. My heart jumped and I whirled back to look at Draven, who was nowhere to be seen. My curtains danced from the outside breeze.

I shut my window and locked it, then stormed to my bedroom

door.

Sterling's hair was tousled in a mess of curls as he rubbed his eye with a yawn. "Sounded like I was hearing whispering or something," he grumbled.

"Yeah, that was my TV. Sorry, Sterling," I said shortly.

*That coward really left without a word.*

"Why don't you try to go to sleep? Tomorrow is important, at least to Astoria. You know she's gonna want you to go with her." His nostrils flared as he fought another yawn.

I frowned and cocked my head. Whatever tomorrow was, I didn't have the time to remember it.

"It's Mom's birthday."

Something in my mouth went bitter. I gave him a stiff nod and closed the door. It took a lot of self-control not to slam it and wake Astoria downstairs.

If I was going to sleep at all that night, it certainly wouldn't happen now.

# 17
# DRAVEN

I STAYED ON THE ROOF JUST ABOVE BRIAR'S WINDOW. THE door creaked subtly, and the drawled voice behind it became clearer. Through the thin window pane, I could still hear their hushed voices.

"Yeah, that was my TV. Sorry, Sterling."

Sterling.

"Tomorrow is important, at least to Astoria. You know she's gonna want you to go with her," he said. I assumed Astoria was the girl who had nearly cried with the police officer a couple days ago.

"It's Mom's birthday."

Judging by what he said, he had to have been her brother.

I heard her door shut, then heavy, lazy footsteps retreat across the house. I would've gone back inside to answer her question, but I didn't think it was a good time. Besides, I wasn't sure what kind of answer I wanted to give anyway.

I lunged off the roof and landed in the street. I glanced back at the house, but Briar was nowhere to be seen from my angle. I pinched the bridge of my nose with a sigh. The guts on that woman... to even attempt to ask a Vampyre to escort her through the city past Gloaming. It was incredible.

I darted back into the heart of Neoterra and waited by a strip mall. I texted Hartley, then flicked my toothpick elsewhere and replaced it with a cigarette, pondering. I watched the smoke swirl and fade into the night air.

If I agreed to escort her, the risk of getting arrested, shot, or bitten would indeed be significantly lower for her. But there was also the risk that Uriah could find out, force her to become one of those *test subjects*, and beat me senseless for letting a witness live or not taking her myself for the experiments. Briar's blood certainly had a unique smell to it... I couldn't pinpoint what her blood type was like the other humans.

Killing Briar was out of the question since her brother was on the force. But dying would be an act of mercy compared to whatever she'd be subjected to in the Nightshades or at White Fang. However... killing her would also be destroying the only human in this cursed world who didn't see a difference between my kind and hers, like picking the only fire poppy that had bloomed among ashes.

The limo slowly rolled to a stop at the curb. The back window eased down, revealing Caspian wiping blood off his face with a handkerchief. I dropped my cigarette and smashed it under my shoe before getting inside.

"What happened?" I asked as I eased into the backseat.

"Arlo was staying in a hotel. He had the money in an envelope. When I reached for it, he smashed a wine bottle over my head. I, uh, I can't remember much after that." Caspian looked down at the floor.

I furrowed my brows. "Did ya kill him?"

Caspian rarely had blackouts, but the last time he did was five years ago, and it ended with twenty Vampyres dead.

"I... don't know..."

His voice trailed off as his eyes grew wider, still staring at the same spot on the floor. I opened my mouth to speak, but my phone started to ring. I leaned to the side to access my back pocket and grabbed my phone to see Uriah's name flashing across the screen. I sighed and closed my eyes briefly before answering.

"Draven," I answered flatly.

"You boys on the way back yet?" I put him on speaker and exchanged a wary glance with Caspian. "I got a job for you with these *guests*. It needs to be done before sunrise."

"Yeah... we're about ten minutes out."

"As soon as you get here, meet me in the cellar and we'll talk more." Uriah hung up without warning. I reached into my front pocket for a toothpick and chewed on it.

⁕

Caspian and I got out of the limo and walked inside. His strides were smaller and slower than mine, the bloody handkerchief still balled tightly in his hand.

"Hey, why don't you go ahead and clean up? I'll cover for ya," I said.

His face stretched in a tight smile, almost grimacing before he took a sharp turn down one of the halls branching from the foyer. I didn't care about Arlo's well-being—not *that* much—but I did wonder if he was truly dead. Caspian was always calm, but like a river, no one ever knew what resided underneath.

Our run-ins with Arlo weren't because he was purposefully holding back payment. He had a real problem with gambling and managing money. Despite the portraits in his house, there weren't any signs of kids or a woman living there. It was safe to assume they'd left him because of it.

Once I reached the basement, I headed straight for the open cellar door. The Sun Dwellers were crowded back-to-back in chains like last time. They were blindfolded but they didn't flinch, only slouched with their heads hanging low as if in prayer. Uriah was sitting on a concrete bench at the end of the narrow cellar with one leg crossed over the other, his metal fingers tapping over his knee.

"Where's Caspian?" he demanded.

"Bathroom," I droned.

"Alright, I'll just explain it to you, and you can pass it along. I need you to take them to this location—"

He pulled out a paper from the breast pocket of his navy blue waistcoat. I walked around the prisoners and took the paper. It was an address I didn't recognize, so I frowned and looked at Uriah warily.

"Is this *their* territory?" I sneered.

"Yes, but they already know you're coming." Uriah tilted his head slightly, his eyes poised with malevolent warning not to question him. I sighed and crumpled the paper in my hand before shoving it in my pocket.

"*Before* sunrise. They close their gates at first light."

Uriah stood from the bench, brushed off his pants, and left the cellar. Caspian was just passing the couches when Uriah jabbed his thumb behind him in my direction, then continued up the stairs. Before Caspian could cross the threshold into the cellar, I met him at the bar and dropped my voice into a low whisper.

"He wants us to go to White Fang territory and drop them off."

Caspian scoffed.

"Did he give you the address?" His face returned to its flat affect, as if his frustration was immediately replaced with acceptance.

"Yeah, but I think we better make sure we're strapped before we go."

The White Fangs. How would I describe them...

If the Devil himself could be anyone, he would choose one of them. Of course, Nightshades were far from saints, but we always kept our word. Uriah was a master of fine writing, but he'd never go back and change a contract after it had been signed.

"I'll get the van ready," he mumbled, then flashed out of sight in the blink of an eye.

"Where are you taking us?" one of the girls asked, her voice so hoarse that some syllables were lost in a vacuum.

"None of ya business," I hissed. I bit down on my toothpick so hard that the wood split, and I spat the whole thing out of my mouth before grabbing one of the frail men and slinging him over my shoulder. He grunted and resisted only a second before slumping weakly. I couldn't help but wonder how long they'd been here to have already lost the will to fight.

I spent roughly ten minutes taking multiple trips to throw them in the back of one of our black vans. Caspian was in the driver's seat. I could hear the clicking of the pistols as he loaded their magazines and chambered the rounds.

Once the prisoners were all buckled in, I double-checked their chains and handcuffs. Finally, I reached in a toolbox and pulled out duct tape to seal each of their mouths.

I stepped out of the van and took one more look at the pitiful souls.

"Any day now, man," Caspian called.

I shut the double doors and jumped in the passenger seat. I took the pistol, still in its holster, from the dash and tucked it in my waistband before readjusting in my seat.

"Don't forget this either." Caspian tossed a black cloth on my lap. I unfolded it, recognizing the half-skull gaiter we used to wear during transports.

I sighed and pulled it over my neck, then stretched it over my mouth and nose. I sunk in the seat a little, staring blankly at the road ahead as we drove deeper into the Nocturne District.

The King Estate was on the edge of the district, right before it transitioned into Neoterra's mainland, where many of our clients and businesses resided. I personally didn't have many dealings in the heart of Nocturne. It was a place of pandemonium, and Uriah preferred "classier" associations. There were Vampyres so unhinged that law-abiding Vampyres would stay home no matter the time of day. The district was plagued with crime. Even the police had mostly given up on the place, although there were rumors that they would crack down on the district. It made sense for snakes like the White Fangs to be this far into the district.

Most buildings were illuminated with red. It made everything look drenched in blood. Some said it was supposed to serve as a reminder of The Cleansing, a day of nothing but bloodshed—when humans still lived in their homes in the Nocturne District and hadn't fully moved to their Diurnal Zones per federal orders. The Vampyres moved in, and the humans were either Turned or drained. I was only six years old at the time. I didn't fully understand what was going on, but I remembered my parents clinging to the television news and ordering me to my room. By the time they died when I was fourteen, I had already been repeatedly warned about Neoterra and its largest district, and had made up my mind to never go there or any other Vampyric territory.

At least, that was before Uriah's men came to my doorstep and drove me straight to the city I feared.

Briar may have been shown mercy in Neoterra, but she most certainly could not survive in Nocturne.

I closed my eyes again, leaning my head against the window and focusing on the unsteady shaking of the van over potholes.

"Hey, pay attention." Caspian nudged my arm and I hissed back at him, but sat up from the window. I just wanted one second of an escape from the reality of giving these humans over to them.

We wound through a hilly area with narrow roads and abandoned factories and warehouses. Then we passed wide patches of land overrun by tall grasses and weeds, but what stood out the most were the twisted poles of wrought iron sticking out of the ground and the countless skulls propped on the tops like flags.

I didn't have a doubt in my mind that we'd officially crossed into White Fang territory.

✳

The road sloped downward, passing a cratered lake partially sur-rounded by pine trees. It sloped back upward, and once we crest-ed the hill, a large black building came into view. Trees concealed the majority of it. The parking lot was empty, encircled by a black iron fence. We entered a circular driveway that led to a gate with two guards standing on either side of it. One had sienna skin with buzzed blonde hair and a pierced eyebrow, while the other had ivory skin with sandy, medium-length hair cut in a curtain fringe. They both wore gaiters over their noses and mouths and held assault rifles. As our van slowed to a stop, they quickly approached with firm, malicious steps. I palmed the handle of my pistol as the one with shorter hair approached my side of the van.

"State your business here." The one with the pierced eyebrow raised his barrel at Caspian, who didn't so much as flinch.

"We work for Uriah King with the Nightshades. We were told to drop off a package."

"What package?" the guard demanded.

"Live cargo," Caspian said flatly.

The guard held the rifle with one hand as he pulled out a two-way radio to announce our presence. Once it was confirmed we were expected, the guard jerked his head toward his partner. The one with shorter hair pushed a button and the gate slid open with a loud groan.

We rolled our windows up as we slowly followed a circular drive-way to the front of a modern laboratory. Large display windows cov-ered the front of the first floor, recessed under a larger rectangular structure with smaller horizontal windows, supported by columns holding up the bottom. The sidewalk was lined by lush green grass and lavender bushes. The laboratory looked very pristine—a stark contrast to the staked skulls.

We pulled around the front. I was the first to get out the van to tend to the prisoners while Caspian watched my back.

I opened the double doors and they lifted their heads from the van's walls. The humans moved their blindfolded faces around to the different sounds around them. I took the women first, slinging one on each shoulder. I glanced back at Caspian, who holstered his weapon to grab one of the emaciated men.

An olive-toned woman with thick, brown curly hair, wearing a long white lab coat and cat-eye prescription glasses, waited for us in the lobby. Her merlot-colored eyes scanned us from head to toe before she extended her left arm toward a door across the lobby labeled "Staff Only."

Caspian and I once again exchanged uneasy glances.

The hallway was initially black, but our motion automatically cut on the bright fluorescent lights along the corridor. We followed the woman down the twists and turns. There were windowless rooms, and then a few with display windows that showed operating tables, monitors, and large lights.

"What sort of experiments do you people do here?" I asked, my voice echoing subtly.

The woman didn't answer, just used a key card to unlock the next set of double doors, revealing a room full of cells. Floating beds were bolted into white cinder block walls, their white sheets neatly tucked into the metal frames. We passed a few humans sleeping in their cells, and stopped in front of a set of empty ones. The woman stopped in front of a block of four.

"You can remove their chains and duct tape over their mouths," she said in a gruff, Romanian accent. "Once you put them in there, we will take it from here."

We started to untie them, and not a single one fought us to escape.

"What are ya gonna do with them?" I asked once the door was shut. She gave me a sidelong glance.

"None of your concern. All our reports are sent to Uriah King." She spoke coldly. "You may leave."

I scoffed and shook my head, then jerked my chin at Caspian and toward the front door.

The guards were still outside, watching through the windows. They eyed us carefully as we got in the van, and followed us until we were completely off the property, once again surrounded by the skewered Vampyre and human skulls.

I glanced at Caspian as the ball of his jaw quivered. The emptiness of the trunk served as a reminder of what and who we were.

I thought about Briar and wondered if by now she'd gone out on her own again. After all, she seemed to want to escape her world as much as I wanted to escape my own. That pure joy on her face... I wanted to know what that felt like. Just a single moment of pure bliss before I had to go back—

I didn't deserve it. Not one second.

The harsh red lighting in the heart of the Nocturne District gradually softened to cerulean, amethyst, and magenta as we drew closer to the King Estate. My body sunk deeper into the seat with the comfort of being as far away from the White Fangs as possible, but the weight of my guilt pulled me further down.

"You want to go out tomorrow night? Invite Delilah, a couple of the guys. Get some drinks?" Caspian spoke stiffly, as if the request were forced. As tempting as it sounded, I needed a night away from Nightshades. A change of pace could make me forget what we had just done.

"Actually... there was something else I wanted to do tomorrow night."

# 18
# BRIAR

I had to take melatonin to douse the rage after Draven left me unanswered. I kept my window unlocked, hoping he would come back after he heard Sterling leave.

Maybe I was being irrational. The guy was a Vampyre who'd only come to apologize, and I may have stepped over the line asking him to break the law with me. But then again, he broke into my bedroom, so it didn't seem like it would go against any values he had.

I only got four hours of sleep. In the past week, it seemed like the new normal. It didn't help my irritability when Sterling pushed me to go with Astoria to the Black Bay County Prison in a city named Helios. It was four hours away round-trip.

Helios was smaller than Neoterra, but it still held its reputation as one of the most successful cities to survive the Crimson War between Vampyres and humans before the new laws took place. Part of its survival was dependent on the fact that Helios was a small island only accessible by ferry. Its location was also a huge factor in choosing where to build the new prison. It made it harder for both humans and Vampyres to escape.

Sterling made breakfast for us, but I only reached for a couple pieces of bacon off the serving platter.

"That's it?" Sterling pouted.

"Yeah, and don't give me that stupid 'breakfast is the most important meal of the day' crap," I grumbled. I savored the flavor and felt my stomach twist afterward. I was hungry and nauseous, so I opted to ignore the hunger.

Astoria eagerly ate her food, then jumped from the table to gather her things. I waited for her by the front door, browsing through my phone. While she was gathering her things in her room, Sterling approached me.

"Hey, try not to make the visit about you, okay? Let her have this," he whispered.

I scoffed.

"I never make it about myself until Vivian says something first. Besides, I don't understand why Astoria is so excited to visit our trash mother anyway."

"*You* haven't seen her in five years. She could be different now."

"We told ourselves she'd be different throughout our childhood. Maybe it's time to wake up," I snapped in a hushed whisper.

Astoria came out of her room holding a little white box with a thin plastic window at the top, revealing a cupcake with rose-shaped icing. She also held a light blue envelope. I tried to hide my sour expression as I imagined the heartfelt message probably written below the generic one on the card.

"I'm ready," she said quietly, almost as if it was more to herself than to me.

"Cool."

I went outside and waited by her car.

"Please be safe! You got that, Briar? Make sure you both get home before Check-In!" Sterling called as he leaned against the porch railing.

"Duh." I rolled my eyes and got in the car. My arm tensed as I gripped the door handle to slam it shut, but I stopped myself.

Astoria carefully placed the cupcake and card on the backseat before sliding behind the wheel. She put on her seat belt and started the car with a sullen face.

✳

We were thirty minutes deep into the trip when I finally decided to speak, mostly to prevent Astoria from turning on one of her boring audiobooks.

"Why do you still care about that woman?"

I propped my elbow against the door and rested my cheek in my palm.

"By 'that woman,' you mean *Mom*?"

I didn't look at her, but I could hear the frown in Astoria's voice.

"You know what I mean," I grumbled as I rolled my eyes.

"It takes more energy to hate her than to forgive her. She wasn't right in the head when she did those things to us. She's still our mom, and we wouldn't exist without her," Astoria said defensively.

"Technically, we could, in a different lifetime with a different household," I snarked.

"With different names, different siblings. Maybe no siblings," she retorted through a tight jaw. "Imagining being born under a different household is like imagining what it'd be like to be an animal."

"I only asked because I'm trying to understand. She beat you senseless when you spilled—"

"I know what happened," she interjected.

The leather of the steering wheel squeaked as her grip tightened around it. Silence returned with a brutal vengeance, and I suddenly craved the stupid audiobooks just for the sake of filling the void. I stared out the window, watching the swamps turn into lakes, then back to swamps, and then into the sea as we crossed a long, two-lane bridge rising into a hill. The horizon was unobstructed, and I wondered what could reside beyond it other than Helios.

I wasn't sure if her general agitation was because of me, Vivian's birthday, or something else. I assumed we would finish the rest of the trip in silence.

"Are you completely done with going out after Check-In?" Astoria broke a twenty-minute quiet streak.

Me, then. I guess that made sense considering she hadn't eaten dinner with us last night.

"Why, Ria?"

"I just... I want to make sure you don't do anything crazy while we're out here or try to make us late getting back home." She tried to soften her tone, as if it'd ease the sting.

"Wow, I didn't realize how low of an opinion you had of me. Why did I tag along again?"

Why would Sterling push me to go? Ever since I'd snuck out that first time, the wedge had been steadily growing between Astoria and me. He may not have known that for certain, but he had to suspect it.

"Because I want you to see she's different. I'm sorry for snapping at you lately. I'm just scared for you."

"The Vampyres aren't what you think," I seethed, turning to glare at her. Draven seemed like a lethal weapon himself, yet he came to apologize like a human. While his kind supposedly didn't have souls, he sure acted like *he* did. Even if he might've burned a house down, there was a speck of humanity there when he saved my life.

"Because you know them so well after two nights, right?" Astoria asked.

"And you do after none?" I retorted, returning my gaze back out the window.

Astoria scoffed and shook her head.

❋

After the most uncomfortable hour I'd ever had to endure, we finally traded concrete for grass, surf shops, and sand dunes. We were still technically in Neoterra, in its northernmost region. The Nocturne District was only thirty minutes behind us, but it was mostly harmless during the day in most recent months.

Astoria parked and we waited on the weathered wooden boardwalk that stretched for miles along the seafront. A Ferris wheel and carousel towered over the shore, hundreds of vendors scattered along the boardwalk. The wind carried refreshing smells of salt, funnel cakes, and popcorn. I inhaled deeply and watched the waves roll and tumble across the sand.

The water was a clear turquoise with patches of darker teal below the surface, which could've been sediment, schools of fish, or coral. I smiled softly, admiring its beauty, and wondered what the boardwalk experience would be like after Gloaming. It had been five years since the last time we'd passed through here, and back then there was nothing but sand, dune grass, and water. It didn't take long at all for this place to turn into a shallow tourist attraction, but I wasn't complaining about the changes too much. It seemed like it could be a lot of fun.

I plopped on a nearby bench with a pout, knowing our brother would never allow us to come here unless it was to see Vivian. According to Sterling's logic, any sort of leisurely activity here would risk being late to Check-In and getting trapped in the Nocturne District. Which, I suppose I could understand. Even with the wild craving to explore the boardwalk, I had no desire to go anywhere near Nocturne as a whole.

I observed the passersby and caught the stiff shoulders, clutched purses, and forced smiles. At first glance, this place looked like paradise, but when I paid attention to the withdrawn or tense facial expressions... only the children had sincere, unfiltered joy.

The boat wasn't far from the ferry slip. It was small enough to resemble a toy in a giant bathtub but gradually growing in size as it sailed toward us.

"We should probably get our tickets and start heading down there," Astoria said flatly.

"Okay." I trailed a couple of feet behind her. I was tempted to let the crowd swallow me and let us separate, but it would've been an act of unforgivable betrayal. Even for Astoria.

So I stayed close, with every fiber of my being screaming and kicking internally.

The line to board the ferry moved fluidly as the skipper checked everyone's tickets with a simple glance. It was a double-decker boat with most people going to the top. I wanted to do the same, but Astoria felt uneasy with the height, so we stayed on the bottom deck.

There were plush white booths and laminate tables lined along the wide display windows that had an unobstructed view of the water. The ceilings were molded in ivory ripples, as if they were modeled after the sea itself. There were menus to order food, although we agreed neither of us wanted anything.

It was going to be an hour-long trip further north, beyond the vast expanse of the sea. Seeing how much the boardwalk had changed made me wonder how much Helios had changed. I wondered if they were still as successful as before, or if they had a steady increase of crime like Neoterra. I tried to focus on the city itself rather than Black Bay County Prison.

As the ferry plodded through the water, I could see a sparkling skyline rise from the horizon. The skyscrapers were a dusty blue against the bright, cloudless sky, and looked like jagged teeth opening up to swallow the sky whole. As we grew closer to the seafront and the ferry slip, swimmers, tanners, and surfers became visible. Umbrellas, towels, and coolers littered the sand; children were running or digging holes; and somehow, their beach seemed full of more life than Neoterra's. I wondered if they had a dangerous district just looming behind them like at home, but judging by the carefree energy of the beach, I doubted it.

Astoria and I were the first to disembark. We moved through the ferry slip and exited onto another boardwalk, where I finally caught Astoria smiling for the first time in a week. The wind carried a more sunscreen-and-citrus scent, mixed with salt. Seagulls squalled ahead and gathered along the shore for scraps.

I frowned as I sulked behind Astoria, looking around. Everyone seemed so... docile. I didn't know how to feel about it. They had curfews too, yet they didn't seem bothered by the time quickly sliding past.

"Briar! Are you coming? The Ryde is on its way!"

Astoria cut into my thoughts. She clenched her phone tightly in her hand and took off her sandals to embrace the sand. Her toes wiggled and I glanced down at my shoes. I wore slip-on skater sneakers and socks. I wanted to experience the beach as she was, I wanted so badly to admire the peaceful beauty of Helios, but Black Bay hovered over my mind like I was going there for intake. I felt like they'd take one look at me and already know my sins, and lock me behind bars right then and there, and Vivian would be my bunkmate—

"Briar?" I flinched when Astoria gently grabbed my elbow. "What's wrong?"

"I can't." My throat bobbed. "I can't face that place."

"Why not?" She tilted her head slightly. All the coldness that poisoned those warm, gold eyes immediately melted.

"I don't want them to take me away and put me near her." Saying it aloud sounded crazy, but the fear still gripped my bones.

"What?" Astoria giggled. "That's not how that works. First of all, the officers can't read minds. Secondly, I doubt they'd even room you two together. If you're really that bothered by it, then..." The smile from earlier faded and her eyes dulled. "You don't have to come with me."

"No! No, I..." I sucked in a breath. "I'll go. Only because I already came all this way. It'd be a giant waste of time if I didn't."

My bones still chattered, but I buried it. I flailed my arms to shake it off.

We trudged through the sand and over a short, narrow board-walk toward a surf shop where the driver would meet us. He wore sunglasses, with grey hair belonging to a seventy-year-old, but there wasn't a wrinkle in sight. I slid across the backseat, but Astoria faltered. She must've noticed the glasses too. She slid into the seat, her hand immediately reaching for her necklace to fidget.

"Where to, ladies?" the man asked by way of greeting.

I slid my hand into Astoria's.

"Black Bay, please." I squeezed her clammy hand, not because we were more than likely in a Vampyre's presence, but because saying that name aloud felt like it would summon Vivian right between us in the backseat.

"Alright." The driver reached for the radio knobs and turned up the volume of pop music to fill the silence, erasing his own burning obligation to speak. I was fine with it, anything to avoid needless conversation.

We were driven roughly fifteen minutes out from the city, where among fields there was a single, hundred-story white tower surrounded by holographic, electrified fences. A single, spherical gatehouse resided at the end of a quarter-mile driveway. Astoria and I were dropped off at the very edge of it, and we had no choice but to walk to the gatehouse.

Out of the SUV, the tower looked ten times bigger, twenty times more menacing, and fifty times more formidable. At the very top, clouds swirled around its peak. My knees threatened to buckle.

I wanted to scream and run back to the beach, to become just as docile and peaceful as its occupants—but I was already here, and Astoria was already pushing forward with that stupid cupcake box. There was no use in running now.

We showed our identifications, signed the paperwork, submitted to a pat down, and watched as the cupcake was searched with a scanner for contraband. A correctional officer escorted us to a room with three rows of tempered-glass cubicles and speakers at the center of each one. Astoria and I sat in two stiff chairs as we waited. The cool metal against my arms was comforting, a brief distraction from the conversation I dreaded to come.

With each step, Vivian's black uniform brushed against itself with the sound of zippers being pulled back and forth. Her wrists were handcuffed in front of her as she sat down on the other side of the tempered glass. Vivian's golden hair was pulled back in a loose, low-hanging bun. Her freckles were stark against her pallid skin; her dark grey eyes were dull like asphalt and her lips were colorless. Vivian noticed Astoria first, her rotted smile full of light. Then her gaze met mine, and the corners of her mouth shrunk back. I looked away as my stomach wrenched itself.

"Ria, wow—this... is this part of a birthday present?" Vivian asked, the seat groaning beneath her as she shifted uncomfortably.

"No, I just wanted you two to have some time together too."

Astoria set the cupcake box down and placed her nimble fingers in her lap, fidgeting. I leaned back in my seat, arms folded and legs crossed.

"How lovely," Vivian purred as she reached through the small rectangular square and grabbed the box. "Now it would be a real party if Sterling was here."

"Sterling would never show up to see you," I blurted. Vivian glared at me as she took a bite of icing. She switched her focus on Astoria.

"How's life? How's school?"

"School's great, actually. I have straight A's, and next semester I'll finish my prerequisites," she said with a small laugh.

"What are you majoring in again?"

"Nursing. I'm thinking about maybe pursuing the nurse practitioner path but I'm not sure yet. I might take a break from school after getting my nursing license and come back later if I still want it."

"Well, whatever you do, you'll be successful at it." Vivian gave me a sidelong glance. "Just stay away from boys and parties."

"You really think you can lecture while in cuffs?" I hissed. "Astoria is good on her own. She's smart enough to make good decisions, she doesn't need any advice from the likes of you, *Vivian*." I spat her name like an insult.

"Briar, please—"

I cut Astoria off with a finger and leaned forward in my seat, bracing my forearms over my knees.

Vivian scoffed, setting down her half-eaten cupcake.

"And what about you, Bri? You think you have any room to give sisterly advice when all you do is fail? You were suspended left and right from fights in school, nearly failed a grade because of poor attendance, snuck out to college parties—need I go on?"

I gripped the chair handles tightly and clenched my teeth.

"At least I wasn't smoking, drinking, and shooting up."

"You probably will one day, when you finally realize what a useless disappointment you are and that's all you have left to fill up the empty shell. You're a lot more like your mother than you'd like to think."

"You're not my mother. You lost that title when you beat us senseless, got Dad killed, and had us split apart in the foster system."

I jumped to my feet, the chair screeching loudly against the tiled floor. I looked down at Astoria.

"I've heard enough. I'll wait for you outside." Astoria didn't protest. I turned back to Vivian. "I hope you choke."

"Astoria turned out fine, so what's your excuse?" she shouted after me. "You know what people do with deadweight? They cut it off!"

I stormed to the heavy metal door, but paused when I heard them speak again.

"I'd hoped this place changed you for the better... but it doesn't look like it, Mom," Astoria breathed.

"I'm clean and I've been taking classes. That girl is a bad influence on you. Don't let her poison our relationship. I was sick before, but I still love you, Ria." Vivian sounded bored.

I scoffed, snatched the door open, and returned the visitor pass.

There was a curved, ivory bench outside the gatehouse. I sat there, leaning into my elbows on my knees. I buried my face in my hands as I began to heave. My eyes burned as my vision crowded with black dots and blurred with tears. I couldn't help but think about how correct she was. I *was* a screwup. I almost dropped out of school, my grades were horrible, I put myself in danger countless times.

She never acknowledged me when I helped her into bed, cleaned her vomit, or tried to give her water to flush her veins. She hardly acknowledged me when I snuck out and came back home drunk myself. No matter what I did, she didn't care. Astoria and Sterling were the only ones that had her heart, but not enough to get clean. The thought of Sterling still being one of her favorites despite putting her behind bars only infuriated me more.

I tapped my heel rapidly as I tried to calm down. Despite being outside, it felt like invisible walls were closing me in.

I flinched when I felt a hand on my shoulder. I dropped my hands to my knees and looked up to see Astoria smiling sullenly down at me.

"You okay?"

A soft, briny breeze passed over my wet cheeks.

"Yeah," I said hoarsely, and wiped my face with the bottom of my t-shirt. "Let's just get out of here."

"Our Ryde should be here soon," Astoria said as she took a seat next to me. "I'm so sorry."

"No, it's fine." I took a deep breath. "You had good intentions."

"They're two minutes away. We should start heading down there." Astoria held out her hand. I grabbed it and we walked down the long drive to wait by the curb.

"I'm sorry, I really thought she changed." Astoria said again. There was a small speck of a car in the distance, heading in our direction. It wobbled in the heat waves hovering over the mirages in the road.

"People never change," I said flatly.

I would probably never change either. If there was anything I knew for certain in my life, it was that I was most definitely a screwup, and even when I tried to do better, I somehow screwed things up again. Maybe I was deadweight that needed to be cut off after all.

✳

The trip back home was rather uneventful. Astoria spent most of the time driving ten miles over the speed limit when the sky started to deepen. I didn't tell her to slow down, but I did remind her that with Sterling's friend Cyrene being our new Check-In officer, we probably didn't have to worry about her being strict. I certainly didn't care about showing up in time. Matter of fact, I contemplated leaving again tonight to pretend everything was okay. I wanted to get lost in the city, the music, the dancing. Lost in a random Vampyre's skin, where he could embrace me as one of his own. Lost from my own life, just for a moment.

As we pulled into the driveway, I saw the flawless, platinum blonde bun poking from underneath Cyrene's patrol cap as she spoke with Sterling, who was also in uniform. They both turned to face us in their masks.

Sterling elbowed Cyrene's arm gently as Astoria and I climbed out of her car.

"See? I told you they'd show up on time." He grinned smugly and strode to his car. With long, dainty fingers, Cyrene tapped her tablet screen and gave us a thin smile.

"'On time' is a bit of a stretch, but I'll give it to you," Cyrene teased. She turned to face us after setting the tablet back in the car.

"How was your trip?" she asked.

I shrugged curtly.

"It could've been a little better," Astoria said, dropping her gaze.

"Have a good night at work," she mumbled as she walked passed and went into the house.

I watched her, then shifted my eyes back to my brother and his colleague. They both had a purpose. Sterling was going to keep the streets in order, Astoria was probably burying her head in her studies, and all I had was the comfort of my bedroom. I gazed at the balcony, at the grey window that led to my room.

Maybe I didn't have a purpose in that clothing store. Maybe I didn't have a purpose anywhere during the day.

I refused to be like my mother.

Maybe I could try to be a night-shifter and live guilt-free after Check-In, because the last thing I needed was for Sterling or Astoria to go searching for *me* and die over it like our father did.

I smiled softly and walked inside with the hope that I wouldn't hate my reflection in the mirror for once.

# 19
# DRAVEN

After our trip to White Fang territory last night, I had plans to spend the day in bed and pretend to dream, then once night fell, I'd venture to the farmlands. Of course, Uriah stopped me right as my hand touched the brass doorknob of my room and lightly slapped a roll of papers against my back. I whirled around to face him.

"How did the exchange go?" he asked with a bright smile. His shoulders were back, his spine straightened, his hair slicked over flawlessly with gel and waves—it was as if he'd had the best night of sleep in his life. If only.

"It went okay. White Fangs ain't have much to say to us." I shrugged.

"That's great. Why don't you try to take the night off and relax? How long has it been since the last time you ate?" Uriah dropped his voice to a whisper and slung his arm over my shoulders.

"I don't know, two days maybe?"

I frowned. The last time Uriah had showed concern for my well-being was when I was a fresh fledgling child refusing to give into my cravings.

"Come to my office."

He pulled away and started walking back toward the white lion sculptures. My back slumped as I followed behind him. Was it too much to ask to be left alone?

When I stepped into his study, my eyes snapped straight to the spot where I'd been beaten. There was a faint blood stain on the floor peeking from underneath a new Moroccan rug that was placed to conceal it but wasn't quite big enough. I sucked in a sharp breath and took a seat in one of Uriah's tufted velvet chairs. I reached in my pocket for a toothpick but was met with an empty box. I sank deeper in the seat, my expression flat.

Uriah walked past my left to a minibar set beneath an oval mirror, then reached into the mini fridge for a bag of blood and a flute glass. My head immediately snatched in his direction the second he twisted the cap. He extended the glass toward me, the ruby in his golden family ring catching the recessed lighting in the study.

"How many years is it going to take for you to accept who and *what* you are?"

Black dots in my vision seemed to gradually grow bigger until the only thing I could see was that glass. I tightened my grip on the armrests before standing up and walking around the room. I paused in front of an abstract painting covered in black, white, and red splotches and shapes. The red was vibrant against the black and white, like the blood in the glass.

"You have a lot of power, Draven. Just think of how strong you'd be if you actually took care of yourself. Imagine where you'd be if these experiments become a success." The scent of the blood grew ever stronger as he held the glass below my chin.

"You may have been a Sun Dweller before, son, but I guarantee that no one cares about what you used to be. All you'll ever be to them is a monster. You've been one of us for thirteen years now... it's time you embrace it. The Sun Dwellers have been embracing it for you already."

Uriah grabbed my wrist and placed the glass in my hand. He patted my shoulder, then left me alone in his office.

I stared at the drink. It was thick and smooth, reflecting the ceiling's lights like still water. Anytime I saw blood, I thought about my parents splattered across the road among the smoke and rubble of the crash. They were long gone, but any time I drank it, I felt like they were watching with disgust.

Uriah had a good point, though. All I ever did was try to help. There was Arlo, a bumbling fool with a gambling problem, yet in the end, he turned on me.

I never felt guilt for any of the Vampyres I had beaten or killed for Uriah in the past, when I knew they were already inherently evil. When the Mandrake Assistance Program started, I tried to help the humans get out, but they never trusted me. One of them even told Uriah, and that landed me in a windowless cell with daily floggings for three weeks.

So why *did* I care? So far, Caspian was the only Vampyre I could trust, and Briar was the only human I'd seen that didn't seem to notice a difference between our kinds. Maybe I would be less miserable if I fulfilled my basic immortal needs.

I raised the glass a little higher, then finally to my lips, but I faltered once more.

*You've been one of us for thirteen years now... it's time you embrace it.*

I was more than just a Vampyre. For thirteen years, I had done monstrous things that chipped away my humanity bit by bit. It was useless to try to regain it back, especially after handing those humans over to the White Fangs to be lab rats. I was a Nightshade, and the only way out was through death.

I imagined my fangs grazing Briar's lithe neck. She breathed softly, awaiting a kiss, only to be met with the unrelenting gnash of my teeth. I pulled back to see her wan face. I watched the starlight die in her eyes, becoming two black holes that swallowed my soul as she sank limply in my arms.

I shook my head, then chugged the glass.

I sat in my room with random movies playing in the background as I spent most of my time watching the sunlight slowly dim to gold, then die out like a flame when Gloaming passed. I got up to brush my teeth, took a shower, and dressed in a black muscle tank styled with tatters around the bottom and baggy black cargo pants with matching sneakers. I gave myself a modest spray of cologne.

Finally, I stepped in front of the plain full-body mirror nailed into the wall next to the window and ran a hand through the longer side of my hair. I bared my teeth to make sure I hadn't missed anything when I brushed them. I turned side to side, examining my overall appearance. It was supposed to be a pleasantly warm night and I hoped that I wouldn't spend it alone.

I ran my tongue over one of my fangs as a craving crept up my neck. I went downstairs to the kitchen, only to find one bag left in the refrigerator and Delilah already reaching for it. She turned away from the fridge as the door shut on its own and froze in the middle of opening the bag.

"Draven? Wow, you look good tonight," she crooned and continued to twist the cap on the bag.

"Thanks." I shrugged.

"You want to go out somewhere?"

"Actually, I have plans." I glanced at the bag in her hand and my stomach gave a nudge.

"Plans? With whom?" She put a hand on her hip and raised an eyebrow.

"Nobody ya know." I turned on my heel, but a gust of wind brushed over me as Delilah flashed to my side.

"Another woman?" She put her hand over my shoulder and I shrugged it off.

"What's it to ya if it's another woman? Ain't like we're anything to each other," I hissed with more bite than I intended. I was more annoyed by the fact that she took the last bag than the line of questioning. She scoffed as I walked away.

I asked Hartley to drop me off in the town square. To his knowledge, I was just on a nightly outing. But instead, I started briskly walking south, toward the farmlands.

# 20
# BRIAR

There were only a few places that were exempt from curfew. There were plenty of other places for employees to have authorizations, but government facilities and hospitals were the only ones where as a *patron*, you were exempt. There were still efforts to avoid exposure across species. For example, a human having a heart attack at midnight would have to disclose their species to the 911 operators so the ambulance would have human paramedics. Anyone seeking certain curfew authorizations would have to go to City Hall, which was a neutral jurisdiction zone as long as the person didn't get caught on the way there if they were outside of their curfew.

I did a bit of research on my laptop, but my plans to become a night-shifter were immediately thwarted when one of the eligibility requirements was to already have a job lined up and show them the offer letter.

The authorization was contingent on consistent employment. In other words, the second a termination, layoff, or resignation occurred, the authorization would expire.

I slammed my laptop shut and put it in its usual spot under my bed. I buried my face in my pillow with a muffled scream.

Then it hit me.

*Sundance.*

They seemed open-minded enough. They didn't turn me away like Chen's Den, or challenge me like The Nightshade bar bouncer. A slim chance was better than none.

I glanced at my closed door. Sterling was working and Astoria was still studying. If I could land a job at Sundance and get that authorization, then this could be the last night of breaking promises.

I jumped from the bed, opening my closet to sift through my clothes to find the most presentable attire. Everyone in that shop was so elegant, glamorous—

"Yes!" I squealed, and snatched a champagne silk trumpet-sleeved blouse of its hanger, and paired it with a black pencil skirt and pantyhose.

* * *

I was an hour deep into getting ready when I heard multiple taps on my window. There wasn't a tree close enough to the balcony for branches to brush against the glass. I paused with one diamond earring in my ear and peeked from my bathroom with a wary frown.

My jaw dropped when I saw the chiseled face, the thick black-violet hair that cascaded like a waterfall over his right shoulder, and the cheeky dimple deepening as a smirk tugged on half of his lips.

"Draven?" I whispered and took a quick step forward, but stifled my excitement and slowed my pace. "What are you doing here?"

I slid the window open but blocked the entrance with my arms folded. I wanted to be mad at him for leaving last time without an answer, but my heart fluttered with excitement that he'd returned. With the hope that he'd decided to help me... which would've been impeccable timing.

"Hey, sorry I left the other night, I didn't want to risk your brother seein' me," he said in a breathy whisper.

A warm breeze carried a fresh cologne scent of cypress and sea salt inside. My eyes trailed the tattoos on his arms and he flexed subtly.

"Ya know... it's a myth that Vampyres need permission to enter."

"I know, but what makes you think I want you around after you left me hanging?" I tilted my head and narrowed my eyes.

"Judgin' by how ya look," Those vermilion eyes scanned the clothes I wore, and I turned my shoeless feet inward as my cheeks warmed. "You *need* me."

"Whatever."

I sighed and stepped aside to let him climb in. I went back to the bathroom to finish putting on my earrings and work on my make-up. Draven chuckled behind me, and I heard the mattress creak as he plopped on it. I watched him carefully through my bathroom mirror.

"Make yourself at home, I guess," I grumbled as I sifted through my bag for a certain shade of nude lip gloss.

"So, what occasion are you dressin' so fancy for?" Draven propped himself on his elbows, turning his head and scanning every inch of my bedroom.

"A walk-in job interview, hopefully." I applied the lip gloss along my bottom lip, then carefully pursed my lips in a line to transfer it to the top.

"You wanna work at night?" Draven snorted.

"Yeah, something wrong with that?" I straightened, knitting my eyebrows together.

"I wasn't tryin' to offend ya. Just... most humans are stuck workin' night shift when they don't have a choice."

"There's always a choice." I smacked my lips and shut off the light. "Has it occurred to you that maybe some humans really don't mind being around Vampyres?"

"No, because even when the system designed essential jobs to force both species to be staffed together to accommodate the population, the staff avoid each other as much as possible. I ain't never seen Vampyres and Sun Dwellers chummy with each other."

I rolled my eyes and grabbed my purse.

"So... where do ya plan on *walking* into?" He rose to his feet with a quiet grunt.

"Sundance," I said curtly.

"Oh, *there*?" Draven scrunched up his nose. "That place is so—"

"It was awesome. They welcomed me there without saying two words about what I am." I clenched my fists. Maybe I didn't want his help.

"Oh, is that where you get your hair done, Sunny?" Draven quipped as he reached to touch my hair. I jerked my head back.

"Did you forget my name already? It's Briar," I griped as I stalked to my window.

"I never forget anything." He extended his clawed hand, which

I didn't notice before, gesturing for me to go first.

"No way, buddy. If my sister walks in here and sees you but not me—"

Draven groaned and waved his hand.

"Whatever." He sucked his teeth and pulled his hand away.

I carefully tried to climb out, tugging on the bottom hem of my skirt so it wouldn't ride up. I immediately regretted my choice in wardrobe, but all my shirts were crop tops or graphic tees and my pants were either shorts, leggings, or ripped jeans.

On the ground, we fell completely silent. Without warning, Draven wrapped a firm arm around my waist and jumped over the balcony railing. It took every brittle bone in my body not to scream, but we landed in the grass with a quiet thud. I straightened my clothes and raked my fingers through my hair as I gathered my rattled bearings. A car was already parked near the mailbox.

Draven took a few steps before turning around when he noticed I hadn't moved. I clenched my fists at my sides.

"What's wrong now?" he groaned, curling his upper lip.

"I don't know you. Who is that?" It was too dark for me to see if it was a regular vehicle or a marked cab.

"It's a Ryde."

Even worse.

"How do I know you're not gonna take me to a slaughterhouse?" I cocked my head as I put my hands on my hips.

"That's a risk you're gonna have to take after Gloaming." Draven plucked lint from his shoulder.

My skin went frigid despite the warm night air. I peered over my shoulder at the golden light pouring through the windows of my home, beckoning me to make the right choice and come back inside. I looked back at Draven, the dark car at the end of the gravel driveway, and the neon skyline beyond the farmlands. Behind me, there was routine and comfort. In front of me, there was risk, opportunity, *freedom*...

I told myself I wasn't going to hate looking at myself in the mirror. I told myself I wasn't going to be a failure like my mother. With that authorization, and a job that would treat me well, I would be on the right track.

I sighed and walked past Draven with my head held high, but I held my breath with each step toward the car.

# 21
# DRAVEN

I DIDN'T EXPECT HER TO FOLLOW THROUGH WITH THE PLAN. Any other Sun Dweller with common sense would run the second I extended my hand or exposed my fangs. The only ones that could tolerate my kind were the ones forced to work alongside us, but that wasn't to say they didn't show up to work in fear of being Turned every night—as if the blood donations weren't enough to allow us self-control.

I grinned and trailed behind her. I looked back at her house. In both instances I'd set foot in her room, it felt like real life occupied it. Uriah's house may have been filled with luxury, but it was always an empty shell, like a frame with the default picture of random people in it.

I wanted to open the door for her, but she'd already let herself in and moved to the other side of the backseat.

"Where to, folks?" The driver had thin tufts of grey hair over a severely balding head, wrinkles in his forehead, and very human blue eyes.

"Sundance on Crescent Street," Briar said quickly.

"Oh, the nice little hair salon? My daughter goes there all the time during the day, but I believe it's called Bethany's Corner."

The man started to punch in the address into his navigation. I could already feel my jaw tighten as I knew he was going to be a talker. Briar kept her face toward the window, and I wondered if it was because she was nervous, trying to hide her eyes, or wanting to be antisocial.

"I guess it's nice. Ain't my cup of tea," I drawled. I shifted in my seat with a grunt. My knees dug into the back of the driver's seat and I had to keep my head tilted forward to clear the low plastic ceiling. I wished I'd ordered a Ryde XL, where the vehicle would've at least been an SUV.

"Sully's is a nice barbershop, it's off of Blackwater and Main," the driver rambled.

"Yeah, I don't really go anywhere. I cut my own hair," I said curtly. Briar turned from the window and looked at me with tight lips, as if she were fighting against laughter.

"Obviously."

"What's *that* supposed to mean?" I consciously put my hand up to my hair.

"I'm just picking," she laughed. "You look cool."

I ran a hand through my hair and looked out the window. I always contemplated cutting it, so I wouldn't look "lopsided" as Delilah once commented, but also I lived by my father's advice to "be your own man."

The trip to Sundance felt never-ending. Briar's remark subtly scratched at the back of my mind, the walls kept closing in, and the driver just never got the hint to shut up. My hand was already on the door handle the second we turned on Crescent Street, and I was immediately outside the second the vehicle rolled to a stop.

There was a bench under a street lamp just outside of Sundance's display windows. I reached in my pocket for a cigarette and lighter, then nudged Briar to go inside while I waited.

"You don't want to come in?" She raised her eyebrows and puckered her glossy lips in a subtle pout. As much as I wanted to help, I had to shake my head.

"Ain't the best idea, Sunny. Knock 'em out." I flicked my thumb over the lighter's wheel until the flame finally ignited.

"Thanks... if it goes well, we should celebrate."

Briar hooked a piece of hair behind her ear. She inhaled a ragged, deep breath. I gave her a quick upward nod with a smile, but my face immediately went slack the second I turned my back. The bell rang as she stepped inside and I took a long, thoughtful draw of my cigarette.

It was several years ago, but I feared some of the beauticians in there would recognize me after a certain... Nightshade shakedown. I didn't want them to think Briar was associated with me or my clan and ruin her chances of getting the job.

The bell rang again after about fifteen minutes, and I looked over my shoulder to see Briar beaming. The starlight twinkle in her eyes returned, matched with her snow-white teeth that were as bright as a full moon.

"I'm assumin' ya got the job." I pulled the cigarette from my mouth and crushed it under my sneaker. Her smile was so contagious, I couldn't help but mirror it.

"Yes! They're going to let me work part-time as a receptionist *and* train me for a esthetician license. A *license*, Draven!" She danced on her toes with a squeal.

"I don't know what an *esketchan* is but I'm happy for ya," I smiled and poked shoulder. She laughed brightly, the sound as lively and peaceful as wind chimes.

"*Es-the-ti-cian.* You do facials, makeup, and all that." She was finally able to get words out once her laughter died. "So um, they printed out an offer letter and everything for me so we can head to City Hall for one of those authorizations, then why don't we go someplace fun after?"

"City Hall?" I echoed with a weak chuckle. "Shoot, if all ya need is an authorization, I can get ya one of those for free." I didn't want to go near any more places where people could potentially recognize me.

"Free? What, you got some black market connections or something?" Briar asked as she narrowed her eyes to slits.

"Nah, it ain't black market—it's legit, I promise. Listen, would you rather do that or spend seventy dollars on a piece of paper that doesn't stick with ya when you're unemployed?" I tilted my head and shoved my hands in my pockets as I waited patiently for her answer.

Much like what she did before we left her house, she stared at me for a few seconds, then looked back at Sundance. She had to be one of the most indecisive women I'd ever met, but I was willing to stand there all night if I had to.

"I don't want to mess up my chances." She spoke in a lower tone, her shoulders slumping slightly as if she felt guilt for saying no.

"Fine, we'll go to City Hall, but I ain't goin' inside."

It stung that she didn't trust me, but I didn't hold it against her. We'd only had three encounters, and the first one was when I stalked and threatened to kill her if she ever showed her face again. Besides... the authorization would've been from some tainted Vampyre police officers lending a hand.

"Why not?" Briar whined.

"I don't get along with bureaucratic pigs." I twisted my lips bitterly.

"It's a neutral zone, though..." she pouted, her voice shrinking in the breeze.

I just shook my head. I observed the Vampyres that walked up and down the sidewalk, moseying to whatever nocturnal business they had going on. Several stopped and stared at Briar, and a few men and women headed in her direction until they saw me. Briar once again gave me that odd look, the one that said she didn't trust me but was still willing to test the water, even though deep down she probably knew there were sharks in it.

"We should probably start heading there then," I said, and started walking further north toward the next intersection. Briar followed closely behind me. The bright star that beamed just moments ago had died out, and I couldn't help but feel responsible.

We crossed the intersection, and when I glanced over my shoulder to check on Briar, I noticed her gaze lingering on a food truck.

"Ya hungry?"

"Kinda, but that owner over there didn't want to serve me before so I'd rather not." She waved her hand dismissively. I gleaned the food truck's details.

"I see..." It was named Chen's Den, which I once heard was one of the top street food spots in Neoterra. I kept her comment in mind, with the intent of paying Chen a visit after getting her home safely.

We walked past The Nightshade bar, where her eyes lingered once again. I only checked over my shoulder again to make sure she didn't wander into the line. We soon crossed a couple more intersections before we reached Town Square, where the large colonial building glowed in its honey-colored uplighting that shone between its numerous Grecian columns. Neoterra's striped flag of tangerine and imperial purple whipped proudly next to the large "City Hall" stone sign that was also illuminated. I stared at all its might as we gradually approached the edge of the wide walkway trailing up the grand staircase that climbed to the heavy mahogany double doors at the top.

"It shouldn't take me too long," Briar said as she walked past me.

I didn't notice how much my pace slowed, but I stopped at the sign and watched her walk up the steps with the offer letter in hand. I leaned against the City Hall sign with my hands in my pockets, patiently waiting and staring at the fountain at the center of Town Square.

"Hey, you!" I whipped my head in the direction of the snappy, gravelly voice. "Get off that sign!"

I straightened as a masked cop came bounding in my direction.

He kept his hand on his holster. I rubbed my nose and scanned him from head to toe, memorizing the golden eyes, the fiery curls framing the mask, the freckles dotting his skin, and the subtle cedar scent that I likened to Briar. He stood at about my height of six-three, with well-developed muscles that matched mine. Were it not for my supernatural strength, we'd have a fair fight. I held my hands up as I took a couple of steps away from the sign.

"Sorry, officer. I was just chillin'—ain't this a neutral zone anyway?" I dipped my head pointedly at the ground, indicating I was still on City Hall's property.

"Yeah, but it's not for loitering. Go *chill* elsewhere." The cop jerked his chin.

"Ain't you got murderers to chase or somethin'?" I hissed. My ears burned, and I contemplated if it was worth dying just to beat the man to death since he wanted to confront me for something so trivial.

"Isn't that what the likes of *you* are, naturally?"

I loosed a wry laugh and shook my head, then sauntered across the street toward the fountain, muttering obscenities under my breath. I glanced back to see if Briar was on her way out, but the officer watched me until I sat at the edge of the fountain. The double doors let out a brief ray of light as Briar stepped back outside, only to instantly duck behind one of the columns.

# 22
# BRIAR

Getting the authorization was a relatively painless process... for the most part. The clerk almost rejected my application because it wasn't essential personnel, but she was impressed enough that the Vampyres were willing to work with me. The clerk asked for the offer letter and typed up the paperwork, she gave me a secondary ID card that I would be required to show whenever confronted by an officer, and then I paid the fee.

The hard soles of my flat shoes echoed through the empty halls of City Hall. I was excited to tell Draven the news, but the vibrant murals of the city's history coating the walls made my loud shoes come to a screeching stop.

In the beginning, there was a serene picture of smiling farmers, hunters, and city-dwellers farther in the background. I lightly traced my fingertips across the wall's trim as the vividly painted sky dimmed to navy blue and yellow swirls of night, showing sickly pale faces, hospital beds, and mass graves. I figured that was about the Red Plague era from 2040 to 2044.

We were told that was when the population was at its lowest, after a new virus spread rapidly and progressed through four stages. First, it caused the body's iron levels to drop; secondly, it turned the skin pallid and frigid; then there were excruciating body pains; and finally the victims would fall into a coma or die. At first, it was believed to be a new virus that caused an aggressive form of anemia, but that was quickly proven wrong in the last year of the Red Plague.

The next phase of the mural had red paint smeared over tombstones. The mural had the pale faces attacking humans with some jumping unnaturally high in the black sky, and figures running in streaks of color that indicated inhuman speeds. Those who fell victim to the Red Plague, who were pronounced legally dead or brain-dead—*came back*. Not as zombies, but instead as sentient savages with an insatiable craving for blood. The virus was dormant in others but would awaken in the survivors of their attacks. They would soon turn into the beasts in a matter of hours, sometimes days. By the end of 2045, Vampyres were no longer a myth.

The black sky in the painting gradually brightened to red, hanging over a mass of figures with guns, explosives, and tanks on one side that collided with the bare hands and fangs of the other side. That was the decade-long Crimson War that occurred immediately after, and Neoterra was shaped in its aftermath.

The rest of the mural showed the Vampyres in chains, some decapitated, and a harsh line of day and night splitting the rest of the wall in half to express the curfew in place. At the center of it all was a glistening tower of marble, glass, and granite known as Mundus Novus—formerly known as the Washington Monument. It was not only the highest-ranking federal government building in the country, but also internationally, as the whole world was under the same order.

It was safe to say I'd reached our present time in the mural. There was still space on the wall, which I assumed was history that had yet to be painted. I sighed and shook my head slowly. I didn't think it was the Vampyres' fault that they became what they were, yet our history was nonetheless saturated with so much blood, and it seemed like they were still paying for their sins sixty-five years later.

I walked outside and my heart instantly jumped in my throat when I recognized the hair behind the mask of the officer standing in front of City Hall. I ducked behind one of the thick limestone columns. My breaths became rough as I sank into a crouch.

*Is Sterling here waiting for me? How did he know? Where's Draven?* The second I set foot off the property—

*Wait.*

I had the authorization card. No matter how angry Sterling could be, he had no legal right to do anything to me anymore.

I straightened and dusted off my clothes with a long exhale. I stepped from behind the column, but his unmarked patrol car was gone by the time I took the stairs. I continued down the concrete walkway and stopped next to the City Hall sign. I looked for Draven among the pedestrians, but none of them looked even remotely similar. I put my hands on my hips with a low chuckle and shook my head, flabbergasted that he'd leave me *again*. Fool me once...

A brisk wave of wind blew my hair to the side. I yelped and jumped back, thinking a car was speeding too close to the sidewalk, only to see Draven just two feet from me.

"Wha—"

"Let's walk and talk, I ain't staying near this place a second longer."

He grabbed my hand and pulled me down the sidewalk. I stumbled at first but reestablished my footing. He didn't let go until we were half a block away from City Hall.

"What's going on? Why did you leave?" I could do all this by myself if my "escort" was just going to keep disappearing.

"Pig of a cop got on me for loitering around City Hall. I saw you hide... you know him, don't ya?"

He gave me a sideways glance that seemed to stab into my side. I looked away with a shaky breath and just nodded.

"I think that was my brother." I hugged myself. "I'm s—"

"Figures. He smells like ya," he said, reaching into his pocket for a cigarette. I scrunched my nose as he started lighting it.

"That's not a weird statement at all," I grumbled uncomfortably. "Look, I'm sorry. What about celebrating? We still haven't done that yet."

"Is your brother always so charming?" Draven asked with a scornful laugh, disregarding my attempt to change the subject.

"I don't know what he's like on duty." The bright tone in my voice finally dropped, seeing as how Draven didn't want to let it go.

"A prick," he said curtly.

I frowned and stopped in my tracks.

"Well, maybe he's had a bad night, alright?" I retorted.

"Okay? Good for him, 'cause I was having an alright night and he ruined it. Go celebrate on your own, maybe tell him the news." Draven flung his arm as if swatting a fly.

"Are you serious? You're going to be mad at me for something someone else did, just because we're related?"

Draven paused and his twisted grimace with slit pupils softened. The crimson of his eyes seemed richer than the last time I saw him, but perhaps I forgot what they looked like. He sighed and ran a hand through his hair.

"I'm sorry," he breathed as he leaned against a brick wall and then took a long draw of his cancer stick. "Where do you wanna go?" Smoke puttered past his lips with each word.

I wanted to go back to The Nightshade, but given his reaction to my presence there before, I figured he wouldn't agree—especially with his current mood.

"You're king of the night, why don't you show me?"

I gazed into his eyes as I smiled coyly, hoping to erase the uncomfortable tension that had shoved itself between us, hoping that I'd see that dimpled smile instead of the furious smolder of a moment ago.

"I ain't one to be called a king, but I'll show you a good time."

He pushed off the wall and walked in the opposite direction. He pulled out his phone, the bright light washing his face in pale teal. His thumbs rapidly danced across it before the screen clicked off again. I stared at the shoulder blades that poked at his tank, my mind wandering off on crazy tangents—like what he did for a living, what his family was like, if he had a girlfriend. Although with that last question, I hoped he wouldn't be out with me if he did.

"Where are we going?" I trotted to catch up to him, then slowed to a brisk walk.

"Ever heard of The Hole?"

"No, but that sounds *exactly* like the slaughterhouse I mentioned before," I quipped with a tinge of fear wiggling under my skin.

Draven released a low, husky chuckle. It was almost ominous, and it sent spiders skittering along my arms and spine.

"I think you'll like it."

My feet were screaming by the time we reached our destination. We had walked out of downtown and into a neighborhood of apartment buildings, scattered houses, and mobile homes. There was a lush park at the center with a playground, small pond, and dog park. It was completely empty, but the skate park next to it carried a low thrum that seemed to beat beneath the surface.

Draven moved closer and I followed, craning my neck to take in every detail. Copious amounts of complex graffiti art littered the sides of the bowls. I stared at the art, jaw hanging. It wasn't the stereotypical random bubble words or derogatory defacements in parking lots or on benches. It was a colorful mixture of portraits, animals, historical figures—a museum of Neoterra's most hidden talent.

At the far side of one of the skate bowls, green light and smoke swirled into the night sky. I pointed in its direction. "What's that?"

Draven flashed a lopsided grin and grabbed my waist again. I yelped as he rushed us to the kidney-shaped bowl in the matter of a second. We landed at the bottom of the bowl where there was a metal trap door. The light and smoke seeped through its narrow wooden slats. I gasped and crouched low to peek through. Bodies were swaying and jumping to an indie band playing synth pop rock music, an energetic contrast to the haunting music that played at The Nightshade. Draven leaned down and swung the door open, and I immediately grabbed the first rung of the ladder to descend.

A fog machine pumped smoke throughout the room. A small makeshift stage held the band. Hundreds of album covers covered the wall and ceiling around them. I lost the rhythm of my heartbeat to the rhythm of their music.

Draven pulled me deeper into the crowd, tightening his grip around my hand so we wouldn't lose each other. I wove through behind him, still taking in as many details of the hidden gem I could. Spotlights swung back and forth, switching to strobe for a moment. Then it switched to black light and everyone inside began to glow. I finally tore my gaze from the band and the crowd to look at Draven, whose fingers finally slipped from mine once we reached the bar. He settled on a barstool with a smug smile.

"This is amazing, I—oh my God, my face hurts!" I laughed as I hopped onto a stool and swiveled to face him.

"Told ya." Draven's fangs glowed blue under the black light. My cheeks heated as I turned around and faced the bartender to order, but he was already sliding two shots our way.

"This is better than any celebration I could dream of." I took the shot, then paused when I noticed he wasn't taking his.

"You're not drinking?"

"One of us gotta be responsible to get you home." Draven shrugged. "Don't worry, I can still have fun without it."

I smiled and took the second one. I bobbed my head to the music, waiting for the alcohol to relax my muscles before daring to grab his hands. His eyes widened as I swayed my hips and shimmied our way to the dance floor. Draven's eyes darted around before he placed his hands over my waist. He raised my hand in his and I spun lazily before he pulled me in close. I leaned my head against his chest as his hands slid to my hips, and closed my eyes to focus on the smell of his cologne—sea salt and cypress—among the sweat and alcohol that engulfed us. He leaned over the side of my head, and his breath lightly brushed against my ear. Here, in this moment, I felt like I was floating without any curfew chains to hold me down.

Draven cleared his throat and withdrew from me. I opened my eyes and spun around, turning my eyebrows upward and poking out my bottom lip.

"I'm gonna get a drink after all."

He rubbed the back of his neck as his eyes darted away from mine. He returned to the bar. I sighed but continued dancing. I didn't quite feel as light as before.

There was a point when the music slowed to a quieter, steady beat as the lead singer took hold of the microphone and switched to normal speech.

"I heard we got a gem hidden down here in The Hole."

His voice was just as smooth and refreshing as when he was singing. All the Vampyres started looking around, mumbling to themselves. I did the same, wondering who else could be playing tonight.

"Now, he might not want to... but it's been years. He's a gent with the piano, a killer on the guitar, and he's got a voice that will make the ladies swoon—"

Draven was facing the bartender with his back against the stage.

"The Hole presents to you... Asher Thorne!" the singer bellowed with a wide grin.

A white-hot spotlight flashed over Draven, shedding light on the tense back muscles stiffening under his tank. He shook his head slowly before turning around. He shut his eyes tightly as he bared his teeth in a pained scowl from the obnoxious light.

"No thanks—y'all carry on!" He cupped one hand around the side of his mouth as he shouted and waved dismissively with the other.

"Naw, man! Bless these people's ears with that voice! It's been years!"

"Well, I ain't been playin' in years!"

"Come on, mate, it's like riding a bike!" the singer coaxed.

"Ash-er... Ash-er... Ash-er..."

The crowd slowly began to chant Draven's alias, gradually growing into a crescendo until they finally erupted into roaring applause when he threw his hands up and headed for the stage. He flashed me a sheepish grin as he walked past. I pushed through the crowd to get to the front, my mouth dry from hanging open so long.

Draven adjusted the microphone to his height as the lead singer passed a transparent and neon-lit electric guitar to him. Draven cleared his throat, his forehead glistening with sweat under the lights. It was hard to tell if it was nerves or the heat. Maybe both.

"Y'all gonna have to bear with me... I've never been put on the spot like this," he spoke lowly into the microphone, so close that it was almost muffled.

"You got this, Asher!" someone from the back shouted.

A heavy silence followed as Draven closed his eyes. His ebony hair hung over half of his face. He took deep breaths before strumming a somber chord that filled the room. He nodded, his eyes still closed, before strumming two more chords. As if on cue, the band behind him began to play a soft melody that married the three chords he'd created.

His lips moved ever so slightly, counting to himself, before his lips parted and a rich, gritty baritone voice poured out. The melody came together so beautifully that I wanted—*needed*—to cling to the edge of the stage, a random person, the wall... anything to keep my knees from buckling. I clenched the front of my shirt collar as if I had a pearl necklace resting there. The way he stood on the stage, shoulders back, fingers nimbly dancing across the guitar strings, it was as if he was alone in the comfort of his home. I closed my eyes to feel the music and nothing else.

A pair of hands grabbed my waist, their cold skin soaking through the silk of my shirt. I yelped and pulled away, quickly peering over my shoulder to see a Vampyre inhaling my hair deeply.

"Back off, man!" I snapped as I shoved him away.

"Aw, what's wrong? I thought you had a cool vibe... you smell awfully good too." He ran a hand through his black hair, greasy and highlighted with green. His eyes floated, halfway rolled to the back of his head—and his breath was rancid. He inched closer to me and I continued to back away until I bumped into a couple of girls. They were so entranced by Draven's voice that they didn't even react.

"I said, *back off*." I put bass in my voice, clenching my fist as I planted my feet and dared him to come closer.

"I never smelled your blood type before, I just need a quick bite.

Come on, it's a win-win, you seem like you'd fit right in."

He smiled, his sharp fangs growing ever longer. He gripped my shoulders, and I winced from the wound that still wasn't completely healed. My vision went white, and all I could think about were the Vampyres who'd circled me when they wanted to steal my bike.

"Leave me alone!" I screamed and jerked my arms away, then swung a fist into his face, bone crunching against bone.

The music stopped on a discordant note.

# 23
# DRAVEN

I FORGOT WHAT IT WAS LIKE TO FEEL COOL STEEL STRINGS beneath my fingertips, to close my eyes and see my mom and dad giving me my first guitar when I was seven, to unleash my caged heart into the wild of song. The rhythm reverberated through my bones, and rolled down my spine like the trill of a xylophone. While it wasn't the pop synth the band was playing earlier, I always found comfort in grunge, punk, or alternative rock. Yet, I could still hear the audience sway and sing with my music. The Hole was meant to be a place for everyone to crawl into.

"Leave me alone!"

A familiar voice, one that was usually steady and alluring but now was in rough, warbling distress. I shoved the guitar back into the lead singer's hands before jumping off the stage without another thought.

I pushed past a few people before snatching the back of the man's shirt and throwing him against the edge of the stage. I bared my teeth with a growl and stepped in front of Briar, who was holding her limp wrist against her chest. I had my claws raised to slice him to ribbons. The man cowered against the stage. A soft, warm hand touched my shoulder and I began to snarl, but softened my features when I caught Briar's large silver eyes looking up at me. A bouncer pulled the man to his feet, then escorted him toward the back exit.

"I'm sorry," I mumbled, then lifted my gaze to everyone else and repeated it louder.

"Thanks, man... that guy was obnoxious all night," a woman in the crowd shouted.

"Killer performance all 'round," someone else slurred.

The lead singer dropped from the stage and put a hand on my shoulder. "Thanks for the show. We'll be fine. Go ahead and handle your stuff, mate. Sorry that had to happen."

I gave him a short nod, then turned to Briar. I placed a hand at the small of her back to guide her toward the rear exit. It didn't look like she'd be able to climb the ladder with the state her hand was in.

The night air had cooled, but it was still subtly balmy. It was grounding. Whatever dreamland I'd visited in The Hole was long gone, and I was back in the bleak reality of Earth. I scanned the park and sniffed the air, searching for the man. Briar started chuckling lowly behind me, then her voice rose to lively laughter. I slowly turned to face her, raising my eyebrows.

I wondered if she hit her head somehow. "Are you... okay?"

"That was so awesome." She still held her wrist, but the pain wasn't enough to sully the beaming glow across her face under the moonlight. "You sound so beautiful! I didn't know you played guitar and could sing! And that guy—oh my God, I punched a *Vampyre*!"

I pursed my lips, slowly shaking my head. I ran a hand through my hair and over my face with a deep breath.

"We can't do this again, Sunny."

Her smile instantly faded like a musical note, replaced by a scowl.

"What do you mean, 'we can't do this again'?" Briar scoffed.

"Do you see this?"

I grabbed her wrist and held it in front of her face, like putting a dog's nose in its own waste. "This wouldn't have happened if you were hanging out with your kind."

She jerked away. "Yes, it would've. Ha, you think humans are such saints? You obviously don't know anything about us."

I opened my mouth to speak, to tell her that I was once like her, but closed it when I remembered Uriah's words.

*You may have been a Sun Dweller before, son, but I guarantee that no one cares about what you used to be. All you'll ever be to them is a monster.*

I bared my teeth as I jabbed my thumb into my chest. "What happened in there is the least of your problems. *You* don't know anything about *me*."

She'd already had a small glimpse of what I turn into when I'm angry. I couldn't understand what was wrong with her, why she'd ignore all the warning signs. Hell, she was in harm's way when we first met.

She didn't even know that I was supposed to be dragging her back to the King Estate to be in the next round of test subjects.

"If you think what I saw in there would scare me, it didn't."

Briar looked down at her hand. It was already swollen and mottled with purple and pink. I reeled back.

"It should!" I snapped, a guttural growl laced in my tone. "How are you gonna explain this to ya darlin' brother?"

"Is that what this is about? You're scared I'll rat about the night at that stupid bar, and this." She looked pointedly at her hand.

The soles of her flats scrapped loudly against the concrete as she stormed away. I slapped myself in the face with a groan. I didn't know how to express my concern for her safety, not my own. Frankly, with the way things were going at Nightshade, I didn't care if a cop executed me. I didn't care if all Sun Dwellers—humans, or whatever anyone called them—were or weren't saints. The fact was that I had killed plenty of them when I was a fledgling, I had killed more by handing the four victims to White Fang for Uriah, and I took from them every time I drank one of those mandated blood bags. On top of it all, I somehow allowed the only human who'd accepted my existence to get injured—when I only wanted to let her celebrate her new job.

"Briar—"

My voice caught in my throat. She was halfway across the turf. I sprinted in a flash, blocking her path and gently holding her in place. "Please. Listen. I ain't gonna fight with ya. This was your night to enjoy and I don't wanna take that away."

"Yeah?" Those grey eyes were roiling thunderclouds, shaking the ground beneath me. "Well, you kinda did."

"I know, I know. Let me make it up to ya. There's an ice cream shop I want to show you and then we can get you home, okay?" Every part of my mind, body, and soul was telling me to chase her away. The little horrors she'd experienced on the streets were nothing compared to the underworld of the Nightshades, and I was a direct link to her life being claimed in an instant.

Briar stared up at me with her eyebrows knit closely, lips tight, and jaw set for a couple of moments. She loosed a sigh, briefly closing her eyes to kill the storm that brewed behind them.

"I don't know if you Vampyres have some sort of hypnotic ability, but I can't seem to stay mad at you," Briar said with a soft grin.

"Never heard of anyone having that. Maybe it's just my irresistible charm," I said with a smirk.

We took seats on opposite ends of a park bench near the street and I pulled out my phone to set up a Ryde. I took comfort in the sound of crickets in the park and the distant urban white noise.

"I tend to throw tantrums," Briar spoke suddenly.

"Hm?"

I glanced at her and she sighed, meeting my gaze with a wince. "I mean... I can understand your line of thinking, I guess. I'm sorry."

Briar swiped a piece of hair behind her ear and scooted closer to me. I looked for any police or Nightshade members, mostly for her sake.

"It's cool," I said, then chuckled a little as I reminisced on our final moments in The Hole. "You did give that guy a pretty nasty right hook." Briar giggled with a nod.

"I did, but you guys are rock solid." She opened and closed her fist, examining her knuckles.

"Worth it," we said in unison, and laughed.

My laughter faded and my face fell into its usual dull rest.

I checked my watch and glanced both ways along the street for the Ryde's arrival. After what felt like an endless moment of silence, Briar turned to me, biting her lip.

"The time at The Nightshade—"

I tensed at the name leaving her lips, but she continued. "What were you referring to when you told me to keep my mouth shut?"

Briar's eyes looked everywhere but at mine. I paused, contemplating telling her the truth. What good would it do either of us if I admitted I was talking about the fire? At the end of the day... I was oil and she was water.

"Just... the whole general thing that happened with the two guys." I shrugged as I slid my arm across the back of the bench. She leaned closer, sensing the subtle invitation. "You ain't gotta worry about that now."

"I wasn't going to. You already know why. I was just... curious." She shivered slightly and curled against me. I pursed my lips tightly, once again looking for a cop nearby to arrest her and shoot me with a silver bullet just for our proximity.

"Briar." I cleared my throat as I looked down at her against my shoulder. "Why aren't you afraid of us? Ya got a death wish?"

It was a question that had burned since the day I laid eyes on her at The Nightshade bar.

Briar shrugged. "I guess I've had worse."

✳

We exchanged phone numbers while we waited for our ice cream at Swirl, then took our seats in a booth. Of course, Briar also treated it like it was the best thing since sliced bread. She swayed in her seat with each bite, twirled her spoon in the air, and hummed the music from The Hole. I watched her closely, wishing I could experience my world through her eyes. I had never seen someone appreciate so many little things before. I craved that experience more than the blood I had yet to drink tonight.

As Briar scraped the bottom of her ice cream bowl with a plastic spoon, I set up yet another Ryde. As much as I wanted her to limit her outings after Gloaming, I knew that'd be impossible once her job at Sundance started.

We took the Ryde back to her house. Across the countryside, I could see the horizon subtly brightening to a pale grey-blue. Sunrise was about an hour away. Briar was sleeping against the door, lightly snoring. I eased her awake when her house came into view. Once we approached the end of her driveway, she yawned with heavy eyelids and didn't protest when I scooped her into my arms and launched us across the yard to the balcony outside her bedroom window.

She lifted her chin to peer up at me with a lazy grin as I set her down.

"Thank you, Draven. You're probably the coolest guy I've ever met." Briar giggled quietly. Her cheeks were flushed, matching the pink of her hair. I chuckled lowly, dropping my gaze to my shoes as my stomach fluttered.

"Yeah? You ain't so bad ya-self." I ruffled her frizzy hair and swiftly jumped on the edge of the railing, then crouched. I peered back at her as she was lifting her window. Words swelled in my cheeks and as much as I wanted to chew them up, I couldn't.

"Hey."

She whirled back in my direction, her leg half risen.

"Good luck at Sundance. Maybe I'll pop around," I said with a soft grin.

"I'd like that." She held her bruised hand close to her chest as she climbed over the windowsill. She closed the window, then waved through the pane.

I gave her a wink, then sprung back to the street, breaking into a blurred sprint to return to the heart of Neoterra, then texted Hartley to pick me up. While I waited at the fountain in Town Square, I gazed at the stars in the waking sky and smiled softly when it gave me more serenity than a cigarette usually would.

Not a bad night after all.

❋

It took Hartley a while to take me home. He was in the limo, which reeked of alcohol, musk, and vomit. I didn't give him a hard time, as the seats in the main cabin told enough of the story. I sat in the front with him to spare myself the scent as much as possible and let him rant about the constant driving and the amount of cleaning he had to do during daylight so the limo was adequate by Gloaming. I zoned out most of it, but I got the gist. I was too busy reminiscing on my time spent with Briar, on my reunion with the guitar and singing. If only I had a camera to record the night, because I would have watched it as much as I thought about it.

I sauntered up the front steps of King Estate, suppressing the smile that kept itching to appear on my lips. It wasn't a challenge anymore when I saw Delilah shuffling across the foyer in slippers and a silk robe, her locs wrapped in a towel.

"Oh, morning, Draven," she said flatly, her dark, wine-colored eyes skimming over my appearance. She cocked her head as her nostrils flared subtly. "Where have you been?"

"I don't answer to you." I stalked toward the grand staircase.

"You smell like a Sun Dweller," she hissed. I continued walking up the stairs. "A *female* one."

I froze halfway up, tightening my grip on the railing.

"I hunted," I said simply, then looked down at her with a more confident smirk. "They have sweeter blood, obviously."

She put her hand on her hip and nodded with a *hmph*, then continued her journey to a connecting hallway without another word.

Once I heard her shut a door, I zipped into my room and quickly jumped in the shower. I let the water soak my clothes for ten minutes before stripping to wash normally. I closed my eyes, whispering the lyrics to the song I'd played at The Hole.

# 24

# BRIAR

I PASSED OUT THE SECOND I HIT THE BED. I STILL HAD MY clothes on from the interview and partying. I was so tired that even my own snoring didn't wake me up as it usually did. I was graced with sweet dreams of life at Sundance and adventures with Draven and his captivating voice and an apartment of my own and—

Biting ice water washed over me, some even landing in my mouth. I woke up in a coughing jolt, frantically wiping my face dry. I slicked my hair back and lifted my gaze to see Sterling hovering over me with an empty bucket. Ice cubes were littered across my soaked sheets.

"Not so fun to wake up with water dumped on you, now is it?" He let the bucket fall to the floor with a hollow thud. He slowly started to pace back and forth.

"You were out last night, don't try to deny it. Nobody goes to sleep in clothes like that, and that's not what you wore when you went to Helios with Astoria." Sterling's voice was low and taut, like a stretched rubber band ready to snap.

I sighed and threw my hands up in a nonchalant shrug.

"So what if I did?" I tugged at the heavily drenched sleeves clinging to my arms with a grimace.

"So what—Briar I have a *legal obligation* to report you for violating curfew. Do you have any idea what you've done and the danger—"

His eyes went straight to my busted hand. "What happened? Who did that to you? See, that's *exactly* what I'm talking about!"

"Oh my God, Sterling, shut up!" I jumped out of the bed. The icy tremors that racked my body were replaced with heated rage. "I have a job *and* an authorization. You can't do anything to me."

I reached in my purse for the card and flipped an obscene gesture at him as I flicked the card in his direction. He stared at it on the floor.

"What have you done?" His voice dropped to a weak whisper.

"I'm finding where I belong and I'm proving to myself that I'm not a screwup." I took out my earrings and padded to my bathroom.

"What do you mean? This is the biggest screwup you've ever done." Sterling laughed scornfully.

I halted in the doorway.

"Get out," I growled, and slowly turned to face him.

"People are going *missing*, Briar," he pleaded as he held out his palms. "It doesn't matter if they were taken during the day, I *know* it's Vampyres doing it!"

"You don't know anything! Get out!" I quickly kicked my shoe off, caught it in my hand, and chucked it at him—but missed entirely. Sterling didn't even flinch. His eyes went glassy as he shook his head.

"Please don't be like Dad. He wasn't invincible, and neither are you," he said somberly before leaving my room, his heavy steps descending the stairs.

My breaths quivered and I inhaled deeply to try to put out the flames he ignited within. I picked up my card and put it safely back in my purse before returning to my bathroom.

After I dressed into a baggy t-shirt and leggings, I spent the afternoon stripping my bed and doing laundry. Once I finally dried my sheets and comforter, I stayed holed up in my room.

I was curled in my bed, snacking on grapes and binge-watching dramas when Astoria lightly knocked on my door before coming in. I knew it was her because she was the only one considerate enough to knock first, especially today.

"I have dinner for you," she said quietly, and moved a plate of chicken breast and asparagus to my end table. The smell of it seemed to awaken my stomach.

"Thanks," I mumbled.

She nodded, then started to head back out, but paused with her back to me. "Why'd you do it, Bri? Do you really feel safe out there?"

"It's the first time I've felt at home in my life." I moved the plate to my lap and then raised it close to my chin to avoid dropping anything. "As far as safety goes... I haven't noticed much of a difference from daylight living."

Astoria nodded, then slowly turned to face me. "I don't like it, either. You know that. But... I'm going to support you no matter what because I love you. Sterling gets to be out there and he comes home every night, and his job literally chases danger, so...”

I could tell she'd spent the whole day trying to justify supporting me. I gave her a tender smile. “Not all Vampyres are savages. Not all humans are innocent. Everyone has the right to be given a chance because deep down,” I said between bites, “we're the same.”

Astoria eased herself onto the edge of my bed.

“I believe in innocent until proven guilty. It's just hard to think that way for Vampyres with how much Sterling hates them. I feel like he sees them act terribly every shift.” Her hand found its way to her necklace and she began to fidget with it.

“He exaggerates.”

I wanted to go into detail about Draven, Sundance, and all the places I'd gone with only a couple of run-ins with rogues. I didn't for two reasons: I still didn't know that much about Draven, and I didn't want Astoria to suddenly become curious and venture out by herself. My chest tightened at my own hypocrisy, but I preferred that she continue to be motivated by her nursing studies. I had nothing to lose.

“How can you be so sure?” Her voice almost came out as a squeak.

“He has to work with some Vampyres too, remember? When you start working in healthcare, you're going to have some co-workers like that too. It's hard for them to get jobs next to humans to start with, why would they do anything to screw it up by attacking us? So obviously they're capable of acting civil.”

My brother and all his genius detective work could never seem to piece that fact together.

"I guess that makes sense. I'm glad you're happier now, though. Do you mind if I eat and watch shows with you?"

I was already halfway done with my plate, but I wouldn't dare refuse such an offer. Astoria smiled and ran to grab her plate, then took her place on the other side of my bed. I switched to a comedy movie because we both desperately needed some laughs.

✳

Sterling was already on the porch when Astoria and I came outside for the usual arbitrary routine. Cyrene pulled into the driveway and adjusted her mask before smiling at us. None of us reciprocated. Not even Sterling, who always seemed to liven up in her presence.

"Jeez, why is it such a morgue here? Are you guys okay?" Cyrene asked as she approached. She didn't ask for our identifications anymore. I couldn't complain about that, at least.

"No." Sterling spoke tightly. I gave him a sideways glance, clenching my fists behind my back.

"How come? What happened?" Cyrene scanned the three of us, I assumed for any signs of physical harm.

"Briar here," he said through gnashed teeth, "got a night-shift job."

Cyrene raised her eyebrows, her icy blue eyes widening. "Doing what?"

"As a receptionist and intern for some stupid hair, nails, whatever. It's not even an essential personnel job, so I don't know how the hell she got it!" Sterling's voice gradually became sharper and more guttural. I waited for him to start growing claws and fur and lash out at me.

"Makeup," I sneered.

"Whatever!" Sterling barked. A vein bulged in his forehead.

"Whoa, guys, let's calm down," Cyrene said with a light chuckle. "Do you have an auth—"

"I do." I saw the question coming a mile away.

She turned to Sterling and bit her lip in a grimace. "She's grown, man. I can't help you with that. City Hall authorized her, and if they approve, we have to."

She shut the tablet off and lowered it to her side. She turned her attention to me, and I lifted my chin defensively.

"Just be careful out there. We're up to ten missing people now, and last night Sterling and I had to take reports from four people who were bitten without their consent. Now they're fledglings. They'll never be able to come back from that."

I didn't say anything, keeping my face neutral despite the queasiness I felt. I wondered if one Vampyre was responsible for the victims or if they were all bitten by different ones.

I wondered if Draven had ever done it before. I wasn't even sure if he was Vampyre-born or Turned. If he was born, the cravings would've been manageable during infancy. Only the Turned had to be closely monitored and hospitalized for six weeks before their reintegration with society. And with how carnal fledglings behaved—

I stifled that thought before I could finish it.

I couldn't always depend on Draven being there for me. He had a life of his own. Becoming a Vampyre wasn't as much of a threat to me as going missing, but if I did Turn, I knew my place in my family would cease to exist.

"I'll see you at work tonight, Sterling," Cyrene said as she tipped her patrol cap and returned to her car.

I was already going back inside and up the stairs. I had to get ready for my first night at Sundance, but I couldn't shake the guilt that seeped through my skin the entire time it took to prepare.

"That's a risk you're gonna have to take after Gloaming," Draven once said. I had to keep telling myself that everything was a risk. I hadn't cared about risks before, I shouldn't care now. Every time someone left their house, there was a risk anything could happen, whether it was a car accident, a shooting, a robbery...

I turned up my music to drown out the thoughts and continued getting ready.

❋

I tried to mimic the general style of the women who worked Sundance. Winged eyeliner, a smoky eye shadow, and dark red lipstick. I styled my pink hair half up and half down, then dressed in a cold shoulder t-shirt with ripped black jeans. Sundance was the first establishment I saw that didn't have a dress code—to promote freedom of expression. It was nice that I didn't have to dip into my savings for new clothes.

I entered Sundance with the bell ringing behind me. I saw Jocelyn in the back busily cutting a fade on a teenager. The same slender model receptionist, whom I could liken to an Egyptian Goddess, greeted me with the her saccharine smile. Today, her locs were woven into beautiful large Bantu knots. Gold bangles dressed her wrists, and a gold choker mimicking melting liquid hugged her narrow neck.

"Welcome to the Sundance family." She extended her hand and I accepted it with a firm shake.

"Thank you so much for accepting me. My name is Briar," I

said eagerly.

"It's lovely to officially meet you. I'm Samara. Some people call me Sam or Mars." She eased onto a barstool with a curved wooden back. "Come around the desk. I'm going to train you, and Jocelyn is going to be the one teaching you for the certification. Although you can learn from all of us too."

My heart skipped a beat as I rushed around the desk. It was just as neatly organized as Samara's appearance, and even the office supplies had an aesthetic of their own. The binders were covered in art like the walls. The sticky notes were black and there were metallic pens dedicated just for them, and even the black stapler looked custom-made with engraved swirls and whorls like lace.

I didn't think I was going to regret taking this risk.

# 25
# DRAVEN

GLOAMING WAS RAPIDLY APPROACHING. BRIAR STARTED HER new job tonight and it was a couple of stores down across the street from the Chen's Den food truck. I imagined her getting hungry in the middle of the night, always curiously gazing at that hunk of junk, wondering what the food tasted like but opting for a longer and riskier walk to the next nearest food place. Maybe even accidentally bumping into a Nightshade because of it.

I dressed in dark green, short-sleeved hoodie with dark jeans. I took the last hour before dusk to clean my guns and tucked one of the pistols in my waistband holster. I put on a pair of black combat boots and left my room just as Caspian was walking down the hall.

"Oh, there you are," he said with a stiff smile.

"Been lookin' for me?" I took a stride next to him down the hall.

"Not really, I just didn't see you all last night. Did you enjoy your night off?" We took the stairs, then stopped at the base of them.

"Yeah, it was actually a great change of pace. What about you?"

Caspian looked over his shoulders before dropping his voice to a whisper. "I went back to White Fang territory in the upper Northside... I think there's something strange going on," he breathed. "I think Uriah might be in over his head."

"Why?" I whispered.

Another voice interjected.

"Going on a hunt tonight again, Draven?" Delilah sneered as she strutted to the double front doors. The loose fabric of her jumpsuit flowed behind her, as if she carried wind.

Caspian exchanged glances between me and Delilah, eyebrows raised. "Hunt?" he echoed.

"You could say that." I licked my lips as I smirked at her.

Delilah sucked her teeth before shoving the door open and letting it slam behind her.

"What was she talking about?" Caspian asked with a tilt of his head.

"I ain't talking about it here and I got somethin' to do."

"Can I go with you? I have quite a bit to tell you too."

"Another time. I wanna hear about it so don't forget."

Caspian's face was always made of stone, but his shoulders sank.

"That's okay. You don't forget either," he pointed at me, then disappeared somewhere in the mansion. Since Hartley was already gone, I went outside and ambled straight to the garage, picking out a sports car with iridescent dark purple paint flecked with blue, then drove downtown.

Neoterra's streets never failed to teem with life. All the neon signs, traffic lights, and street lamps reflected off the hood of my car in stripes and circles. I pulled into an empty parking lot roughly a block away and walked the rest of the way to Chen's Den. There was a line of about ten people stretched along the sidewalk, patiently waiting for their food. Smoke swirled from the narrow windows in the truck as the workers busily cooked.

"No cutting!" a woman snapped, and I released a low, threatening growl before turning back to the truck.

"Hey." I rapped my knuckles against the acrylic divider when the man held his back to me. The back of his grease-stained t-shirt was labeled "Owner" in all caps. Chen turned, revealing a mottled face, stringy blonde hair, and hollow cheeks.

"I'll be right with you," he said irritatingly, then turned away.

"No, you're gonna come outside and we're gonna talk. *Now*," I snarled, my upper lip curling. I wanted to yank him right through the window in front of everyone.

"Who are you?" He sniffed, then ran his nose across his arm as he narrowed his eyes.

"You'll find out soon enough."

Chen looked back at his two colleagues slaving over the stove and spoke in a foreign language. One of them took his place at the register as he stepped out of the truck. I pulled him around the corner out of the view of his customers.

"Time is money," Chen groaned. "Make it qui—"

I swung a knife hand into his throat. He choked and gurgled as he sank to his knees with a hand at his throat. I curled a tight fist and struck the bridge of his nose. He fell back, gasping for air.

"The next time I hear about you refusing your services to any-body, and I mean *anybody*, I'm going to destroy your business—and after I make you watch, I'll cut off your fingers, shove them down your throat, and kill you." I scowled as I leaned close to his face. Condensation profusely coated his forehead as he shuddered. His windpipe popped back into place.

"Okay, okay, I hear you!" Chen shrieked.

I pulled out a cigarette and lit it on my way back to my car. I leaned against the hood of the car, watching him closely. He stayed there for a while before finally getting up and staggering back to the food truck.

I caught myself checking my phone, wondering if Briar would message me on her break. Then my mind wandered back to what Caspian had been trying to tell me. Why on earth would he go back to White Fang by himself, especially when there wasn't a scheduled drop?

I dialed Caspian's number.

"Bishop."

"It's Draven. Where are ya?"

"I'm just going to the store for a blood run since we're out. What's up?"

The mention of blood reminded my stomach to feel pain. I licked my lips and pushed myself off the hood.

"Wait up for me, I'll meet you there."

✳

There were two major grocery chains across the country. Neoterra had both. There was the ordinary Sun Valley Grocers for the Sun

Dwellers and the Lunar Mart for the Vampyres. Sun Valley always closed an hour before Check-In, while Lunar Mart remained open twenty-four hours to accommodate both species.

The store was split in half, with one side dedicated to rows upon rows of refrigerators filled with bags arranged by blood type. There was a difference in flavor between types, which I always regretted to admit. At the King Estate, with fifteen residents living there, whoever went on a blood run had to get enough of every type to appease everyone's preferences.

I recognized Hartley's SUV parked at the far end of the parking lot and pulled up next to it. Caspian got out of the backseat and I shut my engine off to meet him.

"I didn't know the shopping rotation cut to you so soon," I said as I grabbed a cart and passed it to him.

Caspian leaned over the handle as we walked. "Yeah, seems like we both keep getting the short end of the stick this month."

"Yeah, so... what were you gonna tell me earlier?" I stuffed my hands in my hoodie pockets.

"I saw a couple of our own at White Fang." Caspian sucked in a breath as if he was going to say more, but paused.

I sighed. "Okay... and?"

"First, I don't think Uriah fully trusts you," Caspian said coolly.

"What makes ya think that?" I frowned.

We rounded the corner of the first aisle that transitioned from human food to bags of blood. The bags glowed like rubies as the bright white backlighting shined through them.

"Well, they look like they're up to ten Sun Dweller test subjects, none of which you bothered to recruit," he said as we started piling bags into the cart.

"I don't even believe it's gonna work anyway. They can't cure the sun blight. They couldn't even cure the Red Plague. I told Uriah it was a stupid idea," I exasperated in a hushed whisper. We moved down the aisle for the next blood type.

"Perhaps your lack of support in the very type of experiment that allow you to see sunrises makes him question your loyalty," Caspian mused.

"Tch." I sucked my teeth. "If anything that should preserve it. If the White Fangs really are trying to drag us down, why would I warn him about it?"

Caspian only responded with a tight shrug. We started piling the pouches again. I grabbed one of them and cracked it open. I drank it in seconds and tossed it in the cart. Of course, I intended to pay for it. If I remembered.

"Eating more often now, huh? I'm proud."

I shrugged. He continued to push the cart slowly, stopping at the end of the aisle. His expression fell flat again. "As I was saying before... the thing that bothered me the most wasn't the extra Sun Dwellers. It was the fact that the Nightshades who were there were dressed in white gowns. I suspect they want to test on us too."

I stared off into space, trying to piece together the words he was saying. It didn't make sense. For a while, the only sound between us was the mindless music playing over the intercom.

"I can't imagine anybody over here agreein' to gettin' tested on by White Fang," I finally said. "Are you sure?"

"That is the question, isn't it? I don't know if they were given free will or if Uriah is mandating it or what." Caspian straightened and fell silent as people drew near.

We moved on to the next aisle and collected more bags, then passed a shelf of pastries as we made our way to the registers. I stopped, thinking about picking up a cupcake for Briar. They were topped with different flowered icing, and I chose a vanilla one with a red rose. I didn't want to take the chance with chocolate if she didn't like it. While we were in line, I received a text from her that said she had a break coming up in twenty minutes.

Once we checked out, Hartley and I helped Caspian load the blood into coolers in the trunk. With the recent fledglings that had joined our clan finally getting their cravings under control, the next blood run wouldn't be for a while.

"Well, guess this is where we part ways for tonight," I said as I rounded the trunk of my car

"You're not going to help me put this stuff up?" Caspian whined.

"Have Hartley help you. I gotta get somewhere." I dropped into the driver's seat and gently placed the bag with the cupcake on the passenger side.

Caspian leaned over to speak through the passenger window.

"Does that somewhere have anything to do with that very effeminate pastry?" He teased with a thin smile.

"Maybe."

"Have fun!" He laughed, then returned to the SUV.

I waited for Hartley to drive off first before going my own way. I closely watched the clock as I sped through downtown.

I parked the car and made it around the corner where the strip of shops began just in time for her to step outside and sit on the bench diagonal from Sundance's windows. I watched from afar as she yawned and glanced at her phone's lock screen.

With the silence of a prowling leopard, I crept closer from behind and jumped over the back of the bench, plopping right beside her. Briar yelped, then laughed when she recognized me.

"Why are ya so on edge, Sunny?" I poked her arm.

"I'm not, I just didn't expect you to drop out of the sky!" She chuckled, then inclined her head to the bag in my hand.

"What's that?" She pointed with her nose.

"A snack for ya." I passed it to her. I watched intently as she dug through what seemed like endless plastic to get to the box, stressing about the possibility that she might not like cake at all.

Her wide smile shrunk a little as her body tensed. She stared down at the thin plastic window exposing the rose icing.

*I should've gotten a bag of chips instead.*

"You don't like cupcakes... do ya..." I wanted to fuse into the bench and disappear.

"No, no! I do, it just... reminds me of someone."

"I hope not an ex." A lame attempt to lighten the mood.

"A little worse than that but it's okay! I'm still going to eat it."

Briar smiled again and lifted the lid, then unwrapped the bottom. Meanwhile, I was busy trying to think of who or what could have been worse than a bad ex.

"I guess I don't know ya very well," I laughed nervously.

"Back at you. Why don't we fix that, hm?" She turned on the bench, propping one leg on the seat and letting the other hang as she sat sideways.

"Sure..." I trailed off, wary of where this could go. "What's your favorite color?"

"Pink, obviously." Briar flipped her hair with a slight chuckle, then glanced at her watch. "My turn."

"Oh, lord."

"Where are you from?"

My muscles eased a little. That was an easy one to answer. "I spent a little bit of my childhood in the South. A small town called Eclipsis. What about you?"

"I can tell." She smiled softly. "I'm from Helios, but I was very young when we moved to Neoterra, so I hardly remember living there."

Briar tossed the empty box and bag into the trash can next to her. "What do you do for a living?"

*There it is.*

That was exactly what I was afraid of. A question so trivial to anyone else but always carried an enormous weight whenever an outsider asked me. I stared down at my shoelaces.

"I'm a collector," I said simply.

"Collect what? Taxes?" Briar snorted as she braced her elbow on the back of the bench and leaned her cheek into her palm.

"Debts." At the moment, all I could see were the men I'd beaten half to death in front of their families when they didn't pay up for the third time, cutting Arlo's finger off, taking women for Uriah to deal with, and collecting children to initiate so they could work off debts.

Suddenly, I felt sick and the game didn't feel fun anymore.

"Before I knew you could sing, I imagined you to be a tattoo artist. A debt collector would've never crossed my mind," Briar said with a soft laugh. Her face fell when she noticed the lack of reaction on my end. "Are you okay?"

*No, I don't know why I came here. I should be avoiding you.*

"Yeah, yeah, sorry. I just remembered something," I said quickly, waving my hand around.

I glanced back at the salon.

"How's your first night of work goin'?" I stretched my arm across the back of the bench and propped an ankle over my knee. My fingertips were just inches away from her arm.

"It's going great! I'm getting to know everyone, they're all so nice. Although there's one girl in there that doesn't seem too thrilled that I'm there." She scratched the side of her nose and looked down at her chipped nails.

"That's expected. Be glad she's the only one that's giving you a hard time and not most of them. But... if she gets violent in any way—"

"I don't think it's that serious," Briar said quickly. I shrugged.

"Ya got my number now. Any trouble you have, I'm just a call away."

I subtly flinched when my phone rang. I pulled it out to see Delilah's name on the screen and quickly put it back into my pocket. It kept ringing and Briar just stared blankly at me.

"You're not gonna get it?" She stood and adjusted her jeans and shirt.

"No, not while you're on break," I said with a frown.

"Actually... I think I'm going to head back in now. Thanks for the cupcake."

Briar turned away and headed back inside without another

word. My face fell as I watched her walk away. There were still five minutes left in her break. I didn't try to stop her, though I had a gnawing feeling that I should've.

218

# 26

# BRIAR



*DELILAH.*

I hated how nosy I could be.

*Delilah.*

That name was glaring on his phone. I wished he had a picture of her somewhere so I knew what she looked like. I hated that the name kept echoing through my mind.

I had five minutes left of my break and sat in the break room for the remainder of it, marinating in the silence.

I wasn't going to deny that I thought Draven was attractive, but I didn't expect to feel so... *off* seeing another woman's name on his phone, despite never even going on a date with the man. Maybe I was being possessive of our new friendship because he was the only one I could completely be myself around. If he had a girlfriend, we wouldn't be able to spend as much time together as I hoped. The short time we'd spent together left me craving socialization that didn't involve constant arguments like I had with Sterling. Astoria was so deep in her studies that we wouldn't have time for each other until... I wasn't sure. This summer was supposed to be our time together, but she took summer courses to graduate faster.

I hadn't had any friends since foster care. The only best friend I ever had—Quinn Harrison—got adopted and left before we could ever exchange contact information. Neither of us had a phone back then.

Quinn was always in my corner after I had to suffer through various punishments from our foster parents. We played games like hide-and-seek, built forts, and she was the pillar of reason I needed every time I wanted to run away.

I wondered where she was, how she was doing, if she was still in Neoterra or if her new parents had whisked her away to a paradise. I wished we hadn't lost so many years between us, because *she* would've been someone I could reach out to about my problems. I didn't believe Astoria could fully relate or understand.

I scrolled busily through my phone for some form of brain rot and watched the timer on my watch slowly go down. I got up with one minute remaining and returned to the front desk. Samara was assisting a new customer, whose rich hickory skin was so smooth and dewy that she glowed. Her hair was black with white-streaked locs, styled in neat rows that pulled back into the most perfect braided bun I'd ever seen. Her fangs were sharp, her white teeth perfectly straight against her voluptuous lips. She wore a wheat-colored gown with a heart-shaped neckline that cascaded down in a river of chiffon.

My steps faltered as I was taken aback by how elegant she looked, as if she was royalty I was obligated to bow to. The only thing that was missing in her attire was makeup, but she could obviously go without it.

Samara waved me over. I smiled nervously as I approached the desk.

"Hi, welcome to S—"

"Sun Dweller." The woman's narrow scarlet eyes seemed to brighten as she switched her attention to me.

"How—" She inhaled deeply. "Unique."

I forced a dry swallow as my blood ran cold. All the customers I'd dealt with so far merely stared as they spoke with Samara, and the ones over the phone were none the wiser.

"This is her first night, so go easy on her." Samara patted my back with a laugh, then sat on the stool to watch me.

"What services would you like tonight?" My voice warbled in the beginning, but I cleared my throat to stabilize it.

"Makeup. I have an event in two hours. What's your name?" The woman pulled her credit card out of her clutch as I fumbled the buttons on the register.

"Briar..." I trailed off uncomfortably.

"Briar," she echoed. "Briar. Quite interesting."

Her eye contact remained fixed. I only had the courage to meet it for a second. Those eyes pierced my soul, and I was certain she already knew everything about me because of it.

I finally found the correct button and rang her up, then gave her the total. I looked at the list of stylists and glanced back at Samara.

"Go ahead and send her to Jocelyn. It's time for you to shadow her tonight," Samara said as she examined her own nails and picked underneath them.

I turned back to the woman with a small smile. "She'll be right with you in a minute."

The woman gave a slight nod and gathered her dress before strutting to the lounge area. I sighed with relief as the cold aura trailed with her, but still dreaded sticking around Jocelyn during the makeup application.

"Briar, welcome! I'm sorry I haven't said anything yet, I had a couple clients. I'm so glad you're gonna be here with us!"

Jocelyn popped around the front desk and hugged me from behind. I wheezed as she squeezed the air out of me.

"It's been so long since I had a trainee," she beamed. I smiled brightly.

"I can't wait to learn from you," I said as I rubbed my arms. I glanced at the woman and winced when I saw she was staring right at us. I expected her to be looking at her phone or one of the magazines on the coffee table. I quickly turned back to Jocelyn.

"We have a makeup client." I nodded my head in the woman's direction. Jocelyn waved at her.

"Come on back, hon! Ah, you look so pretty! What's the occasion?" she asked as she walked to her booth in the back. I trailed behind both of them.

"A banquet for work," the woman said simply. The fabric of her dress swished as it settled around her in the chair. Jocelyn hit the lever a few times until she was at eye level.

"What kind of look are you aiming for?" Jocelyn scanned her face.

"Surprise me."

I sat in a chair next to Jocelyn's booth, watching her go through her supplies to match the woman's complexion and find the right lip, eye, and blush colors to complement her skin. By the end of the session, the woman looked even more striking than before. Jocelyn stepped out of her way and turned the chair so the woman could admire herself in the mirror.

She smiled serenely and rose to her feet, offering Jocelyn a poised bow. "I feel beautiful, thank you."

I was so thankful the application was finally over. She'd stared at me the entire time and I couldn't decide if it was with hunger, hate, or curiosity.

"I gave you a sizable tip," the woman said.

"Thank you so much, I hope you'll come back! Enjoy your evening."

Jocelyn gave her a final wave before the woman strutted out of the door. Suddenly, the air didn't seem so thick in the salon and I was finally able to breathe.

I spent the rest of my shift shadowing Jocelyn. She often stopped in the middle of what she was doing to demonstrate or explain why she did things the way she did. I learned a lot, and it was a healthy distraction from the rock that sat in my stomach after seeing Draven earlier.

My final task for the night was to help clean the salon. I swept, sanitized the stations, and was finally released to go home around four in the morning.

I put on my helmet before I left Sundance to escape attention as possible. My motorcycle was safely untouched. I mounted it and started the journey back home without trouble.

✴

It was nice not showing up at the same time as Sterling. I could at least go straight to sleep and get a few hours of sleep in without any conflict.

Except when I finally arrived home, dressed down into pajamas, and collapsed in my bed, sleep was distant. Even with the black-out curtains, I found myself staring at the ceiling and mulling over Draven and the mysterious Delilah.

The sun was at its zenith by the when I fell asleep, and it was fitful. I woke up close to dinner time as the sun was melting into the horizon. It still stung my eyes when I opened the curtains.

Astoria was downstairs eating a salad and watching TV in the living room when I appeared.

"Where's Sterling?" I asked with a frown. Not that I *wanted* to see him. But it was awfully unlike him to be gone for this long, even whenever he worked overtime.

"He's probably—"

The front door opened and Sterling manifested in the flesh as if I'd summoned him. He held his cracked mask in his bloodied hands, his hair tousled, and his uniform soiled in dried blood that didn't appear to be his.

# 27
# STERLING

EVERY TIME NIGHT FELL, I WAS LEFT THINKING ABOUT ALL THE demons I was up against. All the vile, depraved parasites that walked among us, talked like us, *behaved* like us. Now, with Briar working with them, I was left thinking about when they would turn on her.

I should've asked where Briar got the job so I could've at least scoped them out. Maybe I would've been more comfortable if I knew the Vampyres were stable. Such a rare collection of them were, after all. It didn't matter how many had jobs and acted "civilized." I knew behind closed doors, they were savages.

I sat in my car in a dilapidated church parking lot with my interior red pilot light on, looking over the missing victims' files for the millionth time. It pained me not being able to show Briar the gruesome details of their abductions—the crime scene photos of their houses and apartments being ripped apart before they were taken, and the trails of blood left behind. These were legitimate victims, not runaways, and their critical forty-eight hours had long gone. The number kept growing, the same pattern every time, without a single witness to give any leads. Their homes and belongings had been scrubbed of their scents, and my Vampyre colleagues couldn't track the victims.

The abductions were organized. The rate at which they were occurring, some simultaneously, had to indicate a group working together. My theory was an underground trafficking ring. There were five women and five men missing, all of varying ethnicities and backgrounds. The only similarity among them was their ages ranged from twenty to thirty.

There was also a growing number of humans being Turned. The victims were scattered across the city.

I shut my eyes tightly and pinched the bridge of my nose as a sharp pang rang through my forehead. I opened them to look at the smiling young photo of my father in his mechanic uniform that I kept on my dash. A deep fold was scored in the corner of it. It was all I had of him.

"What should I do?" I asked him. "What would you do?"

I wished the photo could talk back. More importantly, I wished I'd been there to stop him from going after our mother that night.

It didn't matter how many Vampyres I arrested—it was never enough to put my inner beast to sleep. Never would be until they were all wiped from the face of the planet.

I snapped my focus from the files when a car rolled up next to my window, but relaxed when I saw Cyrene behind the glass. I rolled my window down.

"You picked like... the *worst* area to do your reviews, bud." She put her patrol car in park and unwrapped a sub sandwich.

"Worst areas are the best areas to catch a rabbit." I closed the file I was looking at and moved on to the next.

"Well... if you accepted Chief Duncan's offer for an integrated partnership, maybe you'd get a better insight on the case with another perspective?" Her voice was muffled as she spoke with her cheeks stuffed. I rolled my eyes and shook my head.

I held up one of the crime scene photos and brought it closer to my face. "If I'm going to have a partner, it's not gonna be with their kind."

"That's against policy, you know? They're supposed to be blue before they're Vampyres when they're on the force."

"They drink red. They'll never be blue to me." The sounds of the wrapper crinkling and her quiet chewing cut into my focus as I tried to read the reports, but I still didn't mind her presence. "Besides... old Johnny Briggs died on the force not because of some thug but because his partner bled him out after he got shot."

"That was before you even joined the force." Cyrene wiped her mouth with a napkin and slurped through a straw.

"Doesn't make it less relevant," I grumbled.

"If you get a Vampyre partner to help you on the missing persons case, I promise I'll go on a date with you," she intoned.

I smirked at her and opened my mouth to speak.

The scanner buzzed with white noise before a clearer voice cut in.

"We have two male Vampyre perpetrators engaging in a physical altercation on East and Fifth. Shots have been fired. Shelter in place initiated," dispatch informed.

I burned rubber speeding out of the parking lot and followed closely behind Cyrene, weaving through traffic to rush to the location. I kept listening to the scanner as they described one male being around five foot five and the other six foot two with foreign branding marks along his arms.

Our cars came to a screeching stop. We posted behind our open doors and held out our guns. They were loaded with silver bullets, the new standard ever since the Vampyres' weaknesses were realized during the Crimson War.

"Freeze!" We both kept shouting at them as they writhed on the ground, ignoring us. "Halt!"

The taller Vampyre pinned the smaller one beneath him. I watched in horror as his face contorted, the corners of his mouth stretching to his earlobes and revealing multiple rows of teeth like a shark. The smaller Vampyre flailed and held his attacker's shoulders back. The deformed one snapped at the victim's face as if he wanted to eat him.

"What the hell..." I muttered and fired, the bullet whizzing inches from his arm.

Mutations and this apparent cannibalism were never taught in the Academy. Cyrene emptied her magazine and reloaded without skipping a beat.

The Vampyre jumped from his victim and latched onto a nearby brick wall, then started scaling it like a spider. The victim scrambled to his feet and disappeared in seconds while the abomination gripped a windowsill on the third story and looked down at us, then started shooting his own previously hidden gun.

"Weapon!"

The officers on the other side of the street fired as I ducked in my car for cover, switching magazines in my gun. The Vampyre moved so nimbly across the wall that every bullet missed. He launched off the wall, hurtling toward Cyrene's patrol car. This time I shot him, the bullet slicing through his calf. He roared wildly and landed heavily on her car's roof, caving it in.

"Cyrene, get away from there!" we all screamed as she stood frozen with her gun pointed at him.

She pumped four shots into him, but he didn't miss a beat as he ran across the hood on all fours and ducked behind the car. When I started to shoot again, he lifted the car as if it were made of tin foil and flung it toward the officers on the other side of the street. They scattered frantically as it crashed into their vehicles. Just as I turned away from the lethal disaster that had almost taken out five of my men, the Vampyre snapped Cyrene's arm in two. She dropped her gun as she screamed.

"Cyrene, no!"

I ran across the street and shot at the Vampyre's back, but every single bullet seemed to deal the damage of thumbtacks. I threw the gun aside and pulled out a silver dagger, then charged forward.

Without even looking, he shoved me back with an open palm that carried enough force to send me flying into my car. My head cracked against the window and I slumped to the ground, my mask in pieces. I sat there, helplessly watching as my eyes blurred.

Cyrene's legs flailed as he raised her in the air with one hand, and raked long talons across her abdomen. Her blood rained over him and he held out his long, reptilian tongue as if he was trying to catch a snowflake.

The Vampyre tossed her body aside just as he combusted into flames. He writhed and flailed as he roared and squealed. I weakly looked across the street to see one of the officers had pulled out a flamethrower as a last-ditch effort.

I crawled to Cyrene's body and pulled her to my lap. Her breaths were ragged and shallow, her eyes bulging.

"No, no, no." I started rocking her. "No, no, stay with me. Stay with me Cyrene, please. Please! We—I'll do the integration, okay? I'll take you out to dinner and then the drive-in, we'll even go watch the stupid chick flick you keep talking about—"

I looked down at her stomach. It was completely mangled. No ambulance could get here fast enough, even if the paramedics themselves were Vampyres and came on foot. Cyrene didn't blink. I didn't even notice when her breaths stopped. Rapid footsteps approached as the officers raced to my side, and three of them had to drag me away from her kicking and screaming.

✳

I spent hours at the crime scene, biting my nails and shaking my legs up and down as I sat at the edge of the ambulance. I just stared at the silhouette of her body under the white sheet as camera flashes scattered around the crime scene. I couldn't remember when the media showed up, hawking the tragedy that ensued like vultures behind the yellow caution tape. I couldn't hear what the paramedic was telling me as they shined a flashlight into my eyes. I kept replaying everything that happened over and over and over—

It was supposed to be a disturbance. A simple, routine disturbance between two beasts that could've been under the influence, fighting over drugs, a lover, anything. Not a single person on that radio disclosed that we were facing a monster of unprecedented strength. No one disclosed that we would be racing to our deaths. How could a bystander miss the details of a Vampyre with hundreds of teeth or claws the length of a harpy eagle's talons? No one in history, even right after the Red Plague when Vampyres were at their peak, was reported to have features like that.

I flinched when a calloused hand touched my shoulder and snapped me out of my lost gaze on Cyrene's body.

"Chief Duncan," I whispered hoarsely, then looked down at my lap.

"Are you alright, son? The paramedics said you might have a concussion," he said gruffly.

I jerked my chin in her direction. "A concussion is nothing compared to... to *that*."

Chief Duncan sat next to me on the tailgate of the ambulance truck. His olive skin was rough and porous, weathered from years of being nailed down by the hammers of the city's demons.

"I hate to ask you this but I need you to give a report. You'll also need to speak with one of our therapists and take some time off—"

"No!" I snapped sharply. "Now is *not* the time. That *thing* was no Vampyre. The silver bullets didn't even work on him. We emptied our magazines and he still kept going. We need to learn more about where that thing came from."

We could've started with his branded tattoos, were they not singed off.

"Sterling—"

"No! With all due respect, sir, I can't sit idly by." The shaking started all over again. "I have to keep working."

"Taking time off doesn't mean we won't be working on getting answers. Right now we need to focus on you, the other officers who were in the crossfire, and notifying Ms. Clarke's family. Besides, you of all people should know that victims don't work their own cases."

"This was an act of war," I growled.

"Need I remind you that you have brothers and sisters that are on your side?" He clasped his hands together in his lap and inclined his head.

"Let's not pretend that half of them are corrupt and don't enforce the curfews when they should," I grumbled shakily.

"That is a serious accusation and very low coming from you." Chief Duncan rose to his feet and looked down at me, the wrinkles in his forehead deepening.

"Officer Shaw, I'm giving you a direct order to stand down and go home. Someone will get your report while you recover from your concussion. Officer Hart will be escorting you home after the hospital visit."

Chief Duncan pivoted on his heel as he moved on to the other officers being examined by paramedics. I breathed heavily through flared nostrils and gnashed my teeth so tight I thought they'd break. I rammed my fist into the side of the ambulance and shouted an obscenity.

"Officer Shaw, we need you to get on the gurney so we can get your head looked at." The female paramedic spoke softly, as if raising her voice too loud would finally make me break.

I didn't want to leave. There could be key clues the crime scene investigators would miss. I couldn't trust any of them to do their job right. Not when ten missing people yielded not a single trace for a lead. No Vampyre could be that smart. I was beginning to believe that our police force was growing either incompetent or jaded.

I refused to lie down on the stretcher, so they let me sit with a neck brace on in the back of the ambulance. I watched Cyrene's covered body shrink in the window as we drove away.

✳

I was at the hospital for hours with the other injured officers. While I waited in the exam room for my CT scan results, I stared at my mask cracked in two in my lap. I ran through what happened in my head, falling into the deep pit of hindsight. We should've been better prepared. We shouldn't have let the other Vampyre go. I should've aimed for the head. We should've used the flamethrower first. The lack of detailed communication set us up for fatal failure.

My eyes burned. I wasn't sure if it was from minimal blinking or the constant threat of tears clawing their way through. I lifted my gaze to the sun climbing the horizon, revealing a cloudless cotton-candy sky. Cyrene loved cotton candy. She loved many things. Most importantly, she loved keeping the community safe. She visited her grandmother in the nursing home every chance she had. She had a large, outgoing family that constantly hosted cookouts I was always invited to but never had the time to attend.

"Officer Shaw?"

The thick door swung open and I instantly reached for my gun, only to realize my holster was empty. I blinked as I realized the blonde-haired doctor that entered was human and I was in the hospital, not in the streets. I was safe.

"Yes." My voice was a breathy croak.

"My name is Dr. Blandon. I heard about what happened and I'm truly sorry for your loss." She looked down at her clipboard with pursed lips. "I'm sorry to say your results are positive for a concussion, but it will heal in time. Do you live alone?"

"No. I have two sisters," I mumbled.

"Good. For the first forty-eight hours, you can't drive. You need plenty of rest. That means nothing that requires too much labor, mental focus, or activities affecting coordination. No climbing, jumping, alcohol, or anything of the sort," she droned on.

"My head hurts," I spoke flatly, staring off into space. I was only halfway listening. I rubbed my forehead.

"I'm prescribing you some medicine for the headaches. You'll probably feel dizzy, and have some light sensitivity. Come back to the emergency room if you feel any of your symptoms worsen or you lose consciousness, okay?"

I simply nodded.

I had to wait a couple more hours for the prescriptions to be ready. By now the day was rolling close to Check-In. I figured Briar would be going out of her mind again like before.

I was still zoned out, waiting in the pharmacy on the ground floor when navy blue slacks and a duty belt blocked my view. I raised my gaze to a tall, slender woman with ivory skin and thick black hair pulled into a fishtail braid. A rock plopped into my stomach when our eyes met. Those dastardly garnet irises.

"Are you Officer Shaw?" she asked softly. She had a slight rasp in her voice. I stared at her longer, then chuckled softly. Those bastards.

"Are you Officer Shaw?" she repeated louder. "I'm Officer Hart,

I've been assigned to take you home. You can call me Lyra."

"I'm perfectly capable of going home by myself." I shooed her away.

"Your capabilities aren't in question. I'm just following a direct order by the chief himself."

She sat in a plastic chair next to me. I was slumped in mine, my navy shirt unbuttoned and hanging off of one shoulder to expose my blood-soaked white undershirt. I didn't bother to attempt to straighten anything. I didn't care how brazen my appearance was for other patients in the lobby. Everything felt like a hazy nightmare.

"Number one twenty-seven," the pharmacist announced. Even when I tried to stand slowly, the ground swayed. Lyra gripped my arm to steady me but I snatched it away.

"Don't you dare touch me," I hissed.

Blood pounded in my ears and behind my eyes as the headache intensified from the jarring motion. The light was blinding, and I based my judgment on shapes and colors as I walked to the counter to grab the brown paper bag of pills. I followed Lyra outside to a patrol car parked in the drop-off zone. I got in the front seat and leaned against the door.

"I'm sorry about what happened," she murmured once we were on the road.

"I don't need your sympathy. If your kind didn't exist, it would've never happened in the first place," I shot at her. I shuttered my eyelids when my voice seemed to trigger more crashing waves behind my eyes.

"Humans are capable of murder too," Lyra said flatly.

"Not disembowelment. You weren't there, how would you even

know anyway?" I seethed.

*It should've been you, demon.*

"Cyrene was—"

"Don't say her name. Don't you *dare*," I barked, then reeled back when my voice cracked. Lyra sighed and shook her head. I curled up against the door again, closing my eyes because I didn't know how much longer I could hold back the tears.

# 28
# BRIAR

"Sterling... what happened?" Astoria whimpered as she jumped up from the couch. I probably scanned his body fifty times in a matter of seconds, searching for any possibility that he was injured. As he shut the door in sullen silence, I saw a patrol car back out of our driveway. His car was nowhere to be seen.

Sterling staggered to the staircase and gripped the railing, but I used my small frame to squeeze between him and the wall. I extended my arms to block his path.

"Hey! What *happened*?" I shouted.

He looked up at me from under his brow with a scowl. "Get out of my way," he said slowly through his teeth.

"No! You can't just show up in bloody clothes like this and expect us to ignore it." I pointed at his shirt.

"Briar... please, I can't do this right now." His voice softened with a tremor. "I just want to sleep."

"Is that blood from a friend or a foe?" Astoria cried out.

Sterling continued up the steps, pushing past me like a river around a rock. Astoria and I exchanged wary glances.

I waited a few seconds before following him to his room. When I opened the door, I heard the shower running and quiet whimpering. I bit my lip before slowly closing the door and giving him space. I had to remind myself that whatever had happened was probably extremely traumatic and he needed time to process it himself before he'd be ready to share it with us. Sterling was never one to tell us anything about his work, but this wasn't something he could use to keep us at bay.

Astoria and I agreed we weren't going to let him stonewall us. We both occasionally glanced at the stairs, hoping he'd come on his own terms and explain what happened last night. I checked the clock warily, wondering if he was even in the right state of mind to show up for Check-In.

"What do you think happened to Sterling?" Astoria whispered. "He didn't look hurt."

"I don't know but I've never seen him like that before," I breathed.

Sterling didn't immediately tell us about our father getting killed either. I wondered how many times he'd wept in the shower on his own, losing his grip on the burdens he carried on his shoulders. He hid it so well.

I picked up the remote and flipped through the channels until I found the news. If the incident was big enough, maybe there would be coverage of it by now.

Astoria tucked her legs against her chest and wrapped her arms tightly around them as she watched the screen with big doe eyes.

"Breaking news, in less than twelve hours ago on East and Fifth, what started as an ordinary Vampyre scuffle born from road rage— ended in a fatal tragedy." My eyebrows slowly met in a tight frown. "The Vampyre responsible for injuring five officers and murdering one in cold blood has successfully been put down and is no longer a risk to the community."

"Who died?" Astoria reached for her necklace, sliding the charm up and down the chain.

"Neoterra Police Department has asked us to keep the fallen officer's name undisclosed until the family is notified. We will return with updates as this is an ongoing investigation."

"Whoever it was... they were important to him," I said.

The incident occurred deep in the Nocturne District. I had never so much as gone within a five-mile radius of that area. Yet, somehow guilt and trepidation tried to creep into my gut. I couldn't call out of work on my second day; that was bad for business. Even if I did manage to stay home, Sterling wouldn't let me be his emotional support anyway.

"Are you still going to work tonight?" Astoria whispered. I paused, then nodded.

"Might as well," I said. "Can you keep an eye on him while I'm gone? He's, um... crying right now."

"Aw, that's so sad! I've never seen Sterling cry before..." She peered at the stairs, poking her bottom lip out.

"Come on, let's make dinner before Check-In. Maybe we can get him to eat something... I doubt he had anything all day." Astoria nodded and rose from the couch with me and we started prepping a quick meal of spaghetti.

We sat at the dining table while we waited for the food to cook. I pulled out my phone and opened Draven's texts. My thumbs were positioned to type, but they were frozen as I stared blankly at the screen. I wanted to ask him if he knew about last night, but the only word that came to mind was Delilah's name.

"Are you okay?" Astoria cut into my mind as if she'd read it.

I set my phone on the table face down and forced a smile.

"Yeah, I'm fine. Just... a friend of mine kinda disappointed me last night, I guess."

Astoria raised an eyebrow. "Friend? Since when do you have friends?"

"Haha, very funny." I rolled my eyes. "It's still a pretty fresh friendship. I met him—"

I cut myself off and looked through the archway to see if Sterling was anywhere nearby, then dropped my volume. "I met him while I was out earlier this week."

"*Him?*" Astoria smirked, and then her lips faltered. "Wait... while you were sneaking out? Does that mean he's a Vampyre?" I nodded and her face went pale.

"Sterling would probably kill you," she whispered harshly.

"We're just friends, it doesn't mean anything. He's been keeping me safe while we're out. He hasn't made a single attempt to hurt me." I placed my hand on her wrist comfortingly. She looked down at my bruised knuckles.

"Right," she said dubiously, then went to check on the food. I rushed to her side by the stove and dropped my voice even lower.

"I punched a Vampyre that was trying to bite me and he handled the rest. I'm telling you, Ria. I've had more fun this week than in my entire life. They're not all monsters."

"You keep saying that... but Sterling almost died last night," she said quietly. "I want to keep an open mind, but it's hard to do that when you only see the negatives."

I sighed and shook my head slowly. I might as well have left it at that.

I helped her pile food on plates for everyone except myself. My appetite was still nonexistent. I grabbed a glass and silverware, then took the meal upstairs to Sterling's room.

The shower sounded like it was still going. It had to have been forty minutes to an hour since he'd gotten home. I set his food and drink down on his nightstand and lightly knocked on his bathroom door. I cracked it open but kept the boundaries as steam slapped me in the face.

"Sterling? We made food for you... you really should try to eat." I tried to be gentle, but I was prepared for him to tell me to go away again.

"Thank you," he croaked. His voice was rough, as if his throat were full of rocks and sand. "I just... need another minute."

"Okay. Check-In is in thirty minutes."

He didn't respond, and I closed the door so the warmth would build back up.

Astoria ate on the porch, gently swinging on the bench. I joined her, staring across the fields at the glittering skyline.

"How's school going?"

I didn't realize how long it had been since I asked that. I was so wrapped up in Sterling's life—my own life—that I'd neglected my little sister.

"It's going great. I'm keeping straight A's, and a study group asked me to join them at the library Sunday." Astoria scraped the bottom of her plate before setting it aside. "Finals are coming up fast and I've been studying for those. I got a paper that's due next week."

"That's great!" I reached over and hugged her. "Now... how are *you* doing?"

Astoria shrugged and leaned back. "Stressed. Burned out. A little lonely, but I don't have time to hang out because there's so much to do."

"Well, don't run yourself ragged before you even start." I crossed my legs, allowing my dangling foot to give the swing a nudge whenever we lost momentum.

"So how did your friend disappoint you?" Astoria asked after a brief moment of silence. I gazed at the skyline with my tongue poking my lip ring.

"We've been spending a little time together and I thought he was single, but I saw a woman's name pop up on his phone. I don't know... he never mentioned a girlfriend." I twiddled my thumbs in my lap.

"I thought you two were just friends, though?" She raised an eyebrow.

"We are," I said flatly.

"Then why does it matter?" She frowned.

"Well..." I shrugged. "I guess I preferred to have the option."

A patrol car sped down the road and slowed as it pulled into our driveway. The usual cloud of dust kicked up from the tires. Astoria and I stood up, waving and smiling. The windshield was too tinted to see, but we both expected to see Cyrene's contagious smile.

Our arms and faces fell slack when Officer Kent stepped out of the car. We'd stopped bringing our IDs outside because Cyrene always just checked off our names and chatted with us a bit before moving on to the next house.

"Evening—"

"You have *a lot* of nerve coming here after my brother told you not to show your face again. Sterling!" I cupped my hands around my mouth as I screamed his name.

"Hold on, calm down. None of that is necessary. I remember your names, so I'm going to make this as painless as possible." Officer Kent spoke quickly as he pulled out his tablet.

"Where's Cyrene?" Astoria asked quietly. Her words subtly wavered, as if she was holding back tears. Officer Kent looked up at her with a wince.

"I... can't say," he faltered.

I froze and glanced at Astoria, then back at him. "She's dead... isn't she?"

"I can't confirm nor deny that."

I chuckled scornfully and threw my hands up, storming back inside. Astoria slowly followed behind, shutting the door. I paced back and forth in the living room. Of all officers... of all people, why Cyrene?

The next hour was spent in silence. I couldn't bring myself to listen to music as I got ready for work. I had to keep telling myself to move forward. I couldn't afford to call out on my second day when I could potentially make a career out of this and finally earn a place in my family. When I could finally stop being the middle child bumming off her older brother.

Maybe then Sterling would respect me enough to share some of his burdens.

*

Astoria texted me throughout the night with updates. I was able to check the messages between customers and phone calls. Sterling didn't take a single bite of his food. He spent most of the night working out in his bedroom. The last update I had was that he'd finally passed out in bed next to a bottle of sleeping pills, which she had religiously counted to make sure he didn't take too many.

"Are you okay, girl?" Samara asked as she sat next to me behind the front desk, returning from her thirty-minute break.

"Not really. Someone close to my brother died. She was always nice to me and my sister too." I blurted a lot more than I intended, but I grew tired of saying "I'm fine."

"Oh my gosh, Briar! What are you doing here?" she exclaimed.

"I just started this job, I didn't want to ruin it." The words cracked in the end and I sucked in a breath.

"No! Jesus, we're not monsters. Go back home and be with your family. Hey, Jocelyn!"

Samara waved her over. Jocelyn was hovering over a customer, working on a flawless haircut. She paused her trimmers to look over her shoulder, mumbled something, and gave the customer a pat on the shoulder before walking over to us.

"What's going on?"

"I'm sending Briar home for the night. Her family is grieving."

"Oh! Oh my, darling! Yes, of course. Go home! Take whatever

time you need, okay?" Jocelyn gave me a tight hug, triggering yet another wheeze.

"Thank you." I gave them a weak smile and gathered my helmet, purse, and phone. "I'm sorry."

"No worries. We're sorry for your loss," Samara said. They gave me a couple more hugs and I left, waving briefly before stepping outside. The air smelled earthy and the sky was more dark brown than midnight blue. The moon and stars were hiding, indicating possible rain.

I had parked further away from Sundance under a street lamp since all the closer spaces were in shadow. What happened to Cyrene, even if it was over ten miles away in the Nocturne District, left me a little paranoid.

I took a moment to check my phone again. I didn't realize Draven had texted me four times since Astoria stopped communicating with me.

*Hey, are u mad at me?*

*When is break?*

*I need to tell u something.*

*It's important.*

I turned the corner and the road sloped into a gentle hill. I could see my motorcycle glint under the bluish-white street lamp in a desolate parking lot. I paused and stared at the messages before forming a message.

*Is it about your secret girlfriend?*

I shook my head and backspaced, then put my phone away. I tried to brainstorm my response in the most mature way possible. Those messages had come three hours ago, and I technically would still be working if Samara and Jocelyn hadn't let me leave early.

I put on my helmet as I entered the empty parking lot. I looked around carefully before mounting my motorcycle.

*I'll call you when I get home.*

I was just about to hit send when something hard cracked against my helmet and knocked me off the bike.

Before I could stand up, I was gasping for air from something striking my ribs, my back, and thighs in rapid succession. I curled in a ball, holding my arms over my stomach and relying on my helmet to protect my head, until someone snatched it off. I was blinded by the street light before the rubber sole of a boot came crashing down onto my face.

Everything went black.

# 29
# DRAVEN

I DON'T KNOW WHY I DIDN'T REALIZE IT SOONER, BUT I figured Briar's change in demeanor last night was because she'd seen
Delilah's name on my phone. It was a bad look, but Delilah and I
stopped our fling months ago. I'd never felt the need to mention her.
Besides... it wasn't like Briar and I were dating...

I mulled over how I'd handled the situation as I helped Caspian
organize the refrigerator by blood type. Hartley helped him stock
it, but I took his place so he could return to driving clan members
around.

"So, did the lady like the gift you gave?" Caspian asked as he sat
on the floor to handle the bottom shelves.

"I guess. I kinda ruined it after, though," I griped.

"What do you mean?"

"Delilah called me. She usually texts, but of all nights and moments she decided to call. The whole vibe changed after."

"Wait, don't tell me you *answered* her right in front of the girl?"

"No, she just saw the name on the phone."

Caspian chuckled and shook his head, shuffling the bags around. "I don't get you, Draven."

"What? It ain't like we're a thing anyway."

"Doesn't matter. Women draw up conclusions when the picture isn't fully sketched."

Caspian stood with a soft grunt and grabbed a bag from the top shelf. I finished organizing a minute after and then did the same. I leaned against the counter as we drank. One bag didn't do enough for me, so I grabbed another.

"Who is she?" he asked.

"It'd never work out even if I wanted it to." We tossed our empty bags in the biohazard trash and shuffled out of the kitchen.

"How about a little game of pool to pass some daylight?" Caspian crossed the foyer and stood by the door that led to the basement.

I followed him to the lounge area. It was empty. Most of the Nightshade members were busy recruiting fledglings, searching for more Sun Dwellers for the White Fangs, or conducting other business.

We picked our cue sticks. Caspian arranged the object balls in the rack as I rubbed chalk over the tip of my cue. He was quiet; it could've meant he was calculating his next move in the conversation or just focusing on getting the rack set up.

"Why wouldn't it work out?"

"Hm?" I broke my gaze from the pool table's red felt.

"A moment ago you said it wouldn't work out if you wanted it to. Of course, that was after you ignored my question about who she was."

Caspian chalked his cue stick while I broke the rack. I watched the balls scatter across the table.

"She ain't one of us." I said.

Caspian didn't lift his gaze from the table. He walked around it, almost in a prowl. He chose solids and swiftly made the first three pockets.

"Not a Nightshade or not a Vampyre?" He cut his sharp eyes to mine, and I tightened my grip around the cue stick.

I didn't answer as I took my turn.

We ended the game of pool before the sun had fully risen; I lost interest in it when Caspian tried to press about Briar. Uriah called a clan meeting shortly after, so we stayed in the basement while we waited for everyone to arrive. I found more toothpicks in the kitchenette and came back with one between my teeth. Caspian was lying across the sectional with his head hanging off its edge as he played one of the games on his phone. I slouched in one of the chairs, my head leaning back and my eyes closed to try to clear my head.

"Draven Hawthorne, never thought I'd see *you* again."

The voice made my eyes fly open.

"Arlo? What the hell are you doing here?"

I frowned, but my face softened when I noticed Arlo's entire right arm was missing. Caspian lifted his head and quickly sat up. His eyes widened as if he'd seen a ghost.

"What's wrong? Surprised to see I'm still kickin'?" Arlo jeered. "No thanks to you two, but I am now a Nightshade to work off my debts."

"You can't blame us for that." I rolled my eyes. "Ain't nobody forced you to gamble your money away and not pay back the loans."

"I can blame *him* for taking my arm instead of my life." Arlo glanced pointedly at Caspian. "I ain't rich like Uriah, who can just buy a new arm."

I guess I understood now why Caspian seemed so disturbed the night we split up. Something had broken inside... while Caspian was trying to kill a man, I was apologizing to the very human I was supposed to either kill or send to the White Fangs. I was even more convinced to never tell him about Briar.

"I was following orders," Caspian said softly, more to himself than to Arlo.

"Ah, yes, the Golden Boy of the Nightshades. Uriah must be proud." Arlo spat on the floor next to Caspian's polished shoe and walked across the lounge toward the bar.

I leaned over my armrest and dropped my voice to a whisper. "Don't feel guilty about him, man. If he was responsible like our other clients, none of it would've happened."

"He has two kids. We burned his house down and he has children," Caspian whispered harshly, then buried his face in his hand.

I leaned back in my chair and sighed. I remembered seeing the photos upstairs. Caspian never went up there. I wondered if he would've been as calm during the arson if he had known.

Delilah was the last to come downstairs before we'd have to wait for Uriah's arrival. She was busily chewing gum and twirling a manicured finger around a loc. I met her by the staircase.

"Hey, did ya call me last night? What did you want?" I narrowed my eyes, especially since the past couple of days had been nothing short of unpleasant between us. She blew a bubble and popped it before she resumed chewing. She shrugged with a small smirk.

"You'll find out soon enough."

She brushed past me and joined the group of Vampyres crowding near the pool tables. I frowned, the gears in my mind quickly turning as I tried to understand what she meant. Was she going to give me a heads-up about whatever this meeting was about?

Uriah shortly came downstairs and moved to the bar. I dreaded another reveal of the cellar.

"Good evening, family." He adjusted his sand-colored tie in his olive green suit and cleared his throat. "There was an incident last night involving one of our members. He's fine, he's in hiding. However, he reported he was attacked by a Vampyre of inexplicable strength."

"Sounds like bro just needed to lift more," someone quipped, followed by brief laughter.

"No, the Vampyre in question had multiple rows of teeth, and his claws grew to five-inch talons. He described him as a beast." Uriah cut his eyes in the voice's direction.

"Where did this happen?" I called out. I wondered if it had anything to do with what White Fang was doing in their labs.

Uriah glanced at me, then scanned the rest of the crowd.

"In Nocturne. Now, the Vampyre was burned to death by the police, but we did find out that their silver bullets didn't work on him." His lips slowly crawled into a sly smirk. I squeezed my phone in my pocket, itching to warn Briar about the anomaly. Maybe I could convince her to go back to day-shifting.

"So what does that mean for us?" another Vampyre chimed in.

"It means that whatever White Fang is doing, they need to keep doing it. The silver bullet immunity is the first step. Just think, sunlight immunity can be next. We would be unstoppable!"

"Fire still worked on him," someone else pointed out.

"Who's to say that they can't stop that too? Science brings on a whole world of possibilities." Uriah's thin smile stretched like a snake. Everyone began murmuring among themselves until he spoke again.

"With this spectacular milestone they've reached, there's going to be more trials. I need volunteers to participate." He clasped his hands together and scanned the room, expecting people to already have their hands up. "I would *prefer* volunteers, but I can easily make it mandatory."

For a moment, I was tempted to volunteer. Being immune to silver bullets sounded great, but the possibility of sunlight immunity sounded like a dream come true. I'd practically feel human again aside from the dependency on blood. Maybe they could cure that too. But that Vampyre sounded like a real freak of nature and I didn't want to risk becoming worse than I already was.

I looked around as three Vampyres slowly lifted their palms. Caspian and I exchanged wary glances. Whatever theory he had about Nightshades being tested on was true. However... as Nightshades, we were supposed to trust that Uriah knew what he was doing *and* that it was in our best interests.

"Just the three of you? Alright, that'll do for now, but we'll need more by the next clan meeting," he said, then extended his arms. "You're all dismissed! Draven, Caspian, I need a word with you two."

Uriah hung back to speak with the volunteers, possibly detailing what they should expect.

I groaned under my breath. Caspian was already on his way up the stairs. I faltered a moment, then followed behind him.

We settled in the wing-backed velvet chairs in Uriah's study and waited for him. My stomach flinched when the door finally opened.

"I have an assignment for you guys. It's highly sensitive, so I know you're the ones I can trust to take care of it. As long as you promise me no slipups this time." He slid his gaze in my direction.

"Yeah. What is it?" I asked curtly. I just needed *one second* to shoot Briar a text.

"Careful," Uriah warned. He slid a paper with an address and two portraits—a man and a woman—across the desk. I leaned forward, snatched it, and sank back in the chair.

"Solaris Theatre... what's there?" I frowned as I examined their headshots. The man had medium-length salt and pepper hair and the woman had brassy blonde hair that washed out her rosy skin.

"Are you two familiar with Nathaniel and Helene Barnaby?"

Uriah propped his elbows on the desk and wove his fleshed and metal fingers together before resting his chin over them. I shook my head with a frown. I couldn't keep up with the hundreds of clients we had. It wasn't my job and I had never been an overachiever.

"Mr. Barnaby is one of the wealthiest and formidable arms dealers in Neoterra, right?"

I instantly passed that title to Caspian.

"Correct. He and his wife will be at Solaris Theatre for an opera showing at ten o'clock tonight." He swiveled in his chair, turning his attention to the map of Neoterra behind him. "He has an encrypted passcode on his phone that gives access to his arsenals and armories."

I held my breath.

"I need you both to kill him and his wife tonight and obtain that passcode." Uriah said, plucking a piece of lint from his shoulder.

"Done," Caspian said.

"Wait, hold on." I leaned forward and held out my hand as if I could freeze time. "What do we need access to that for? We tryna start weapons trafficking? What about the Neoterra Police Department? If he's that big, what makes you think he doesn't provide their weapons too, and if we kill him—the NPD turns against us?"

"It's above your pay grade to know what it's for and all the logistics. I just need you to do your task," Uriah said harshly, then leaned back in his chair and shooed us away. "As far as the police goes... I wouldn't worry about it."

Caspian left without question, while I stayed to toe the line of getting battered again.

"The experiments... the Barnabys... what are you planning?" I dropped my tone.

He stood from his desk and walked behind my chair. I tensed when he slammed his metal hand over my head and squeezed my skull. I squirmed in the chair, my hands shooting up to his wrist.

"You seem to have forgotten your place, my boy." His tone was calm but thick with malice, like an ocean teeming with sharks.

Black dots spotted my vision and my head felt like it was splitting. I released a growl as I tried to twist away from him, but his grip was unyielding. I shut my eyes tightly as I gnashed my teeth, held my breath, and suppressed tears.

"Question me again, and it'll be the last time you speak." He roughly pushed my head forward as he let go.

"Sorry." My voice was strained. I didn't dare reach to rub my head until I left his study. The pain subsided in seconds, but the fear lingered like fog.

✳

Caspian had already packed the duffel with weapons, gloves, and everything else we needed by the time I linked up with him outside. Hartley was made aware of the situation and Uriah ordered him to exclusively drive us around the entire night.

Hartley was waiting for us in a new, unassuming black sedan with false license plates. It would be taken to the junkyard to be scrapped after the mission.

Caspian and I got in the backseat with our gaiters in hand. I pulled out my phone to text Briar, as I knew this was the only time I had to do it.

*Hey, are u mad at me?*

I waited a few minutes, then sent another text when I didn't get a response. Even though I understood she was at work.

*When is break?*

I wanted to tell her in person, but maybe I could find the time to call her after the mission.

No response. I figured the salon could be busier than usual. It was Saturday, after all. Regardless, I sent two more texts.

*I need to tell you something. It's important.*

I stared at the screen for a moment, realizing I probably could've condensed all of that information into one text. I cringed as I let the phone screen go black and looked out the window. I adjusted the beanie over my head and put on sunglasses when we were halfway to Solaris Theatre.

We drove by Sundance, where I saw Briar talking on the land-line and writing on a notepad. I smiled softly, a little relieved that I wasn't being ignored and she truly was busy. Maybe she wasn't even mad at me and I was overthinking the whole phone call situation.

Either way, it was the least of my problems. I needed to focus on the mission at hand.

"When we get there, we need to get to high ground through the backstage access," Caspian said. "If we can post up somewhere above the stage, we'll have an open view of the audience. Depending on where they're seated, we can take our shots from there."

"That sounds like a great plan if they were gonna be the only ones in the theatre, dude," I droned as I rolled my eyes.

"We don't have many options."

"I say we post on the rooftop of the building across from Solaris Theatre and wait for the play to be over," I suggested with a shrug. I wasn't as bothered by the assignment as I was by the big picture.

"*I don't think Uriah fully trusts you,*" Caspian once said. There was a time when Uriah trusted me with a lot of sensitive informa-tion. One mistake with Arlo and all of a sudden it seemed like I was almost a fledgling again. It gnawed at me. I wanted to get this assassi-nation right and take back my place as a right-hand man so I could at least stay informed. I didn't want to return to my past, when I spent most of my adolescence in the windowless cells of the basement be-cause I wasn't "ready."

I started to chant the Nightshades' manifesto softly under my breath. Caspian joined in shortly after and we spoke in quiet unison.

"We will crush the bones of our enemies. We will bathe in the blood of their descendants. We will poison the weak, and nurture the strong. We will rise and conquer, for the world is ours."

I only said it once, although Uriah always expected us to say it three times if we had to. Caspian continued while I reeled from the words. I'd repeated that manifesto a million times in my life, with the enemies always referring to humans. But I could never view Briar as an enemy. Saying it felt like a betrayal.

※

"Did you guys decide what you wanted to do?" Hartley slowed to a creeping roll down the street. We were an hour early, with Solaris Theatre less than a mile away.

"We'll try Draven's plan," Caspian begrudged.

We pulled our gaiters over our noses. I dragged the duffel bag into my lap and held onto the car door handle, waiting for Hartley to stop behind a six-story bank across from Solaris Theatre. We quickly got out and Hartley drove off without skipping a beat.

Caspian swiftly banked off a street lamp, onto a windowsill, and then straight to the roof. The tails of his trench coat whipped wildly, then disappeared over the edge. He poked his head over the roof and held out his hand. I threw the duffel bag up and he caught the strap. I launched straight from the ground to the roof, leaving small cracks in the sidewalk. When I landed, Caspian was already setting up the sniper rifle on its tripod over the edge. I crouched next to him, peering down at the line of suits and gowns flowing into Solaris Theatre.

Once he finished setting up, I sank and lay prone behind the scope next to Caspian.

"We could probably take the shot when they arrive rather than wait until the end of the performance. Get it over with," Caspian muttered.

"Yeah. Most of the cops are still finishin' their Check-In rounds right now," I responded, staring intently through the scope. "The crowd will be more dense with everyone leavin' the theatre at the same time."

"Once you kill them, I'll go get the phone."

I adjusted my gloves with a nod. "Yeah, sounds good."

I was a better shot, but Caspian was a lot more agile.

A convertible pulled up and parallel parked flawlessly in front of the theatre. I saw the salt and pepper hair rise from the driver's seat, then move around to the passenger side to open the door for his wife. His head was leaned downward, but as he threw his head back with a guffaw, I pulled the trigger. The barrel quietly spat the bullet right between his eyes.

He crumpled instantly.

A shrill cry rang from his wife's throat but it was silenced abruptly when I shot again. She fell forward next to him. Caspian leaped from the roof as the blood crept from their heads, and bystanders scurried inside nearby businesses. His gloved hands were blurs of black as he sped through Mr. Barnaby's pockets. I started packing the duffel bag swiftly, then took the gaiter, sunglasses, and hat off. Caspian launched back to the roof with the phone secured in his hand.

"Hartley's on his way to the pickup point," he breathed as he removed his gaiter from his narrow nose. I slung the strap of the duffel over my chest. We removed our gloves and I shoved everything into a side pocket on the bag. We jumped off the back of the bank building, landing in a wide alley one street over. We casually strolled toward a gas station as if the distant screams were caused by something else.

"That was too easy," Caspian said. I shrugged.

"I'm glad we got it done. I got other things to worry about." I broke into a brisker gait once I saw the black sedan sitting next to an air pump. We jumped in the backseat and Hartley started rolling before we'd completely closed the doors.

"Did you two get it done?" He glanced at us through the rear-view mirror.

Caspian held up the phone with a blank expression. "It's done."

Hartley gave him a short nod and fell silent.

I eased the stiffness in my shoulders, but the tension in my neck remained as I looked down at my phone in search of any texts from Briar. She still hadn't responded. I released a quiet, drawn-out sigh and decided I'd try harder after we reported to Uriah.

# 30
# BRIAR

VIVIAN SCRATCHED THE CROOK OF HER ARM WHILE SHE PACED
back and forth in the living room. Her voice was frantic as she spoke
on the phone. She threw her hands around as she pleaded with them
to give her a quarter of something and she'd pay them tomorrow.
My dad was at work. I was sitting at the table racking my brain over
the math questions I needed to answer for my fourth-grade teacher.

"Mom, can you help me?" I whined, swinging my legs back and
forth.

"In a minute, Briar," Vivian hissed as she pulled the phone from
her ear and covered the microphone with her hand. She returned to
her conversation at normal volume. "Reggie, what's it gonna take?
I'm down bad."

"Mom, *please*?" I drew out the word in a prolonged syllable,
changing the pitch of my voice. I took a breath and sucked in a lot

of air so I could continue extending my "please." I hoped that if I was obnoxious enough, she'd hang up. Whatever it was she was talking about, it didn't sound like business. I certainly didn't know who Reggie was.

"Mooooooom?" I whined, then repeated her name over and over until the bottom of a pan struck my cheek and all I saw were stars in a night sky.

✳

I jolted awake and hit my head on a metal bar. I groaned and winced, reaching up to rub my head only to realize my wrists were bound together. I opened my eyes, but I was still greeted with an inky abyss, as if I was staring into my eyelids.

The air was thick and acrid; it smelled of rust, rubber, exhaust, and heat. Loud rhythmic thrums were muffled through the wall and seemed to echo my heartbeat. I felt around and my fingers met cold metal above and plastic below. I tried to open my mouth to scream, but duct tape sealed my lips together. Panic rippled along my body, leaving goosebumps in its wake as I realized I was in the trunk of someone's car. I rolled to my side and tried to kick at the door, but every movement pierced my body with sharp agony.

I huffed through my nose as I reached for the corner of the tape and braced myself to rip it off. I yelped. My skin felt hot and cold at once, like it had split in half and bled. I touched my face. There wasn't any fresh blood, but there was a line of dried flakes above my mouth. When I touched my nose, it felt like shards of glass were slicing through it. My lips felt like bubbles ready to pop.

The trunk jittered and jerked from the bumpy road. Neoterra's roads were horrible aside from the higher class areas. The countryside had smoother roads too, so I knew we weren't going in that direction at least. I only hoped I wasn't being taken to the Nocturne District.

I frantically felt my front and back pockets for my phone, but it was gone. I felt along the ceiling for a string or lever, but there was nothing. I even felt around for a weapon, but the trunk was empty, like its sole purpose was to be my coffin.

"This isn't happening," I whispered as tears welled. My chest caved in and the heat seemed to only make the air thicker.

In the seconds I'd taken to respond to Draven's texts, I could've been on the road, on the way home. All the warnings Sterling gave me... the two close calls I had going out... what a fool I was.

I wondered if whoever took me was the same person who'd taken those other people. Was I the eleventh victim? They were still missing... were they all dead?

Before the blood donation mandate, Vampyres would hunt and kill right on the spot. Kidnappings were rare if not nonexistent. I couldn't even fathom what a Vampyre would want from me if they didn't kill me in the parking lot.

My knees ached and burned as they stayed tucked against me in fetal position. I pressed my ear against the plastic floor of the trunk, listening to the tires' roar. We hadn't hit any bumps in a while.

My body shifted against the back wall of the backseat as the brakes were heavily pressed to slow the car. The vehicle quivered when the engine was cut off and the doors slammed shut. Leaden footsteps dragged around the back and my stomach wrenched as I braced for the trunk to open.

Cool, limpid air washed over my damp skin as the door swung

open. Two men in gaiters hovered over my body, with one grabbing my bound wrists and the other my ankles. I bucked and kicked as I released a piercing scream. They both dropped me from chest height and I slammed on my back on the pavement. I wheezed as my breath was shot into oblivion. They picked me up again while my lungs still barked.

I could only see out of one eye. The other one felt like a tight bulge being sealed shut, like forcing a zipper over a stuffed bag. The men carried me into what looked like a mansion. The landscape was pristine with under-lighting emphasizing the spackled siding. What caught my attention the most was the fact that I couldn't find an address number anywhere. Not on the mailbox, the columns near the front door, or any of the walls at the front of the house.

As soon as the door opened, the men threw me on the floor in the foyer. My legs flailed as I rolled and slid, hitting my back against the bottom of a grand marble staircase. I tried weakly to sit up, but one of them swiped my elbow with their leg and chuckled as I flopped back flat. The lights were so blinding, I couldn't get a full look at their features.

I cried out as one of them took a fistful of my hair and forced me to stand. I staggered behind them with my palms over his hand to try to ease the pain from the pulling. As we walked across the mezzanine, I caught a glimpse of two white roaring lion sculptures settled on either side of mahogany double doors. I planted my feet and the rug beneath my soles buckled, but they continued to drag me along without skipping a step.

One of the men gripped the doors and swung them open as the other one threw me inside. My head whipped forward as my body plunged roughly across another rug. One of my elbows stung from a nasty burn. I lay there for a moment, quivering. I was afraid to get back up. I was weightless, powerless, and could probably be thrown across the ocean if they wanted to do so.

"My, what a surprise."

A smooth, aged, sophisticated voice like bourbon.

"I thought spending some time in Helios would've softened you two, but you proved me wrong."

Slow, prowling steps rounded a heavy desk and approached me. I opened my one good eye and peered at a man with the complexion of morning light, salt and pepper hair gelled in a swoop, and a trimmed beard and mustache. He wore a dark violet pin-striped waistcoat and slacks. The ruby in his fat gold ring caught the light at every angle. As he crouched in front of me, I could smell subtle cologne. I tried to move away, but every bone in my body had turned to stone. I lay before a man who looked like he had the power to command the wind and sea. He grabbed me by the chin with his metallic hand and turned my face from side to side.

"She had a cute face, did you have to go wailing on her there? Poor thing is all bruised and bloodied." He leaned close, so close that I could feel waves of ice emitting from his skin.

"She was a fighter, sir," one of the men answered.

His crimson eyes met mine again. "We can't send her over there looking like this. She'll have to stay here for a little while until she heals."

"You must be Briar." He caressed the side of my cheek and I jerked away.

I couldn't figure out how he could possibly know my name. I

started to worry if he knew about my family too.

"A thorny bush of wild roses. Did you know that's what your name means?"

I glared at him, twisting my lips in a bloodied grimace. It didn't matter how terrified I was, I wasn't going to entertain him. I swallowed the blood that kept filling my mouth as I fought the temptation to spit it in his face.

"It's quite fitting... seeing as how you've been a thorn in one of my men's side without him knowing it." He finally let go of my chin and stood straight, adjusting his waistcoat.

"Go put her in one of the cells downstairs," he said as he returned to his seat behind the desk. I glanced at the cell phone that sat there, then back at the men stalking toward me. If I could just send Draven a quick text, he could track my scent—

I shot to my feet and lunged at the desk to snatch the phone. One of the men struck me in the jaw with his elbow before my hands even reached halfway.

※

I woke up in a narrow, windowless room completely covered in grunge concrete from the ceiling to the floor. A single, recessed light hovered above me, revealing a twin-sized bed in one corner and just enough room beside it to walk in. At the foot of the bed, there was a plastic bucket. Near the barred door, there were two dog bowls. I crawled backward until my back hit the wall and curled into a ball. I thought about Cyrene and how unstable Sterling was as he mourned. Was I going to meet the same fate? Would Sterling try to find me, or would he let me suffer the consequences because I didn't listen?

*Ya got my number now. Any trouble you have, I'm just a call away.*

Why didn't I call Draven and tell him to meet me after leaving Sundance so early? He could've escorted me to my motorcycle. Instead I had been petty to answer his texts over something I didn't have the right to be upset about.

*We can't send her over there looking like this. She'll have to stay here for a little while until she heals.*

At least I could find a little solace in knowing that I wasn't going to die *here*. Yet the uncertainty of wherever they were planning to send me still loomed over me.

I'd observed everything in the cell in one blink. There was nothing I could use to escape. I even checked under the mattress for something to pick the lock, only to realize that there wasn't a slot in the door to pick in the first place.

My head was pounding. It weighed ten times more than the rest of my body. I leaned against the cold wall, staring at the door until my vision blurred.

❋

Vivian and Dad had been screaming at each other in the living room for probably an hour now. He kept pleading with her to get help, she kept insisting she didn't need any.

Astoria and I were hiding in the closet beneath the staircase, watching through the thin slats in the door. I had my arms wrapped protectively around her, as if she were the teddy bear I always went to sleep with when I was scared of the dark. Astoria was sniffling quietly in my arms, hugging me back. Her hot tears soaked through my favorite glittery princess dress. We were just playing dress-up before chaos erupted.

"Where did you hide my keys?"

Vivian tossed the couch cushions in every direction. She began pulling Dad's books off the shelves, checking the bottom of lamps. She constantly screamed at him as she ripped the place apart.

"You're drunk right now, Viv. I'm *not* letting you go anywhere!" Dad reached for her arm to pull her away from the fireplace mantle, and she shoved him away.

"You can't hold me hostage!" she shrieked.

"Vivian, *please* calm down! The children—"

"Did you give my keys to the girls?"

Vivian's voice was suddenly lower. She looked directly at the door under the staircase. I shrunk to the farthest corner in the closet, pulling Astoria with me. She whimpered, and I quickly pressed my hand against her mouth as I tried to hide us behind a vacuum cleaner.

I jumped out of my skin when the door burst open and Vivian's gnarled hand reached in and snatched Astoria's ankle. She dragged her out and I held tighter, trying to pull her back in with all the strength my frail eight-year-old arms could muster. Vivian's hand flew out of view as Dad snatched her away.

The front door opened, and our fifteen-year-old brother instantly dropped his book bag to jump in and help Dad hold Vivian down. Astoria was sobbing loudly now, and I rubbed her back as I hyperventilated and hiccupped uncontrollably.

✳

I jerked awake when the heavy metal cell door grated against the floor. I gasped as an unfamiliar Vampyre stood at the door, holding a tray of grey paste—maybe mashed potatoes. He was bald with tattoos of skulls and flowers flowing across his scalp and down his neck. He had large plugs in his ears and his eyes were such a light red they almost appeared pink. His tattooed black sclerae made his irises appear luminous. When he smiled and licked his lips, he revealed a split tongue, and every single one of his teeth was sharpened into fangs. I shrank further against the wall as he crouched to scoop the potatoes into one of the dog bowls. He poured water into the other, then set the tray aside.

"Are you calm now?" He tilted his head slightly.

I couldn't stop staring.

"Why don't you come over here and eat something?" A soft, cold smile.

"I-I'm not hungry," I breathed.

"It's okay, I don't bite." He grinned wider, baring his shark-like teeth.

"I don't believe you."

He chuckled and walked deeper into the cell, crouching in front of me. He was inches away from my face and I pushed my head tightly into the wall. I wished it would absorb me and get me away from him.

"You smell like some kind of sweetness I ain't never crossed before."

He reached in his back pocket, then flicked open a pocket knife next to my face. I flinched and stared at the blade as it glinted. He lowered it to my neck, the blade just barely kissing my skin.

"Somebody like you would probably have a high price on the market."

My lip trembled as he put more pressure on the blade.

I cried out as he left a short, deep cut on my neck. I cringed as his slimy tongue ran across it. I pressed a hand over my mouth to suppress vomit. He pulled away, licking his lips with an even sicker smile than before.

"Woooo!" he crooned. "I feel like I just experienced what a billionaire would probably taste like. Such a shame you ain't here to stay with us. You and I would get acquainted real fast."

He caressed my cheek with claws painted black and I flinched away.

"Please go away," I pleaded quietly.

"Look who's humble now," he purred. "Since you said 'please,' I'll see you later... *sweet* heart."

He backed away and shut the cell door. I filled the space with shaky breaths, then quickly crawled to the bucket before hurling up my insides.

# 31
# DRAVEN

HARTLEY DROPPED US OFF AT THE EDGE OF THE KING ESTATE before driving to dispose of the vehicle. I ambled behind Caspian as we trudged along the driveway, then froze.

An airy waft of cedar and rose.

*No.*

My chest heaved as my breaths quickened.

Caspian turned when my footsteps halted.

"What's wrong?"

I inhaled sharply and shook my head. I adjusted the duffel over my shoulder.

"Nothin'..." I trailed, then pressed forward, picking up my pace into the house.

*It can't be.*

My eyes went straight to the small drops of blood splattered on the floor. I had to keep swallowing as my mouth watered from the scent. I followed the drops up the marble staircase, dropping the duffel bag. I continued to trace the blood to Uriah's office and froze at the door. My ears started to ring as everything in my peripheral vision blurred.

I was reaching for the handle when Caspian gripped my shoulder roughly and pulled me from the door.

"Hey," he whispered firmly. "Pull yourself together before we go in there. I don't know what your problem is, but Uriah can't see you acting like this when we give him this phone."

"You don't smell it?" I said breathlessly.

"I do. So what? They got another human to transfer to White Fang. Let's go before he smells us hanging around his door." Caspian's crinkled forehead smoothed as he gripped the brass handle, then pushed the door open.

"Wow, you two sure got back fast. I hope it was a success," Uriah said as he counted money.

"It was." Caspian set the phone on the desk.

I stayed near the door, staring at the blood that now stained the floor.

"Aw, the screen is cracked," Uriah pouted as he examined the phone.

"It must've happened when he fell after Draven shot him. It's still functional, though."

Caspian clasped his hands behind his back and glanced at me. I glowered when I noticed a few strands of wispy pink hair scattered on the rug.

"How long is this going to go on?" I cut in, approaching the desk quickly.

"What do you mean?" Uriah tore his gaze from the phone. The light in his eyes dulled to boredom.

"We're still doing the White Fangs' dirty work," I growled through clenched teeth.

"This was a special order." Uriah put the phone in the safe, then leaned back in his chair with a smirk. "She's quite exquisite, according to Wraith."

"Wait... Wraith's back?" Caspian interjected, eyebrows raised high.

I curled my fists, knuckles cracking. Uriah nodded proudly, adjusting the gold watch on his wrist as he stood from the desk.

"Wraith *and* Larkin. The Nightshades are beefing up the artillery since we've been falling short." He patted Caspian's shoulder and cut his eyes at me. "There's going to be a change in some dynamics around here."

I didn't take my gaze off him until he left the study, whistling a light tune.

"What's going on, man?" Caspian asked.

Delilah's voice echoed in a coy melody from downstairs before I could answer.

"Draven, did you see the present I left you?"

I snapped my head toward the door with wild eyes. In a blur, I flew out of Uriah's study and jumped over the mezzanine's railing, landing on the bottom floor. I didn't care that Caspian chased after me. He couldn't hold me back if he tried.

I shoved Delilah into the wall, and she laughed. I snatched her by the neck and raised her higher. She coughed, but the sardonic grin didn't falter.

"I guess you have," she said, her voice was strained.

Caspian yanked me away. and she landed gracefully on her feet as I lost my grip.

"Get off me, Caspian!" I roared.

"Draven, think!" Caspian snapped. "She's not worth it and you know it! You're in enough hot water as it is. Are you *trying* to get killed tonight after you just had a successful mission?"

He dragged me outside to the veranda. I grabbed one of the wicker chairs and threw it across the yard. It blew into splinters against a palm tree.

"I can't help you if you don't tell me what's going on, Draven."

Caspian folded his arms, leaning against one of the veranda's beams. The pool's webbed reflections swept over his blank face, making his skin appear teal. I paced under the veranda, into the grass. I looked up at the bleak, black sky as distant thunder rumbled.

"I need to see her. *Now,*" I growled.

"That isn't smart." Caspian said.

I ran a hand over my face with a groan.

"This is all my fault. That human girl... I ain't kill her. She's who I've been seeing this past week," I said. "Delilah smelled her before I could wash her scent off. She must've set this whole thing up."

The phone call... Delilah could've been watching from across the street to make sure Briar saw it. She could've seen her walk into Sundance, the perfect spot to watch her and then take her once she got off work. I didn't understand how she could pull it off unless Briar was taken during her break, but why would she risk going out alone without me?

"Unbelievable." Caspian dipped his chin with a soft chuckle, shaking his head slowly. "I knew it. I knew you wouldn't have been able to do it," he sighed.

"Excuse me?" I tilted my head, raising my voice.

"Ever since you opted to cut off Arlo's finger instead of killing him that night, you've been on a steady decline." He sat down in one of the wicker chairs and it crackled as it settled beneath him.

"Yeah? What about you? Obviously you didn't manage to kill him either," I spat.

"Maybe you're rubbing off on me then," he said as he crossed his leg over his knee and gazed out toward the ocean beyond the hill.

"If Delilah told Uriah and he arranged her abduction, this whole thing is a test to see where your loyalties are." Caspian's gaze hardened. "If I were you, I'd think long and hard about where they lie... and choose wisely."

I ran a hand through my hair and chewed on my inner cheek. The past week flashed through my mind like a film as I tried to decide where I'd gone wrong. She didn't deserve to die. She never did. I cursed her life the second I set foot in that bedroom and apologized to her. I didn't even have the willpower to push her away and ignore her request to help her around the city. That had been the point of no return.

*Caspian was right all along. You are weak.*

I couldn't go guns ablaze without a plan. They could use her against me now. They could find out about her family.

"I know you want to see her, but I don't think it would be a good idea to do it tonight." The chair crinkled as Caspian rose to his feet. "I'll check on her condition."

"No—"

"Don't worry. You're not the only one with a strong willpower against feeding."

I narrowed my eyes.

"Why do you care?" I barked, sharper than I intended. Caspian was like a brother to me, but I knew how he felt about humans. If he harmed a hair on Briar's head—

"You don't trust me?" He tilted his head. "I know it's bothering you, so I want to help. To this extent, anyway."

I pursed my lips and slumped in a chair, then pulled out a cigarette. "Thanks."

If only Vampyres slept... then I could visit her.

Caspian gave me a nod and then made his way back to the house, the damp grass rustling under his brisk footsteps. I gazed at the sky through the slats in the veranda. I weighed whether it was worth burning the house down, getting Briar out, and spending the rest of my life with a target on my back while we looked for a place to lie low in.

Raindrops gently filtered through the vine branches that wove through the veranda beams. I let them pelt my face, wishing I could drown in them.

# 32
# BRIAR

After that *monstrosity* tasted my blood, I had four other Vampyres cut all over my arms to sample my blood. I kept my face glued to the cold, cement floor. I tried to keep my nose close to it, hoping the mildew would mask the smell of vomit emitting from the bucket in the corner. My disheveled hair hung over my face, a few strands moving with my shallow breaths. I could still feel the Vampyres' tongues over my arms and the tip of one's nose pressed against my scalp as he savored the smell of my hair.

I had been such a child.

Too childish to understand the true gravity of the danger my brother always warned me about.

Too rebellious to consider the likelihood of this happening with the recent abductions.

Too blind to see the red flags that even Draven tried to warn me about. All for what? A little excitement? A little enjoyment? To prove to my brother that I wasn't some fragile thing, and to prove to my mother I could do a better job with my life than she did with hers?

"Life is too short," I'd once heard. I laughed weakly. I single-handedly shortened it all on my own. Even my younger sister had more common sense, and she was the most naïve seeing the world in black and white.

The door slid open with that roaring scrape. I didn't bother to move.

"I don't have anything left to give," I implored in a weak rasp.

"I'm not here for your blood," the voice spoke coolly.

I tried to lift my head and swiped the hair out of my face.

I recognized that face from somewhere. The ghostly ivory skin with the hair and eyebrows to match. He wore a black short-sleeved turtleneck and slacks. The only color present was found in his deep sangria eyes. His expression was hollow and indistinguishable as he glanced at the filthy bucket.

"How are you doing?"

He took a step closer, stiffly crossing the threshold of the metal door. I frowned, forcing myself to sit up and lean against the wall.

"Why do you care?" I asked with indignation.

He glanced at the dog bowls, which were still full of food and water. He sighed softly and took another step closer. His nostrils flared and his Adam's apple dropped.

"Your well-being is important to someone."

He grabbed my wrists with only his thumbs and index fingers, as if he didn't want to touch me. He started to lift and rotate my arms. He sucked his teeth as he examined the fresh wounds. His movements were graceful, but the way he moved his head felt... feral.

"This is unacceptable."

"I've seen you somewhere before," I said softly. My mind was so muddled that I couldn't even try to visualize everything that had happened before my abduction.

"I'm sure you have." He rested my limp arms in my lap. "We have a medic. I'll send her to tend to your wounds."

He stood quickly and took two long, swift strides to reach the door.

"Wait!" My voice cracked.

The door was almost closed when the man paused. Half of his face was concealed behind the door, with one eye sharply piercing mine.

"What's your name?" I drawled.

There was a long pause that probably lasted a full minute. I expected him to shut the door at any moment.

"Caspian."

Then the door shut completely, leaving a booming echo.

A few seconds later, I heard muffled voices. I crawled weakly and pressed my ear against the door. I stared at the dog bowls as I listened.

"They've been sampling her like she's a buffet. I assumed she was here to heal before we sent her off, right?" It sounded like Caspian.

"You're correct. Was she able to describe who did it?" It vaguely sounded like the man with the metal arm, but that particular memory was already distorted.

"I didn't ask, but I can find out for you," Caspian said.

"Excellent. Where's Draven?"

"Last I saw him, he was out back, sir." A pair of footsteps retreated.

It all hit me. That familiar face Caspian possessed... I recognized him from when I saw him and Draven running from the burning house. They knew each other. I covered my mouth as I stifled a cry. My eyes burned, and then the whole room started to ripple as tears flooded my vision.

The door slid open again and I crawled backward to the farthest wall. Caspian kept the cell door cracked as he walked further inside and crouched in front of me.

"Who did this to you?" He tilted his head downward but gazed intensely at me through chalky eyelashes.

"I-I don't know..." I sniffled, my chest overwhelmed with hyperventilating hiccups.

"P-Please... let m-me go..."

"Describe them," Caspian demanded, ignoring my cries.

"One—" I sucked in a breath to reign in the hiccups. "—guy had a bald head and tattoos. A girl with brown hair. Two other guys, one with sandy blonde hair and a gold fang and the other with black hair."

"Helpful," Caspian groaned. "I know two of who you described, but the other two sound like half of the people here."

"I never said anything about the fire," I said. "Y-you can let me go, I promise I won't say anything about this either."

"It's not up to me." He stood and rolled his neck, effectively cracking it. "Someone will be here to clean your cell before the medic gets here."

He turned away to leave. I didn't stop him this time.

"They're not all monsters," I once said.

That was the biggest lie I'd ever told myself.

⁕

I cried myself to a nightmarish sleep. I couldn't remember when I fell asleep, but I woke to the sound of sweeping outside of my door. I smacked my dry lips and glanced at the dog bowls again. I crawled to them and examined what I had. The food was dried out, hardened to gunk that caked around the sides. I still couldn't tell what it was, but it had once been a soft grey paste. I couldn't salvage that even if I wanted to. Particles floated in the water, but I swallowed my pride and raised the bowl to my lips. I drank most of it, then splashed the remaining on my face.

I didn't know what day it was, but I hoped enough time had passed for Sterling to realize something was wrong.

I pushed myself off the floor and crawled into the bed. At least the mattress was somewhat comfortable. The pillow was practically devoid of feathers or filling, but at this point, I would take whatever I could get.

It could've been hours, it could've been five minutes. My stomach was in knots by the time the door opened again. A petite, rotund woman wearing a light blue dress and a beige apron shuffled inside, grabbing the bucket and dog bowls. She grunted as she slid the door shut. I slowly sat up on the bed.

*I could take her,* I thought. Though with the red eyes, I knew she had inhuman strength. Nonetheless, I was confident I could build myself a small window of opportunity to run. She didn't seem like her job was to guard me, only to ensure the cell was clean.

I mustered what little energy I had and dragged the blanket off the bed, then hid in the corner next to the sliding door. I held the blanket open as I waited.

The door opened with that same strained grunt. The woman didn't even look around before she leaned down to set my dog bowls on the floor.

*Go.*

I lunged forward, wrapping the blanket tightly over her head and arms. The woman cried out, thrashing her arms. She hit the wall. I ran down the short hall of the cellar—and didn't stop to process much. The little kitchenette, the felt tables, and the pool at the far end of the room were mostly blurs. I ran until I saw a staircase tucked away.

I took the first step, but my heart jumped when I heard footsteps pad above, shadows shifting through the crack beneath the door above the staircase. They paused. I watched the door handle slowly turn and frantically looked around the basement for a place to hide. They could smell and track me anywhere.

I ran to the pool and eased myself into it to avoid splashing. The cold water crawled up my body as I slowly submerged myself. I pressed against the wall, then sank under the water when I heard the steps descend the stairs. Above the water were muffled voices.

My chest burned. As every second passed, it felt like my heart was racing faster to the finish line. They could detect the slightest movement if I wasn't careful. I leaned my head back to expose my lips above the water and carefully controlled my breaths.

The muffled voices grew louder. Maybe they were yelling. I tried to hold my breath a little longer, then carefully raised my head above the water to peer over the edge of the pool. The servant woman and the two men who'd dragged me here ran upstairs, shouting obscenities.

My clothes clung to me as I climbed the ladder to get out. My hair stuck to my forehead and cheeks, water dripping into my eyes. I slicked it back as I took a step. My shoes squelched. I promptly took them off, and my damp feet slapped across the floor as I hurried to the pool tables. I grabbed one of the cue balls. I tossed it in my hand to test its heft and tightened my grip around it as I ran back to the staircase. I stuck to the edges of the steps to avoid creaking. Yelling and rapid footsteps ran back and forth above. My knees felt weak as I neared the door. If the hinges made any sound, this could be where it all ended.

I pressed the handle down completely before pushing forward. There was a soft *click* as the door swung open. The foyer was empty, and the double front doors were right in front of me. I looked up the marble staircase I'd been dragged across. To my right, lied a veranda, pool, and beyond the property—the beach. The sky was creeping into periwinkle and coral. If I could stay hidden till daylight, I could survive this.

I darted to the sliding glass doors and opened them just wide enough for my body to fit through. Blades of grass brushed the soles of my feet as I darted across the yard.

"Briar, what are you doing?"

A harsh whisper.

I was so close to the crest of the hill. I didn't stop to look, and when I felt hands grab me, I screamed and swung the cue ball into their temple. We both tumbled to the ground. The ball was still in my grip and I quickly rolled over to strike again, then froze mid-swing when I saw Draven beneath me.

The bloody gash on the side of his head slowly closed. My heart quaked. I bit my lip roughly as I continued to swing, but he caught my wrist and flipped me onto my back. He pinned my arms down, straddling me with solid weight. The ball rolled from my palm and my chest heaved as more sobs threatened to come.

"How could you do this to me?" I whimpered.

Draven looked down at me with soft, dull eyes, but he didn't hold the gaze for long. His eyebrows were pinched, lips pressed into a thin line that subtly curved downward.

"You have to trust me," Draven whispered as a group of five Vampyres flashed into the yard behind him. He forced me to my feet by my wrists, then gripped the back of my neck so I couldn't run. I wished I could kill him.

"Good catch, Draven," a woman purred with her hands on her hips. Her familiar black and white locs swept over one shoulder, and she wore a crop top exposing a belly-button piercing and denim shorts. I knew that face from anywhere.

The woman stepped in front of the other Vampyres with a sly smirk. The wind dried my widened eyes as I gaped in horror. She slinked closer and grabbed my chin, forcing me to look up at her—the customer from Sundance. The one that had made my skin crawl.

This must be Delilah.

"Lovely *Briar*."

I winced as her manicured nails dug deeper into my skin.

"It's a shame you have to be in tip-top health when we send you away—otherwise I'd bury you alive." She spoke with a saccharine tone, her smile laced with poison. The grin instantly shrunk to a scowl when she noticed Draven.

"Let's go inside. It's starting to get uncomfortable out here."

She strutted back to the house. The other four lingered for a moment, then followed. Draven started to move forward, still pushing me to walk with his hand on the back of my neck. A small part of me hoped that he would wait for them to go inside and help me escape. That he had some kind of elaborate plan to infiltrate whatever gang this was, that he lived a double life as an undercover agent. I desperately wanted to believe he hadn't set me up. As we drew closer to the house, my hopes faded like a dying song.

I wanted to go back to that euphoric night we had at The Hole, when I still believed that not all Vampyres were monsters.

# 33
# DRAVEN

Briar's neck quivered beneath my palm, and I wondered if it was because she was drenched from the pool or because she was afraid. With the bold attempt she'd made to escape on her own, I assumed the former.

I wanted to sweep Briar off her feet and run away with her. But Uriah had too many connections across the country and too many underlings with undying loyalty to risk it. We would spend the rest of our lives on the run.

Yet, running away from Uriah with Briar at my side sounded more peaceful than living with the thought of her hating me.

I led her inside and took her to the basement. I walked as slowly as I could, but it probably would've been easier if I just rushed her down there. Every waking step was like walking on knives.

Goosebumps prickled Briar's skin, making it rough like a cat's tongue.

"You sure got a pair on ya, tryin' to escape a den of Vampyres," I said once I confirmed we were alone in the basement. "You're lucky they need you alive."

She walked into the cell silently and kept her back to me.

"Debt collector, huh," Briar rasped. She scoffed softly.

"That was true. I... was supposed to kill you from the beginning for witnessing that arson," I said, still looking over my shoulders and sniffing the air for any onlookers.

She turned to face me, her eyes bloodshot and glittering from the tears that coated them. "Why didn't you?"

"When ya went to the Nightshade, I just... I don't know. I never seen a human willingly put herself among Vampyres for *fun*. You looked so comfortable. Anyone else either fears or hates us. Killin' ya would've been like plucking the only flower in the rubble."

I held out my palms, then let them flop at my sides.

"I was stupid." Her face contorted as she sniffled. The cracks in my soul steadily grew into chasms.

"Briar, I-I need you to understand this ain't the life I wanted," I pleaded.

"Then change it." She clenched her jaw, her words sharp.

I flinched at the sound of one of the steps creaking and glanced across the basement. Caspian stood near the staircase and pointed at his watch. I exhaled softly through my nose.

"I never had a choice."

The words tasted severely bitter, but they were true. The day my parents died was the day I became a Nightshade fledgling.

"Everyone has a choice... and you clearly made yours." Briar reached for the door and slammed it shut. I stood there, stunned.

*I promise I never wanted you here, but I needed to keep appearances*, I wanted to say. *It was Delilah, it was all her!*

Briar screamed furiously with thuds in rapid succession as if she was punching the mattress. The bucket crashed against the wall with a hollow thump. I walked away from the cell door and allowed the cellar to close behind the shelves of liquor. Her screams were silenced through the thick wall.

I met up with Caspian, my head hanging low.

*She hates me.*

I retreated to my room and collapsed on my bed, staring at the ceiling.

Briar was going to be here for a couple of weeks while her wounds healed. If I proved my loyalty up until she had to be transferred, I could volunteer to transport her to White Fang and help her escape. Whatever they were doing there was probably ten times worse than what could happen to her here.

Then again... with Wraith and Larkin back, I wasn't so sure how accurate that thought was anymore.

Light knocks tapped against my door. I sat on the edge of my bed and braced my elbows over my knees.

"Who is it?" I sighed.

The door creaked open and Wraith's lips stretched into a jagged smile. Larkin hung around behind him. He also grinned, his teeth normal aside from gold-plated top fangs.

My upper lip curled with disgust. "What do ya want?"

"I just wanna congratulate you on recruiting such an entertaining Sun Dweller. I forgot what it was like to have a good chase."

Wraith licked his lips, as if a fat ham were displayed before him.

"Stay away from her," I snapped.

"Oh? You got a soft spot for her, bud?" Larkin cut in behind his brother. Wraith opened the door wider and they both blocked the walkway.

"No, I'm just saying she's here to heal so the White Fangs ain't got a problem with taking her in."

I tensed as they entered my room without asking. Larkin perused the band posters on the walls. Wraith shuffled around and stopped at my old, dusty guitar case.

"Does your little girlfriend know you play?" He tilted his head curiously as he poked the leather hardshell.

"She's not my girlfriend." I scowled. "Get out."

Wraith's eyes lit up, the slick grin stretching wider.

"So you wouldn't mind if I had my way with her, then?"

He glanced at his brother, his shoulders beginning to shake as a laugh prepared to erupt. I lunged across the room and snatched his neck, then shoved him against the wall.

"Oops, did I push a button?" he asked coyly. I shoved him toward the door, almost lifting him entirely off the floor. He laughed—that twisted, giddy *laugh*—as if everything was some sort of game.

"Get out." I whirled to face Larkin. His hands were in his pockets, but I didn't trust whatever trick he might have up his sleeve. "I won't ask again."

Wraith raised his arms in a shrug and jerked his chin toward the stairs. Larkin followed behind him, cutting a glare as he walked past me. I slammed my door shut and sifted through the contents of my top drawer for a list of clients. A collection was coming up soon, but

I decided that now was the time to show up early. I needed to get out of this house—I didn't care if the sun was high in the sky.

If the Nightshades weren't such a complex network, maybe I would've been able to protect Briar. If her brother wasn't a Vampyre-hating cop, I would've been able to nudge him in the right direction to rescue her without putting my own life at risk. If I wasn't so *weak*, maybe I would've had the strength to sacrifice myself.

But I wanted to be able to see the sun again, *truly* experience life in the light without it hurting me. I wanted the White Fang experiments to work, and a very small, cruelly selfish part of me was curious to see if Briar could make that possible.

I brushed past Caspian as I descended the stairs. He didn't say anything, but I felt his gaze burn into my back as I burst outside. I walked along the narrow shoulder of the road that wove up a steady incline. I hoped a car would careen around the corner a little too short—but then I remembered I was a freak of nature that would just heal after the impact. Six cars drove past, all were cruising as if it was Sunday morning anyway.

I slowed my pace and gazed up at the houses littering the small mountain. It finally hit me—

If I took the time to find multiple humans to take Briar's place, maybe they'd let her go. A sharp pang seared through my chest for fathoming it in the first place, but it was the only option I had where everyone was a winner—mostly. To give White Fang what they wanted, to regain my place with the Nightshades, and to free Briar from the horrors of my world.

# 34
# DRAVEN

By the time I returned to the estate, got dressed, and gathered weapons, the sun was at its peak. The rays beamed violently as I cruised around Neoterra in search of Diurnal Zones to scout. The last thing I needed was to accidentally break into a Vampyre's house.

I observed Sun Dwellers milling around town through heavily tinted windows in the van. The traffic was thick from the morning work rush. I glanced at myself in the rearview mirror, double checking that the brown contacts were dark enough to conceal my crimson irises. I tugged at the gaiter over my nose and mouth and put on sunglasses.

I wanted to find someone who deserved being prodded at like a lab rat, but it was impractical. I would've turned around, but Briar's freedom lingered in the back of my mind.

I drove the van until I reached a less densely populated area. Most of the driveways in the suburban neighborhood were empty. I was left to wonder if the residents were gone or if their vehicles were tucked away in garages.

I wondered if the police still suspected humans were behind the abductions.

A group of three kids rode their bicycles around the neighborhood. Sprinklers spat against grass, flowers, and bushes. A young woman in a sports bra and leggings walking alone.

I didn't allow myself to think as I reached into a duffel on the floor and pulled out a cloth soaked in chloroform. I climbed into the passenger seat and waited for the woman to walk closer. Her shoulders were relaxed and her hips swayed casually as she strutted by with headphones over her ears. There wasn't a single muscle tensed as she passed my foreign van. I quickly jumped out and wrapped my cloth-covered hand over her mouth from behind. Only a short yelp escaped her throat before her body slumped against mine.

Rather than take the time to put her in the trunk, I pushed her into the passenger seat. I allowed her limp body to lean against the door, then rushed to the driver's seat. I left the neighborhood and pulled onto the shoulder of the road to place a blindfold over her eyes and bind her wrists behind her back, then buckled her in.

As I drove back toward the King Estate, I'd glance at the woman whenever her breathing hitched. She was still unconscious, but I didn't want to risk her waking up too soon. I chewed on my bottom lip as I fixed my gaze on the road ahead.

※

The rest of the day passed in a blur. I had to dissect myself, pulling my mind and heart apart as I went house to house in different Diurnal Zones. The last victim, a boy just barely out of high school, was tied up in the trunk with duct tape over his mouth. I spent most of the drive back home wiping his blood off my knuckles. I gave up when all it did was smear. By then, the sun's rays were dimming like dying candlelight.

I dragged my feet to the trunk and opened the double doors. The boy twisted onto his back and released muffled screams beneath the duct tape. He bucked his legs as I reached for his ankles. I wrenched them until he stopped screaming. Tears streamed down his cheeks.

I hoisted the boy over my shoulder and carried him into the house. I kept my face blank as I gripped the railing and trailed upstairs to Uriah's office. For once, it was empty. The next place to look was the basement. I lifted the boy again and carried him down there.

The basement was empty aside from Uriah, Wraith, and Larkin standing around the pool table. Uriah was leaning over, eyeing one of the balls before sending it flying into a pocket. Wraith's cue stick was propped over his shoulders, his arms dangling from it. Larkin leaned against the wall, picking his nails with a needle. I wondered if it was laced with poison, as his needles so often were. They were always his weapon of choice above anything else.

The Kline brothers simultaneously looked over their shoulders as I entered, their eyes instantly falling on the young boy when I tossed him on the sectional. The boy shrieked before the air was knocked out of him.

"Wow, Draven, you actually contribute to the family?" Larkin gibed.

I kept my gaze fixed on Uriah, who straightened. He observed the victim, his forehead winkling with raised eyebrows.

"This is the sixth one today. What's gotten into you?" Uriah cocked his head.

"This is the last one for today." I pulled my gaiter down and hung the sunglasses over my shirt collar. "I'm just looking forward to what White Fang has to offer."

*I have six bodies, now trade Briar for them*, I wanted to demand.

Wraith's lips stretched into a sly smirk, his eyes narrowing.

"That's a lie." Uriah was calm as he rubbed chalk over his cue stick. He reached for a glass of blood that rested on the bar counter and chugged half of it. "What are you *really* after?"

"Can we talk in private?"

The last thing I needed was Wraith and Larkin knowing I cared for a human, even if it was arguably worse for Uriah to know. If Delilah arranged Briar's capture, he probably already did.

"No, you can say it here. We're all friends." He leaned against the bar, setting his cue stick aside. He braced his elbows on the edge, his watch and ring catching the recessed lighting.

"I want Briar to myself." I fought the urge to shove my hands in my pockets. Fought the urge to claw the nasty grin off Wraith's face.

"Oh?" Uriah lifted his eyebrows. "What do you want with her?"

I opened my mouth to speak, but Wraith and Larkin burst into guffaws. Larkin held his stomach as he doubled over while his brother wiped tears from his own eyes.

"I can't blame you, brother," Larkin said breathlessly as his laughter died. "Her blood is some of the sweetest I've ever had."

I shot him a sharp glare, clenching my fists tightly.

"Why does it matter?" I challenged, prepared to take a beating if it meant keeping my intentions quiet.

"If you want her to yourself, I'd suggest Turning her. If it's to help her escape, well..." Uriah chuckled softly. "We'd have to kill both of you."

Wraith ran his index finger across his throat with a grin.

I scoffed and shook my head as I stormed back upstairs, ignoring the hyena laughter that erupted once again.

✳

I stormed through the mansion to the Nightshades' little armory upstairs, huffing through my nostrils like an enraged bull. I was fully prepared to load a fully automatic rifle and make it rain throughout the house, even if it cost my life—

Caspian slammed his hand over my shoulder and hauled me into the kitchen before I even got to the stairs.

I jerked away. "What are ya doing? I ain't got time to talk."

"Draven, take a second. I overheard what went on down there. You're off to a really reckless start." Caspian dropped his voice to the volume of a butterfly's fluttering wing. "I wanted to tell you Briar's okay and the medic visited her. But... I'm not sure if she'll last long here."

"Why? Did Wraith do something to her?" I whispered, the rage roiling more violently.

"Well, the others keep trying to sample her blood before she can even heal. With her blood type—"

"What's wrong with her blood type?"

She had a unique smell, which was why it was so easy for me to detect her relationship with her brother. I'd never sensed a human even remotely like her, but it never triggered red flags.

Caspian's eyebrows knit together. "She's AB negative, Draven. Do you realize how rare that is? She's driving everyone crazy."

*Rare.* That explained why I didn't recognize her smell. That explained why Wraith and Larkin laughed at me, and why Uriah wanted to know. They'd all known before I did—it didn't matter if I captured the whole city and brought them here. They would never let Briar go.

Unless...

Her brother smelled similar. He could've had the same blood type, and I could trade his life for hers.

I would been doing everyone a service if I got rid of him.

"She has a brother," I murmured. "He could have it too."

"Uriah would stop at nothing to get to him then."

I stepped further away from the archway. "What if I offered him in exchange for Briar?"

"She'd *really* hate you then." Caspian poked his head outside of the archway to make sure the hallway and foyer were still clear.

"She doesn't have to know I did it." I shrugged.

"It wouldn't be rocket science to figure it out." Caspian shuffled to the bay windows and sat at the bench. I followed him across the kitchen and took a spot at the dining table directly in front of the windows. "Besides, I'm pretty sure Uriah would just want both of them. So you would not only fail to get her out, but you also land someone she loves in an early grave too."

"Then what other options do I have?" I sighed.

Caspian shrugged apathetically.

"There are none. Just forget about her, man. She's just a Sun Dweller. She's not worth the trouble. If you went in there and tried to kill everyone, other Nightshades across the country would stop at nothing to kill *you*."

He reminded me of my father when I was a kid. I was crying over a puppy that had been hit by a car, and his response to me was, "It's okay, I know it hurts, but there's plenty of other puppies. We'll get another one."

Briar was someone that made me feel human again. Most importantly, she was someone who still wanted give me a chance after watching me burn a house down. I couldn't even imagine anyone else having the ability to do that. She was worth every bit of trouble.

Caspian was right, though. Going in guns blazing wouldn't achieve anything.

"Well, if they're not down there anymore, I'm going to see her. Don't try to stop me." I quickly stood, the chair scraping loudly against the tile as I pushed it with the back of my knees.

Luckily, Uriah, Wraith, and Larkin were gone. I pulled the lever to the cellar, watching the liquor bottles tremble and clink together while the shelves shifted into the wall. I squeezed through the space as soon as it was big enough to let me through. The shelf was still dragging across the floor when I slid open Briar's cellar door.

Briar popped her disheveled head from the pillow and curled against the wall.

"What do you want?"

White gauze patches were scattered over her arms, and one poked out from under her hair. I sat on the edge of the bed and reached for her neck, but she slapped my hand away.

"Were you bitten?" I asked, reeling my hand back. It wouldn't have made sense. The White Fangs needed humans... biting her would have eliminated—

"No, I wasn't."

Her voice was as sharp as knives, cutting into my train of thought. I rubbed the back of my neck, then bit my lip, trying to hold back the words that tried to claw their way out.

"Would ya wanna be?"

I couldn't look at her as I lost the battle to my own words. I didn't want that life for her—stripped of the ability to see daylight comfortably, the privilege of growing old with her family, or suffer the plight of eternal blood dependency. Yet, it seemed to be the lesser evil compared to whatever the Nightshades or White Fang would subject her to.

"What kind of question is that? Of course not," Briar scoffed. I released a short sigh of relief, but somehow still felt a small sting in my chest.

"I ask because you'd be useless to these people if you became one of us," I said.

"You really believe that? 'Cause the way I see it, they'd just force me to be a part of whatever group this is. No matter how you look at it, I know too much." She hugged her knees to her chest, her nails digging deeply into her palms.

"I'm trapped, no thanks to you," she mumbled against her knee.

"You watched me run from a burnin' house, I threatened to kill ya if I ever saw ya around that bar again, and yet all it took was one apology to ease your mind." I slowly rose from the bed. "You knew

I was a snake when ya picked me up."

"Maybe so. Maybe I was stupid." Briar's eyes glazed over as she lifted her trembling chin to meet my gaze. "I thought the snake wasn't poisonous since he'd helped me so many times."

I sucked in a ragged breath. "I'm not the snake that bit you."

If she viewed me as a beast no matter what I said, what reason did I have to try to be a better person?

*All you'll ever be to them is a monster.*

Those diamond eyes lost their glimmer, replaced by cyclones. She pursed her lips into a thin line as Uriah's voice continued to scratch at my mind.

*You've been one of us for thirteen years now... it's time you embrace it.*

Without Briar, I was like the rest of them. Without her, I was nothing.

"Please... I *swear* I never tried to trap ya. Delilah smelled you and tracked you all on her own," I pleaded once more, on the edge of dropping to my knees.

A sardonic chuckle puffed from her lips. "What did you need to tell me that was so important while I was at work?"

"The Vampyre that killed one cop and injured a bunch of others had strength that no one in history ever had," I said. "I wanted to warn you."

"I already knew about that." Briar buried her face in her knees. "I hope you know a war is coming now."

"Is that a warning... or a threat?" I tilted my head slightly. Perhaps if Delilah had realized Briar's brother was on the force, she would've left her alone.

"Both." She gazed at the open door behind me and I slowly inched backward, stopping right at the threshold. "I don't care if you planned my demise or she did... you should've told me what I was really up against."

"I'm sorry... I'm trying to figure out how to get you out," I whispered.

"Take your sorry and choke on it."

She lay back down and buried her head under the thin sheets. I shut the door and leaned against it, staring at the ceiling.

Was Briar's hatred toward me reparable? If I captured her brother, she'd never forgive me for certain.

I stayed in the lounge for hours, ruminating.

When I finally emerged out of the basement, the sky was already in its dusky ombre. Near the veranda in the backyard, the fire pit was ablaze. I stepped outside, hoping it was Caspian tending to the flame. As the angle of my view shifted, I saw Wraith, Larkin, and Delilah circled the pit instead. Larkin and Delilah lounged in the chairs while Wraith leaned back on his palms in the grass. They erupted into guffaws as I stepped outside. I loathed the Kline brothers with every fiber of my being, and with what Delilah had pulled, she made the list too.

"Hey! Come join us!" Larkin waved, shadows dancing across his sharp face. I paused mid-stride, contemplating going back inside. I had too much to mull over to be distracted by them.

"He won't," Wraith said. His teeth glinted in the light of the fire as his lips stretched. "He's too busy looking for his backbone."

I loosed a low, guttural growl as I changed course and accepted his challenge. As I approached, I noticed the empty beer cans.

"Isn't it a bit early?" I glanced at the horizon over the beach. The sun was barely treading above it.

"We're just spending some much needed *family* time." Larkin crushed a can and tossed it into the fire. His forehead shined with sweat and his pupils were dilated so wide, his eyes appeared black.

"You are part of the family... right?" Wraith was lying on his back, picking at his nails.

I sniffed. "I think the crest tattoo says enough."

"Sure, you can have the tattoo. Don't mean you're really one of us," Wraith said.

Delilah scooted closer to the armrest of her seat and patted the space next to her.

"Why don't you sit down?" she purred.

"I'll pass. I was about to head out, actually." I took a side step but paused when I heard the grass rustle beneath Wraith.

"And what's more important than family?" he asked as he snapped upright.

"Probably more Sun Dweller fraternizing," Delilah snorted.

"No, I was just going to get away from the house," I scoffed. I patted the carton of cigarettes in my pocket as tremors rippled underneath my skin.

"We'll tag along and have some fun, then." Wraith jumped in a springy kip-up. "Let's go on a hunt."

# 35
# STERLING

IT FELT LIKE A TRUCK HAD RAN OVER MY BACK WHEN I AWAK-
ened. My cold sweats had permeated through the sheets. My body
felt like it was sinking deeper into the bed as I tried to sit up. I turned
to my alarm clock. It was only noon. My eyelids hung heavy. Sleep
whispered my name and I craved the dreamlessness from the pills.

I heard the front door open downstairs and a heavy bag drop on
the floor. I assumed Astoria was returning home from her classes.
Nothing came from Briar's room across the hall, but with her new-
found status as a night-shifter, she would most likely sleep through
the afternoon like I would.

I didn't want to get up. God knew I didn't. But Astoria would
just keep checking on me and I couldn't keep putting her in that
position. Besides, I was always supposed to be the stable one in the
family.

I had my time to mourn Cyrene's death in the shower. I couldn't let it pour over into a second day.

I kicked the rest of the sheets off the bed and started my workout routine, which I would usually do before going to work. Since I was on mandatory leave, it didn't hurt to switch things up. A change of pace could be something I needed anyway.

I tried to be positive—everything happened for a reason. Maybe this was a lesson to appreciate life more and focus on my sisters instead of work. Perhaps Cyrene's soul was in a safer, better place, away from the beasts of the world today. Although the world wasn't better for it.

I took a shower after working out for an hour. I intended thirty minutes, but time slipped through me. By the time I dressed in a relaxed white t-shirt and grey basketball shorts, Astoria was coming up the stairs with a plate of fish and roasted vegetables. I gave her a small grin as I took the plate from her hands.

"Aw, Ria... I was coming down there," I pouted.

She shrugged, clasping her hands behind her back. "I wasn't going to take any chances."

"Well, did you eat yet? We can all have lunch together."

I carried my plate and crossed the hall, opening Briar's door to see her bed neatly made. Astoria's soft steps padded closely behind me. I frowned and moved to the window to check the driveway. Her motorcycle was gone.

"Did Briar stay late?" My throat tightened as I fought to keep the invasive thoughts at bay.

"She didn't say she would, but the last time she responded to me was pretty early last night." Astoria reached for her necklace, her round eyes growing wider. "I'll text her again."

We went downstairs and I set the plate on the dining table in the kitchen. I called Briar, but the automated voice answered. Her phone was either off or she sent me to voicemail... but if she was busy working, it would've kept ringing.

I tightened my grip on my phone.

"What's the name of the salon she's working at?" I turned to Astoria, who stood in the archway's threshold to the kitchen and tried to call. She received the same automated response. She shook her head and raised her shoulders.

"She never told me."

Astoria's voice softened, almost a squeak. That hand never left her necklace. She jumped aside when I broke into a barreling gait, running upstairs and bursting into Briar's room. I rummaged through all her drawers without a specific item in mind. I was playing tug-of-war with panic and its grip was getting stronger by the second.

I quickly moved on to the nightstands. Those drawers were mostly empty aside from phone chargers and family photos. I grabbed a recent one that showed her hair dyed pink. I paused, staring at how Briar beamed with her arm thrown across Astoria's shoulder. I remembered taking this photo when we had taken a trip to Helios for leisure. It was one of the rare occasions where she wasn't bored, sullen, or angry.

I checked her closet, which was a chaotic mess. I searched the top shelf, but it was lined with nothing but shoes. I switched to her bookshelf and sifted through her vinyl records. My heart jumped when I found a paper sandwiched between a couple of them. I snatched it and smiled as I unfolded the offer letter. She needed it to get the authorization, and naturally, the company name would be on there.

Sundance sounded familiar.

*Everything happened for a reason*, I thought again. Suddenly, taking leave from work wasn't so bad, because I could focus on finding my sister.

I could be overreacting. Maybe she was just shopping, but how could she have the energy to stay awake after a long night? It was Briar... she was always unpredictable and flighty. I couldn't completely knock the possibility.

"Ria, call me if she comes back!" I put on my sneakers, grabbed my badge, Astoria's keys, and a notepad. I carefully tucked Briar's photo in my wallet. "I gotta take your car, sorry!"

"I don't care, please find her!" she whined. She paced in the living room, biting her nails and still blowing up Briar's phone despite being sent to voicemail.

✳

I walked into Sundance and paused by the door to scan the shop. There were six stylist stations, three on each side, lined against the walls. The vanity lights were bright and glimmered against polished concrete floors. The walls were filled with local art and band photos. It started to make more sense for Briar to find comfort here.

"Welcome to Bethany's Corner!"

I flicked my gaze to the front desk, where the receptionist gave me a charming smile. She was petite with a blonde pixie haircut and bright blue eyes. Her features reminded me of Cyrene. I looked down at my shoes for a moment, swallowing the knot that formed. I cleared my throat and looked back at her with a bland grin.

"I'm sorry, uh, do I have the wrong place? I thought this was a hair salon named Sundance," I said as I approached the desk.

"Oh, no, we only share the space. We're not associated with that company, they're exclusively Vampyre. What services are you looking for? We're running a special on cut and wash bundles today!" She gestured to the menu on the wall.

"Actually, I'm here to ask you guys some questions." I turned in a small circle for another look and clicked my tongue. If this place was open twenty-four hours, why on earth couldn't she work the day shift? Both companies were identical, aside from the names.

"This girl—" I held up the photo. "—she started working there two days ago. She was here last night, do you know where she could've gone?"

The woman leaned forward with a squint, frowned, and shook her head. "She's human?"

"Wholeheartedly."

"And she worked *here*, last *night*?" She scrunched her face. "They're all Vampyres, sorry. I don't even know how that's legal."

I nodded, chewing on my lip as I pondered. I figured this search wouldn't work out during the day, but every hour that passed was vital.

"You don't have access to any security cameras?"

I showed her the badge in my wallet. She pursed her lips and shook her head.

"We use different systems." Her smile weakened to a sheepish grin as her eyebrows curved upward. "I'm sorry."

"No, it's fine. Thanks."

I backed away from the desk and walked out. I scanned the store strip, then went into each shop to ask the employees if they had seen her inside this morning. Once I'd exhausted my options on that street, I rounded the corner and did the same for the next set. I tread the street's gentle slope. There was a sparse parking lot ahead with people parked there to either avoid the meters or the parallel parking.

I stopped asking after the first store on the next street. The rest of the shops would've been closed last night—they were exclusively human. I continued my trek to the parking lot, wondering if anything could've been left behind if she'd been taken.

There was nothing other than glass shards, empty take-out cups, cigarette butts, and gum wrappers across the lot. I stared at the glass. I imagined Briar's motorcycle being pushed over or her helmet's visor shattering as someone blitzed her. I flinched back into reality when a beer bottle crunched underneath someone's car tires as they parked.

I dialed Astoria's number with a shaky sigh.

"Did you find her?" she asked by way of greeting.

"No, have you heard anything?"

"No... I think her phone is off," she whimpered. "It's never off, Sterling. *Never!*"

"I know, Ria, I know. Let's not freak out yet, okay? I'm looking for her now."

I didn't want to reach out to the precinct. Chief Duncan would send Officer Lyra Hart or another Vampyre, as if they were the only options we had. On top of that, he always made us wait seventy-two hours before searching for adults when they went missing. I believed it was partly why all our trails ran cold.

I went back home, though I hated returning empty-handed.

Astoria was in her room, buried under her covers. I could hear the sniffling. I sat on the edge and she flung the covers off of her head with bright eyes, but they dulled again when she saw I was alone.

"She might not be missing, Ria," I murmured, but I didn't quite believe it myself.

"No, she *is*," she croaked. "It's normal if she ignores your calls but me? She *never* ignores mine."

"I'm going to go back to Sundance tonight. I can trace her steps that way." I felt uneasy letting so many hours pass without investigating. But since none of the humans in the immediate area had any relevant information, I didn't have a choice.

"Why don't you get one of your Vampyre officer friends—"

"They're not my friends, and they're part of the problem. I won't," I said firmly. Astoria pursed her lips and looked away.

"Even if they have the power to help? You're really gonna let your pride get in the way of finding Briar?" Astoria's voice slowly rose.

"It's not getting in the way. I *know* I can find her." I jabbed my thumb into my chest. She scoffed.

"That's crazy."

She reached across her bed for a pair of headphones and her novel. She slumped into her pillows and opened the book, shutting me out as she covered the view of her face. I sighed and stood up, leaving her alone and returning to my room upstairs.

I opened my laptop and began researching Sundance. Its business profile appeared, but below it, the first thing was an article about a robbery. The store had opened five years ago, then closed for a year after it got held up by two masked men. Then the owners withdrew their charges before they reopened and refused to disclose why. The robbers were never found. Sundance had an extensive renovation that appeared to cost more than the revenue they brought in. The source of the extra money wasn't in the article either.

I narrowed my eyes.

Hours passed as I scribbled my findings in my notepad. I didn't peel my eyes from the screen until the Check-In alarm rang on my phone. I met with Astoria downstairs. She clenched her ID in her hand and went on the porch.

"I don't need to tell you that you need to report her missing, otherwise she'll be flagged." Astoria's gaze was fixed on the patrol car pulling into the driveway. My mouth went dry as I hoped for Cyrene to step out of the car, only for Officer Kent to appear. Just another reminder of reality.

"I thought I told you never to show back up here," I said tightly.

"I understand, sir, but I've been assigned here. I'll be out of your hair as soon as possible," he swore with an open palm before unlocking the tablet. His gaze flicked between me and Astoria. "Where's the one with pink hair?"

"Missing," I said curtly.

"*Missing?*" Officer Kent echoed.

"Yes, but I want you to mark her present, alright? I'd rather handle this situation on my own."

"You're on leave and I could get fired." Officer Kent shook his head and only tapped the screen twice, then the screen blackened.

"Listen, rookie." I stepped down from the porch and only allowed a couple of inches between us. "I can make your life a lot harder than it needs to be if you don't."

The only sounds were distant birds, ghostly wind, and a passing vehicle down the road as we stared each other down like two dogs on the street.

"Fine," he said, then turned the tablet back on and marked her name. "I don't understand why you wouldn't want to report her missing. The amount of manpower you'd have looking for her—"

"Chief Duncan would just assign Vampyres on the case and they would drag their feet to look for her." I knew I would be working alone the second Chief Duncan forced me to go on leave instead of letting me continue my cases. *Cyrene's* case.

"I guess that's fair." Officer Kent shrugged, then walked away. I knew he and Briar had clashed often in the past, so I figured he didn't care either way. He was only trying to keep his nose clean to climb the ranks, like we all did when we were fresh on the force.

I turned to Astoria. "I need your car again." She gave me a stiff nod.

"Take whatever you need. My head hurts... I'm going to go sleep."

✳

I dressed in a white button-down, navy slacks, and a dark blue blazer. As I loaded my pistol with silver bullets, trepidation crawled along my spine. I'd never felt insecure around these bullets until I discovered there was a creature they couldn't put down. I kept a silver bullet in its chamber, then holstered the pistol at my hip. I looked down at the cracked mask on my dresser with a sigh. The lack of anonymity only added to the uneasiness I already felt, but I didn't have time to worry about such things.

The city was coated in scarlet and violet as the sunset deepened. I parked a block away from Sundance and trekked on foot, pausing across the street to observe them. The stylists and receptionist were busily setting up the shop. From what I could see, everyone had the Devil's eyes.

I stalked across the street, and my jaw tightened as I yanked the door open and entered.

"Hi, welcome to—"

"I need to know where this girl has been."

I held up Briar's photo to the receptionist. The bangles on her wrist jingled as she grabbed the photo and examined it. She eyed me warily before handing the photo back.

"She was here last night, but we sent her home early." She put a hand on her hip and scanned me closely.

"She never made it home," I said, flashing my badge at her. "I need to see your security cameras."

Her bronzed skin seemed to lose all its color. "W-we don't have access to whatever cameras are outside."

"I can have this whole place shut down a second time for having a nonessential human employee on your books," I spoke low, my tightened fists on the counter.

"I can show you what we have in the salon." She slipped from the desk and led me to the back room. There were several monitors across the wall. A security guard fused to a rolling chair that hugged his hips ate a bowl of instant noodles. He choked and coughed, setting the bowl aside and wiping his mouth with a napkin as we entered.

"Hey, Fred, it'll just be a minute," the woman said.

I pulled out my notepad. "What's your name?"

"Samara." She pointed at the top screen and directed Fred to rewind to the previous night's recordings. I wrote her name down, then switched my focus to the monitor above, taking note of the times.

There was a black-and-white tape of Briar walking inside from the north, the same direction I came from. She set her helmet and purse down at the desk, then got right to work.

"Fast forward," I said, leaning closer to the screen. People were in and out of the salon, zipping around the screen three times the normal speed.

"Stop the video," I said once I saw one of the stylists hug Briar. Samara waved goodbye to her, and Briar left, heading back north.

I desperately needed access to the street cameras. She might have been in that parking lot after all. It was the only one close enough to walk to Sundance, though far enough from most operating businesses that no one would witness her abduction.

"Why did you send her home early?" I put the notepad back in my pocket and kept my hands tucked away. Samara kept her wide gaze on the screen.

"She said someone close to her brother died, and we wanted her to spend time with her family." She peered back at me over her shoulder. Her eyes softened. "You two share a resemblance."

"Yeah... that's my sister."

Samara's explanation was like a hot blade seared through my lungs. I hadn't realized Briar was bothered by what happened to Cyrene. I was too busy wallowing to ask how either of my sisters were doing with the news.

I walked out of the security room and Samara followed, closing the door behind her. Fred remained seated.

"What is *your* name?" She tilted her head slightly.

"Uh, Detective Shaw," I replied hesitantly.

"Are you aware of the Nightshades?" She dropped her voice to whisper.

My eyebrows knit.

"What is that?" I frowned. Samara shuddered.

"Not what, but *who*."

# 36
# STERLING

Samara explained what happened to the Sundance hair salon five years ago. The previous owner loaned over a hundred thousand dollars to get the salon started, but profits were slim. A couple of men came in and demanded money through force. The damages were so extensive that it took them a year to rebuild.

A shorter stylist inserted herself into our conversation and introduced herself as Jocelyn.

"I'm pretty certain The Nightshade bar belongs to them," she whispered as she pointed across the street with cherry red nails. "I'd check over there for anything suspicious. It's right by that food truck."

"If the Nightshades—"

The two women hissed loudly at me. Samara held her finger over her lips. Jocelyn frantically looked around, as if saying their name would summon their presence in seconds. She clutched Samara's arm like a security blanket.

"If the Nightshades are as formidable as you make them sound, how is it that I've never heard of them before?" I dropped my voice to a near indistinguishable murmur.

"They cover their tracks. They disguise their dealings as territorial Vampyre squabbles or human activity. It's just how it is, love," Jocelyn said, then rushed back to her booth.

"You never know who's associated with them either—unless they bear their crest and show it to you as a warning. The tattoo is always somewhere hidden, but with easy access. I wouldn't go around saying their name out loud... *especially* as a Sun Dweller. You're not supposed to know they exist," Samara said.

As I was about to ask what the crest looked like, the shop phone rang. Samara flinched, then eased her shoulders before picking it up. She brightened her tone when she answered, as if we weren't just talking about the Boogey Man. I gave her a silent wave and left the salon with enough information for a lead, aside from the crest.

I peered at the Chen's Den food truck and the alley that emitted an ominous red light a few stores down from it. I didn't bother walking down to the intersection to cross the street.

Vampyres lined up to enter. I waited at the end of the line like I was a patron. The bouncer allowed five of them inside and I tried to slip through, but he put a hand on my chest and pushed me back. Searing heat rose along my neck from his touch, but I tamed my anger when I observed his skeletal features. He held the threat of death in his eyes.

"Sun Dweller. Move along elsewhere," he threatened. I stared him down. If I showed my badge, he'd have to let me in... but then he could notify any Nightshade members inside about my presence.

"Do you have a hearing problem?" the man sneered.

"No." I took a step back and reached for my wallet. I pulled out Briar's photo and held it up. "I'm looking for this human girl. Have you seen her?"

The bouncer looked down at the photo for a moment, then his lips curled into a sinister grin.

"Yeah, she was here last week with her boyfriend." The bouncer unhooked the velvet stanchion and extended his hand toward the door. "Be my guest."

*Boyfriend?* Not only was she breaking curfew, but she was illegally dating a Vampyre?

I frowned and entered into a narrow hall washed in alizarin. The music drowned out my thoughts as I entered the main clubroom. I stood in the back, taking a moment to watch all the Vampyres drinking and dancing. They were living their lives like how humans used to. No one wanted to go to a bar or club during the day, so the Vampyres' very existence took that leisurely activity from us. I sucked my teeth as I imagined slaughtering every single one of them, and destroying the building too. I didn't understand how Briar could even stomach being around them.

I moved closer to the bar to question the bartender. She was stretched thin between patrons crowding the counters. I wedged myself between two women, one of whom scooted away with a grimace to preserve her personal space.

"Sterling?"

A loud, feminine voice.

I whirled around and scoffed at the familiar ivory skin paired with garnet eyes.

"Lyra?" I curled my lip up, her name leaving a bitter taste in my mouth.

"In the flesh."

She tilted her head, her diamond earrings catching the light of the pendants above. Her hair, styled in luscious curls, cascaded past her shoulders and down to her lower back. She wore a fitted black cocktail dress with a plunging neckline that exposed a long, white-gold lariat. It was safe to say that she was here for pleasure rather than business.

"How did you get in here?"

"The bouncer let me in. Apparently my sister came here with some secret Vampyre boyfriend." I pulled out her picture from my wallet, hoping Lyra came here often enough to point me in the right direction.

"Hm." She took a sip of her half-empty cocktail. Her dark, plum-stained lips remained flawless as she licked them. "You're the last person I thought I'd see here."

"Yeah, me too. I'm not here for fun though." I placed my thumb and index finger in my mouth and pushed a quick whistle. The bartender held up an impatient finger before serving drinks to the patrons near her.

"What are you here for?" Lyra asked.

"My sister." I didn't take my eyes off the bartender.

"Well, she's not here. Trust me, if a human was in here, I'd know." She raised her glass again.

"Are you sure?" I looked at her drink pointedly. She didn't

appear drunk—not even halfway—but I was well aware of how much more sensitive Vampyres were to alcohol compared to humans. She probably couldn't smell a thing from one drink, let alone however many she'd already had.

"Yeah, I'm sure." She slid the empty glass away from her.

The bartender rushed to our side of the bar, wiping her damp hands on a towel.

"What can I get ya?"

"Any identification on this girl?" I held up the photo, cutting right to the chase.

"Not tonight, but she was definitely here last week." She took Lyra's glass and started washing it in a mini sink.

"Do you remember who she was with?"

The woman briefly looked up at me and frowned. "You cops starting heavy investigations on Sun Dwellers that break curfews now? Ain't that like arresting someone for speeding yesterday?"

I straightened, tucking Briar's photo away and returning my wallet to my back pocket.

"How did you know—"

"Come on, honey. I wasn't born yesterday. She's a cop too." She pointed at Lyra.

"Then you should know that I'm here on serious business. I'm not going after her for breaking curfew. She's *missing*. I need to know about everything and everyone she was around. Starting with her boyfriend."

The girl on the other side of me finally left and I took her place on the barstool. Lyra choked on her drink.

"I wouldn't say boyfriend. They bickered the whole time—she

kept trying to get away from him." The bartender shrugged.

*That's it.*

"Describe him."

"Listen, I really should get back—"

"If you know something, I can have you arrested for obstruc-tion." I scowled. "Let's start with *your* name."

"Stella. And the guy looked like everyone else. Black hair, half shaved, neck and arm sleeve tattoos..." Her voice trailed off as she started mixing a couple of cocktails.

"You know him, don't you?" I challenged.

"N-not personally," Stella reassured me. "He's a regular here. One of the VIPs. I just make the drinks."

"Feel free to describe his tattoos," I said as I pulled out the note-pad and waited. "I got all night."

"He's..." Stella sighed and rubbed the back of her neck. Her face fell into pallor. "I don't wanna get killed, alright?"

"You won't."

"You can't promise that. Neither of you." She frowned at Lyra.

"He's a Nightshade... isn't he?" I looked up from my notepad. It seemed like the only thing a Vampyre could possibly fear was that group.

Stella pursed her lips and looked down with a sheepish nod.

"Describe. Him," I demanded slowly.

The suspect had a deep bronze complexion and stood at my height. He had black hair, geometric and floral tattoos around his neck, and dragon sleeves on both arms.

"He's usually in the VIP lounge," Stella finished, pointing across the dance floor to a curtain guarded by two armed bouncers.

"Thanks."

I took a step away from the bar, but Lyra gripped my arm tightly and held me in place.

"Let go of me," I snarled.

"If you walk over there, it's suicide," she said.

I snatched my arm away from her. "You know about the Nightshades too?"

"What sort of Vampyre would I be if I didn't?" She stood from the barstool and dusted off her dress. I released a harsh, derisive laugh.

"What sort of *cop* are you knowing they exist and not doing a thing about it?" I shouted over the music.

Lyra yanked me by my shirt collar and dragged me away from the bar and the dancing patrons, all the way to the back hallway where the bathrooms were. Bass thumped through the walls, the surrounding chatter growing more indistinct.

"If any of us had the power to stop them, we would. Don't you *dare* suggest anything otherwise." She whipped her hand away from my collar, almost throwing me against the wall. I straightened out my shirt and brushed off the ghost of her hand.

"Suggest what? That your kind look away while they probably fill your pockets?" I scoffed.

"You're an ignorant scum bag, you know that? You know how to kill us, but you know *nothing* about how we live," she muttered harshly. "It goes far above my pay grade. I don't have a say in what goes on. I'm not *allowed* to say anything. It's more than losing my job—I can lose my life. If your sister got caught up in their circle, she's as good as dead."

"That's for me to find out on my own," I said as I planted my feet and folded my arms. She chuckled and put her hands on her hips, glancing at people going in and out of their respective bathrooms.

"You'll get yourself killed the way you're doing things." Lyra flipped some of her hair behind her shoulder. "Let me help you."

"Not in a million years," I scoffed.

"Then prepare for your sister's closed-casket funeral."

Those words clawed my skin like nails on a chalkboard. Lyra started walking away and I quickly jolted ahead of her, blocking her path.

"Fine! Fine, please." I huffed air heavily through tight teeth. "Just this once."

"You're in our world now. So you need to let me take the lead," she said, then held out her hand.

*Anything for Briar. Anything to bring her home.*

I stared at Lyra's hand for a moment, then shook it firmly. Her palm was like ice, its coldness sinking into my bones.

I had a sickening feeling I'd just made a deal with the Devil.

# 37
# DRAVEN

Wraith walked ahead of me while Larkin and Delilah trailed behind. Being sandwiched between the three of them felt like being escorted to a prison cell. I had to tread lightly and do whatever task that waited for me if I didn't want to risk being sold out to Uriah for good.

A hunt could mean a couple of things, though it usually meant finding a human to Turn without their consent. It also could mean finding clients who owed money or recruiting fledglings to join our clan. Recruitment was the only option that didn't require spilling blood. With Wraith being the one leading this little *excursion*, blood had to spill.

"What are we huntin'?" I finally said, my voice booming against the silence in the garage. Wraith circled each car like a vulture, scratching his chin pensively while his brother packed his needles in a small leather case.

"Just pick one, man," Larkin whined, then shuffled to the rack of keys.

"We need something with a big enough trunk." Wraith smiled when he stopped at one of the four-door sports cars.

"Not this one." I grimaced at its bright orange paint.

"Why not?" Wraith frowned as Larkin tossed him the keys. He caught them and hopped in the driver's seat.

"Gee, I dunno, maybe it's because it stands out?" I asked.

"Shotgun!" Larkin shouted and jogged to the passenger seat as Delilah settled in the back.

That left me with the spot behind Wraith. I grumbled obscenities under my breath even as they ignored me.

As the garage door gradually rose, Wraith revved the engine. The tires squealed and left a thin swirl of smoke as he shot out of the garage. I tensed, but I didn't dare grab the handle on the ceiling or put on a seat belt. As he swerved around the bends, gravity pulled me to either side of the backseat.

Delilah glanced at me from the corner of her eye with a smirk, and I bared my fangs at her.

✳

Wraith took us downtown and parallel parked in front of The Nightshade.

We skipped the line and I stopped at the door for a moment. The last memory I had of this place was getting lost in Briar's smile as she watched Until Dawn perform for the first time. Yet there was a bitter taste in my mouth.

Delilah's slender hand pushed me inside.

"Why would we hunt here?" I shouted over the music.

"We ain't, I just wanna holler at Stella!" Wraith shouted.

I rolled my eyes. She hated him, much like everyone else who crossed his path aside from his little posse.

We entered the main clubroom and Larkin paused, sniffing the air.

"What are you doing?" I scrunched my nose as his nostrils flared.

"You don't smell that?" He was going toward the bar but changed course. "It's... similar..."

I pushed a couple of people aside to follow him. Delilah drifted behind.

"Similar to what?" I shouted. I tried to filter out all the different scents hitting me at once. There was a faint smell of musk and wood. My heart iced over as I followed Larkin to the narrow hallway in the back. There, standing in front of the bathrooms, was the freckled, copper-haired cop—now unmasked. He was talking to a Vampyre woman, surprisingly with a softer demeanor. His light brown eyes were still cold and narrowed, but at least he wasn't harassing her like he did me at City Hall.

"Well, well, I knew I smelled a human 'round here," Larkin intoned. I grabbed his shoulder and pulled him back.

"Don't." I spoke firmly and didn't take my eyes off Sterling. He peered up from above the woman's head and our shrewd gazes met. The woman followed his attention to us. I sniffed and rubbed my nose.

"Come on, man. Let's go," I insisted, tugging on his shoulder once more. Larkin shrugged it off quickly.

"He's just a human." Larkin slithered toward Sterling and the woman. "Perfect timing considering what we're out for."

"Stop!" I barked.

"Why don't you two come with us?" Larkin lifted the flap of his jacket, allowing the stainless steel of his gun to glint at the man.

"We were just leaving." Sterling did the same, opening up his blazer to reveal a pistol. I was certain it was loaded with silver.

Larkin laughed contemptuously, then stepped aside. Sterling and the woman stalked off, but his gaze lingered over me as he passed by. I kept my head held high and my chest out. He spit on the ground next to my sneaker before rounding the corner, and I gave him one last scowl before disappearing. He had to have remembered me from City Hall. I'd never forget him either.

Delilah put a hand on her hip. "Let's follow him."

"Are you crazy?" I exclaimed.

Larkin ran his tongue over his teeth. "No, she's right. Ain't no human gonna punk me out all 'cause he's carrying too. I'm getting Wraith, you two go ahead." Larkin stormed out of the hallway.

Trading Briar's brother in exchange for her freedom didn't seem feasible anymore. The opportunity presented itself as if it were a supernatural sign, but I didn't want it anymore. Not if I could still prove to her that I wasn't the monster she thought I was.

Delilah and I left the bar, tracking their scent down the street and around the corner. We passed multiple vendors, some even calling out for our attention. It wasn't long before Wraith and Larkin caught up with us. I fell back a few feet, silently hoping Sterling and the woman got away. I wondered if she was an officer too, seeing how easily they got along.

"Somebody tell me what happened? I was too busy trying to get

Stella's number." Wraith yawned and sniffed the air.

"We're huntin' a Sun Dweller that thinks he's a hot shot 'cause he got a gun," Larkin said. "He thinks he can swipe up one of our ladies and get away with it."

"The man is a cop," I cut in finally. "If you attack him, you'll start a war."

Wraith and Larkin burst into maniacal laughter. Wraith held his stomach as tears squeezed out of his eyes. My gaze bounced between them as heat crawled from my gut to my ears.

"Is everything a joke to ya idiots?" I snapped. "I'm serious!"

"Do you live under a rock, bro?" Larkin asked between dying chuckles.

"Ah, don't you know that's what Uriah *wants*?" Wraith tilted his head condescendingly. "Or did he just... stop sharing informa-tion with you?"

"Uriah isn't that stupid," I hissed, then started walking the oth-er way. Delilah flashed in front of me and folded her arms. Wraith and Larkin snaked their way to block the rest of the sidewalk.

"Since when do you turn down smoking a pig?" Wraith's head dropped to a feral tilt. Larkin rolled his neck, cracking it.

"I'm down to hunt, just not that one. He ain't my blood type." Wraith narrowed his eyes.

"No, I think he's the perfect blood type. That smell... it's awful-ly like Briar's, no? Matter of fact, why don't we bring her a friend?" Wraith shoved me back, but I barely moved. "Better hurry, their scents will fade soon."

"No." I planted my feet and bared my fangs.

"If you don't help us go after him, Uriah's gonna hear about the

Sun Dweller lovin' traitor he has." Wraith smiled thinly.

"I ain't no Sun Dweller lover," I snapped, then pushed forward. I led the way since the three of them refused walk ahead until I moved. I didn't like having my back to them, but at least I knew they wouldn't do anything to me yet if they wanted to see if I'd follow through.

Voices were within earshot, like crackling fire in silent woods. We paused in front of a bus stop. There was a parking lot and a strip of more shops lining the far side of it across the street. Sterling stood at his car, talking to the woman over the roof of it.

"What are you waiting for?"

Larkin pushed me and I stumbled into the street. I hissed at him, then dashed across the intersection. I leaped over five cars and kicked Sterling in the sternum. He crashed against the car next to him. I listened to the air shoot from his chest, a flicker of pleasure leaking into mine. The woman shouted his name but was later cut short as Wraith, Larkin, and Delilah came to hold her back.

Sterling scrambled for the gun in his holster and I kicked it out of his grip before he could aim. I leaned down, snatching him by the neck. Blood leaked from his temple, his scent permeating the air. It was much more similar to Briar's than I thought. My mouth watered and my lengthening fangs poked the insides of my lips.

"Run," I growled, before yanking him to his feet and shoving him into the street.

"*Run!*" I howled, just before something sharp pricked me in the neck. I grunted as my hand shot up and plucked a needle out of it. A bright green substance oozed from its tip. Sterling's body became distorted and blurred, stretching and swaying with the tilting street as he ran away.

"What—"

My legs collapsed beneath me. My arms were anchors. It didn't matter how much I told myself to stand up—nothing happened. I opened my mouth to speak, but only strained grunts came out.

Delilah, Wraith, and Larkin stood over me, with Larkin's smile stretched the widest.

"How do you like my new project?" He held out five tiny needles, each with a small green vial the size of a fingernail attached at the end. "A new paralytic agent for Vampyres. It can't be metabolized so quickly without an antidote. Best part? You get to stay awake and feel *everything*."

"Thanks for giving us the hunt we hoped for," Delilah gloated as Wraith and Larkin lifted me. I imagined myself scowling at her, but the only muscle tic I could muster was a blink.

# 38
# BRIAR

Grey. So much grey. I never knew I'd crave *color*. I never knew the desperate lengths I would go until I pulled chunks of my hair out so I could at least see pink. The medic said only a few hours had passed. Caspian said it had been two weeks. I wasn't sure who to believe, but two weeks seemed the most realistic.

The cleaning lady refused to come in without an escort because of my escape attempt. Even if I had the will to fight, I wasn't going to try the same strategy twice.

I didn't get any more visits from the creep and his brother. Delilah hadn't visited, but that was no disappointment. I was so angry at Draven that I pushed him away, so I should've been happy that I hadn't seen him in a while. Yet... my heart ached with his absence. A part of me desperately wanted to believe he was telling the truth.

I was lying on the bed, counting the strands of my hair over and over again. I counted my breaths. The scars on my arms. The number of creaks the bed made each time I moved around. The footsteps that walked through the cellar. I tried to memorize everyone's gait. The cleaning lady had quick, short strides in sneakers that always squeaked. The medic wore heels that carried firm steps with confidence. Caspian's footsteps were impossible to hear. If the door suddenly opened, I would know it was him by the lack of sound.

I watched a spider crawl on the wall and sat up. My head felt heavier than the rest of my body. I squinted, unable to tell if the spider was black or brown in the dim lighting of the cell. It crawled a never-ending trek along the wall toward the narrow vent in the ceiling. I stood from the bed and chuckled before pressing the tip of my index finger on the spider, smashing it against the concrete. I stared at its curled legs and guts against the wall.

"If I can't get out of here, neither can you, friend," I whispered.

I heard the main cellar door groan and creak outside my door. I quickly dropped to the floor and crawled under the bed when I didn't recognize the footsteps.

Another cell door next to mine opened and slammed shut. Voices were muffled, then a quick burst of laughter. I didn't dare press my ear against the door this time. I hugged myself under the bed as I curled my knees to my chest, praying that those Vampyres weren't returning to cut my arms again.

Caspian promised me no one would do that again... but it happened twice more after.

Sometimes I wished I had taken Draven's offer to Turn me. I would've been equipped to get myself out of this situation. However, there was no guarantee that he wasn't asking that just as an excuse to drain me completely. Once a human consented to a Vampyre, any death that followed couldn't be considered murder. The human was always expected to know the risks of a Vampyre losing control. I already didn't have control of my situation and I couldn't trust Draven. So that option was foolish no matter how desperate I was.

But now? If he offered it to me again... I probably wouldn't even let him finish the sentence before saying yes.

To have the strength to bust down that cell door—

The door slid open and I hesitantly poked my head from under the bed before reeling back against the corner.

"What are you doing under there?" Caspian murmured before entering and crouching. He peered at me with his head tilted upside down.

"Hiding." I loosened my fetal position.

"From me?" He raised his eyebrows, but the rest of his face remained unchanging.

"From whoever else. Is there a new prisoner?" I asked. Caspian's face fell, wrought with an exhaustion I'd never seen him display before. As if my question made his burdens all the heavier.

"Yes, unfortunately," he said, then extended his hands.

"Why unfortunate?" I slowly crawled from under the bed. I placed my hands in his clammy palms. My knees wobbled as I rose with him.

"Nothing. I've been sent to take you to get ready," Caspian said flatly. "A couple of the servants will be preparing you."

"Preparing me for what?"

I frowned as he pulled me toward the door. He reached into his pocket and took out a black cloth.

"Your stay with us is ending. I'm only following orders," Caspian said gently.

I could never tell if he felt any remorse beyond that blank expression. But I appreciated the fact that he treated me with dignity even as he blindfolded me. I tried to see through the fabric, but he wrapped it twice and it turned opaque. He tied my wrists behind my back, but he didn't snatch me by the arm or throw me around when he led me out of the cell. I wished he gave me the time to put my shoes on.

I savored the change in texture, from the lukewarm roughness of the concrete to a cool, slick flooring. I dragged my feet across the grout and figured it was some sort of tile. I couldn't remember what the floors looked like when I tried to escape—I had been too focused on trying to live.

I counted my steps.

*One, two, three, four, five...*

"There's a little step up," Caspian muttered. I lifted my leg higher than necessary and wobbled forward. As he guided me through the house, he mumbled little warnings so I wouldn't stub a toe or knock an elbow. He counted each step aloud so I knew when to change my gait. He led me to a second set of stairs that were colder than the last. I vaguely remembered a marble staircase when I first arrived.

My stomach twisted as I realized we were heading to the same floor where the man with the mechanical arm was.

*Sixteen, seventeen, eighteen, nineteen, twenty...*

"What's going to happen to me?" I whispered shakily.

"You're going to a different group of people that need your

blood," he replied as he pulled me along. "Turn left."

I staggered but cooperated.

"This is where it ends between us," he said flatly. I flinched as he knocked on solid wood. My heart trembled in the rhythm of the shuffling on the other side.

"You didn't seem so bad... for a Sun Dweller," he said finally. "I guess I can see why Draven took such a liking to you." A rush of cold air washed over me as a door swung open and a new pair of cold hands took hold of my arms to pull me in.

"Wait—" My breath caught in my throat and I dug my heels into the floor. "Wait, wait! No! Caspian?!" I started to scream when I felt his presence leave my side like a ghost.

Something cracked against the back of my head and sent me stumbling forward. My hands were still tied behind my back and I couldn't cushion my fall as I plummeted onto my stomach. I gasped for air.

"We have permission to sedate you if you give us any more problems," a seasoned, elderly woman warned.

"Don't get brave now, girl," a younger, monotoned woman said. They dragged me across the floor and into another room, where they shut the door and began to undress me.

Goosebumps prickled my skin. I crossed my arms over my chest and slouched. I yelped as they hoisted me up with ease and dropped me into scalding hot water without warning. I screamed and tried to stand, but a hand with the strength of steel held me down by the shoulder.

They started to roughly scrub me down, further agitating my already burning skin. My blindfold became soaked with tears as I bit down on my lip and dug my nails in my palms. They tugged at my hair as they washed and scratched my scalp raw. Then they kept a hand pressed against my eyes as they leaned me back in the water and rinsed my hair. I didn't expect it and swallowed a mouthful. I coughed as my nose burned.

The bathtub burped and gurgled when they unplugged it. As the scalding water sank below, cold air replaced it and sent my body into violent shivers. The women forced me to stand and rubbed a towel over my hair and body. I bit my lip to suppress any more winces.

"Keep your eyes shut," one of them snarled as she took the soiled blindfold off and replaced it with a dry one. They temporarily unbound my wrists and dressed me in a baggy shirt and pants made of a soft but papery material. I imagined scrubs like doctors wear as they retied my hands and put some sort of thin slippers on my feet. Damp, stringy strands of hair snaked around my ears and cheeks, and felt like bugs crawling.

They led me back downstairs, but they weren't nearly as helpful guiding me as Caspian. I tripped over multiple steps. I felt like my arms or shoulders would snap in half as jerked me back to prevent me from falling. I tried to remember the amount of steps I counted going up, but my mind was buried in fog. Every step became tentative.

We stopped and I could hear a door click, then sigh as it opened. Mild humid air washed over my stinging skin. I heard the hissing of a nearby sprinkler, the hum of an engine, and the car doors swinging shut. I shuddered when the front door slammed behind me and the women disappeared. I wriggled my wrists in their bindings before a calloused hand grabbed me. I staggered over two—no, three—steps and walked over a bumpy ground. It wasn't jagged enough to be gravel. The grout lines underneath the thin slippers' soles felt relatively uniform. I could've been cobblestone.

No one was speaking this time. There was the sound of metal being dragged against the ground, then the frigid metal was wrapped taut around my torso and ankles. The ground left from beneath my feet and then I was sitting. I moved my head around according to the sounds, trying to keep my breaths steady.

*Zip, click.* Seat belt.

*Clomp, clomp, thud.* Heavy boots, then dropping down from the vehicle.

I could be in the back of a van.

*Knock, knock.* The thin metal around the vehicle shook. I jolted to the side as we started rolling.

All I could think about were the decisions that had led me to this point. I wished I could've traded places with that spider in my cell.

Twenty minutes or so had passed when we finally rolled to a stop. The same calloused hand grabbed me and slung me over a bony shoulder, carrying me back outside. Once he set me down on my feet, the blindfold lifted.

I squinted my eyes at the bright white light pouring through rows of display windows. The building was six stories tall and resembled a hospital, and all sconces illuminated modest parts of its white walls. A woman in a white lab coat stood at the entry's sliding glass doors with a fanged smile. Two armed bodyguards in black suits stood at her sides.

My eyes darted around for clues to signal where I was. I wasn't even sure if I was still in Neoterra.

One of the men from the van chuckled as I tried to squirm and twist out of their grip. I screamed once they passed me to the foreign Vampyres at the door. I thrashed and kicked until I felt a pinch, then a burning sensation under the skin of my shoulder. My body slowly fell limp, my eyelids heavy as if someone were tugging strings on them. The last thing I heard before everything turned into a sable void, as if I dove head first into a still lake at midnight—

"Welcome to White Fang, human."

----•◆•----

# Enjoy A Sneak Peek of

# The Bleeding Hearts
### Book Two of the
### "Until Equinox" Trilogy

----•◆•----

I INSTANTLY REGRETTED ALLOWING THOSE WORDS ESCAPE my lips. I stared at my friend sitting on that degraded mattress, his sickly ashen skin slowly deepening to a bronze. I dipped a glance at the blood bags in my hands, wondering if our friendship was truly worth the risk of losing a secure place here at the Nightshades. If it was worth potentially falling into the same trap Draven was in, after all they had done for me.

Briar wasn't a depraved Sun Dweller like most of them, but she wasn't enough for me to risk my life. I couldn't quite wrap my head around why Draven was so desperate to save her. Of all the humans we had to kill or capture in the past, not a single one had such a pull on his heartstrings like this woman.

Any time I couldn't understand his line of thinking, I brushed it off as a result of his Sun Dweller past.

"Thank you," Draven whispered, his voice subtly cracking. I gave him a stiff nod in response before shutting the door. I wanted to take the promise back.

But if there was anything positive I'd learned from my despicable father... it was that a man's word held the most value.

The Nightshades who volunteered to participate in White Fang's trials had yet to return home. With Draven going there—without anyone having reported their activities—they could be slaughtering us in disguised science experiments, and the rest of us would be none the wiser.

I felt like I was balancing on a tightrope hundreds of feet in the air, waiting for it to snap.

I stuffed the empty blood bags in the waistband of my slacks before I sped out of the basement. The cellar door was still groaning shut by the time I reached upstairs. I glanced at the wide picture windows lining the far wall and the French doors that led to the backyard. The crescent moon was a tiny smile in the sky, mocking me.

I stalked toward the front doors with the intention of disposing the bags far from the King Estate, but Larkin swept through the foyer and snapped his fingers at me as if I were a dog in the street.

"Where are you off to, Ghost Boy?" He poked my shoulder. I glanced at the spot he touched, and slowly lifted a disgusted gaze to meet his.

"You were never much of a talker, were you?" Larkin pressed. He took a step back and hooked his thumbs through the belt loops of his jeans, puffing out his chest like a proud state trooper.

"Not to irrelevant people," I said calmly, though I felt the beast begin to stir in the pit of my gut. I glanced at his throat, imagined ripping it out with my bare hands.

Larkin folded his arms with a proud smirk. "Irrelevant? Haven't you heard? Uriah's got me and Wraith as his top Watchmen while he's in Helios for the week."

I blinked, then turned to open the door again. Larkin rammed his shoulder into it, forcing it shut. I took a step back with a quiet inhale.

"This is the smallest amount of power I've ever seen get to anyone's head," I said, brushing a hand over my shoulder to wipe away the ghost of his finger poking me moments ago.

"Yeah? Well, I don't think you should be allowed to leave without telling me your whereabouts. Wraith would be interested to know too, seeing as how you're friends with a traitor."

Guilt by association already, but I saw it coming. I paused for a moment, thinking up a story that could be deemed satisfactory just to get him out of my way.

"Very well." I ran a hand through my hair. "I'm tracking down some potential test subjects. We're still keeping White Fang stocked, are we not?"

Larkin's eyes darkened as the corner of his mouth pulled into a sinister smirk.

"Of course," he said. "Just... let us know if you find anyone good. It'll be hard to top Briar's blood type."

"I'm sure," I said, and turned away to continue my path to the garage. My body was rigid as I expected Larkin to follow me or Wraith to wait around the corner and grill me about the same issue. But I didn't feel or smell either of their presences once the garage door opened.

Nonetheless, I chose a blacked-out SUV and set the back seats down in case they decided to watch. Why would I choose a sports car with minimal trunk space if I was hunting for more Sun Dwellers? Perhaps I was being too cautious… but being that way was what had kept me in Uriah's good graces all these years. I wished Draven wasn't so careless.

As I climbed in the driver's seat, my eyes swept over a new motorcycle with LED lighting around the rims across. I frowned as I remembered Delilah once boasting that Briar's abduction had come with a bonus ride. Delilah never rode motorcycles, but it wasn't hard to assume she took it out of spite.

I kept an eye on every vehicle I passed and especially on any that found themselves snaking behind me. Even with enhanced Vampyric sight, blinding headlights at night concealed the vehicles' makes behind me. My mind would play tricks on me as I imagined clan members tailing my whereabouts.

I loosed a relieved breath each time the vehicles turned on a different street.

I drove further north, toward a gated apartment complex known as Crow's Nest. It resided on a hill overlooking the beach and was just one street away from the Nocturne District.

I approached the gate and triple-checked my surroundings before I punched in the four-digit code, then waited for the iron gates to slowly open. I drove through, glancing at the group of Vampyres lounging around a fire pit and several others swimming in the pool. I could smell the grill and hear the laughter, and I sucked my teeth at their obliviousness to the world around them.

I went to my building at the back of the property and climbed the stairs to my fourth-floor apartment, hoping my nosy neighbor, Nadia, was buried in hers. She was always conveniently leaving when I arrived, and vice versa, or poking her head out her front door when she heard mine open.

I heard paper crinkle at my shoe as I worked to unlock my door and looked down to see a cupcake with a smiley face on a sticky note that said, "Hope you had a good night!"

I growled under my breath and picked it up, only to immediately toss both items in the trash when I went inside. I just wanted to be left alone.

As much as I wanted a high-rise, keeping a low profile was more important. This was the last place any of the Nightshades would be willing to look for me because Uriah detested the Nocturne District. I supposed I should've opted for a cabin in the woods to avoid people like Nadia.

I finally pulled the empty blood bags from my waistband and tossed them in the biohazard trashcan at the edge of my kitchen. With an exhausted sigh, I shuffled across the apartment and stepped onto the balcony. I peered down the rocky hills and at the black sea subtly glittering beneath the crescent moon. I listened to distant cries and car alarms, shutting my eyes. The sound reminded me of Briar's screams when I took her to be prepared for the White Fang transport. No one had ever been so desperate for my help before, not even Draven.

I pushed away from the railing and went back inside to research the yellow house on a satellite map.

For the past few weeks, I couldn't figure out how she ended up in Pelican's Crossing and witnessed our arson. Finding out that she lived on the south side of Neoterra only nourished my confusion.

I plopped on the couch and swiped through the map on my phone. Once I felt confident I'd found the right area, I switched to street view and followed the road until I saw the yellow house. I pressed my lips into a thin line and ran my hands through my hair.

Approaching the brother directly would be too risky. I would be implicated along with the entire clan, especially with his reputation of sharp investigative skills. There had to be a way to get the message to him without the Nightshades being exposed and there had to be a way to stop the White Fangs before they could hurt Draven and—free Briar. I stared at the ceiling with a developing headache until an idea hit me, and the corner of my lips ticked upward.

⸺•⸺

**Thank you for reading!**
**If you enjoyed this book, please consider leaving a review on Amazon and/or Goodreads. Reviews are golden for indie authors and they encourage more exposure!**

⸺•⸺

# AUTHOR'S NOTE

LOOKING FOR THE NEXT BOOK? IF YOU'D LIKE SIGNED copies with extra goodies like bookmarks and stickers, you can find them on my website: *www.taliawall.com/book-store*

If you are interested in monthly updates for upcoming projects and events, you can also sign up for my newsletter on my website.

# ACKNOWLEDGMENTS

First, I want to thank God for giving me the strength and the imagination to write again. It took seven years to recover from college burnout and life distractions to start reading again, as well as regain the attention span to sit through writing a full manuscript.

I want to thank my husband and the rest of my family for always being in my corner, no matter how dark it seemed. They always helped me stay encouraged and focused on the light at the end of the tunnel.

I thank my friends who didn't abandon me during the antisocial moments when I prioritized my work over socializing.

I give thanks to my editor. She gave such gentle and constructive criticism as well as encouragement I never expected from a stranger. The experience has expanded my mind to think outside the box, and I can't wait to use the knowledge I've learned in my next projects.

Finally, I give thanks to my readers. None of this would have been possible without any of you. I have so many stories to tell that have been collecting digital (and physical) dust. Thank you for joining me on this journey!

# About the Author

Talia spent most of her life in North Carolina and had the lifelong dream of becoming an author since she was five. She not only loves to write but also to draw and paint. She has a loving husband and Persian cat named Thor who often interrupts her writing sessions. She writes young and new adult, paranormal, urban fantasy, and dystopian genres with the intent to send powerful, relevant messages and warnings through fiction.

## Social Media Handles

### TikTok | Threads | Instagram

@fromdreamstopaper

### Website:

www.taliawall.com

www.ingramcontent.com/pod-product-compliance
Lightning Source LLC
Chambersburg PA
CBHW071751110726

47908CB00006B/1771